COME OUT
AND PLAY

Seph Pelech

American Grizzly Publishing

CONTENTS

For you, Gus Fleck.

Come Out and Play

Seph Pelech

CHAPTER 1

Today's the first game of the season and I swear I'm gonna burst! I can't wait to get out in the sun after a long winter. I wanna feel the pine tar on my bat and the dirt beneath my cleats, fine as powder and red as rhubarb. When there's an incoming pitch, I'll swing and send the ball flying over the center field fence. The crowd will go wild as they jump to their feet and cheer my name.

That's not the whole story, though, is it? Whatever, I'm not gonna say it.

I just gotta get through school first. My calculus and French classes pass relatively painlessly, but time starts to drag in English and almost crashes to a halt in creative writing. It doesn't help that I have Ms. Cooper for both and she started each class with the same presentation about her spring break volunteer trip to Lima. I had to look at the photos of her posing with the small Peruvian children twice.

I find my way to the team's table at lunch and to no one's surprise, all we can talk about is today's game. The Fair Grove team doesn't stand a chance! We're bigger, we're stronger, we've trained harder! We're gonna hand them their asses!

Seriously. I'm not gonna say it. Just forget about it.

In history class Mr. Thomas drones on and on about

some president who got shot. I forget which one, I wasn't paying attention. I'm just waiting for school to get out.

In chemistry, I can't help but check my watch at every idle moment. *Almost there... Almost there... Almost there...*

The bell rings and before Mr. Holtz can say goodbye, I bolt out the door and race down the hall. Once outside, I hurry to my truck and burn rubber to get out of the parking lot before the after-school traffic jam begins. As I speed towards my house, I can't take the grin off my face. *It's finally here! The spring opener!*

My parents are still at work when I get home, so there's no one to distract me or slow me down. I run upstairs to my room and pull my uniform out of my closet, eager to put it on for the very first time this season.

I have to say it, don't I?

All right, fine. I'm gay.

Happy now?

My bright red jersey looks sharp, the white pants are snug, and the brim of my hat is perfectly flat. I look like an athlete, a real athlete. No one would ever look at me and think... well... they wouldn't think anything.

I grab my bat bag and head downstairs to make myself a sandwich. Peanut butter and jelly. I have to have one before every game. Or else.

No one knows. And I mean no one. Not my parents, not my teammates. Not even Brody. But why does anyone need to know? It's none of their business.

After eating, I throw my bat bag in the bed of my truck and drive back to school. Most of the parking lot has cleared out now and I can drive to the baseball diamond with relative ease. I park my truck and as I get out of the cab, Brody pulls his Subaru hatchback into the spot next to me.

"It's finally here!" he shouts as he turns off the engine. "Spring opener!" He stands out of his car and swings his bat bag over his shoulder so effortlessly, like there's nothing in it.

"Can I borrow your eye black?" I ask. "I can't find mine."

"Yeah, let me put it on first." Brody pulls out the black tube and looks into my truck's side view mirror, carefully drawing two neat lines under his amber eyes, straight as possible. "Okay... I think that's good," he says after double checking. Always the perfectionist. He hands me the tube.

"Thanks!" I say, quickly smearing two lines under my own eyes without looking in the mirror.

Brody laughs. "They're a little crooked."

"That's okay. No one pays that much attention anyways."

Brody and I drop our bags in the dugout and then begin our warm-up stretches in right field. After some sprints and leg stretches, we throw a ball back and forth, taking a step back after each toss. Once we're warmed up, Brody goes back to the dugout to do his obligatory dozen cartwheels on the third baseline before the game starts. The first baseman, Parker, counts for him when we hear an old engine roar and belch. We turn our heads to see a blue school bus pulling into the parking lot behind the diamond. It's our rivals for today—the Fair Grove Foxes.

The Foxes shuffle off the bus and into the visitors' dugout. They look real cute in those blue uniforms, but they

4

don't stand a chance against us. I adjust my red jersey, flick a bug off my white pants, and take my place at third base.

By the way, when I said they looked cute, I meant that ironically. I was trying to belittle them, I'm not actually attracted to them. God, not everything I say is about, well, you know.

The top of the first inning is three up, three down. Our pitcher, Blake, is really talented. Coach Cole scratches his beard and pats Blake on the back as he runs into the dugout after the first half inning. He shoots me a wink as I squeeze my hands into my batting gloves.

Bottom of the first. The whole team is in the dugout, leaning against the railing and standing on their toes, cheering for each teammate who walks into the batting box. We've already got our center fielder, Josh, on first base. I'm outside the dugout taking practice swings as Brody walks up to the plate. He draws a spiral in the dirt with his left foot—his own superstition, in addition to the dozen cartwheels.

Brody swings and misses on the first pitch but knocks the second one into left field. The Foxes' left fielder can't get the ball fast enough and Brody gets on first while Josh moves to second base.

All right. My turn.

I hear Kev, our announcer, shout, "Batting next for the Trojans, number twenty-two, Derek Milligan!" My teammates cheer for me as I take home plate. Before I begin, I use my left foot to draw a smiley face in the dirt. The Foxes' catcher chuckles. The first pitch is a swing and a miss. The second is way outside the strike box and it zooms right past my crotch. I have to take a couple deep breaths after that.

I raise my bat, waiting for the third pitch. I make eye

contact with the pitcher for a moment. Just a moment...

He lifts his front leg, twists his body, and releases the pitch. I pick up my right leg and swing!

I hear a loud *ding!* and watch the ball sail over the right field fence. The first homerun of the season and it's got my name on it! Josh and Brody run the bases and when I finish my victory lap Brody hugs me off the ground. The score is 3–0 Trojans and I know it's gonna be a good game.

CHAPTER 2

My truck roars to life in our driveway the next morning. I back out and begin my drive through my neighborhood's wooded streets.

They say Oak Ridge is a small town built on red dirt and dreams, but it's mostly red dirt. The dreams died a while ago. Now it's just a tiny town in the middle of nowhere whose suburbs sprawl outwards from the town's center until they intertwine with the forest on the north side. That's where my family lives—in the middle of a neighborhood where trees line every street, a massive oak stands just outside my bedroom window, and thick woods crowd alongside the rear of every house. Sometimes deer wander through and eat our garden. My mom hates that.

I coast down the street a couple miles then swing my truck into the student lot, choosing a spot near the back. Even though it's a longer walk to the school, which is especially crappy in winter, the back of the lot is almost never crowded. Plus it's closer to the baseball field across the street, so I don't have to carry my bat bag as far every day.

I check my watch and pick up my pace. The last few students are filtering into their classes and the first bell of the day is about to ring. I don't care if I'm late for calculus as long as I don't get detention. Coach Cole will kill me if I miss practice because I can't manage my time well enough. I scurry through the classroom door and slide into my seat just as the bell rings. Mrs. Garcia turns around from the blackboard where she was writing up math problems. Her eyes do a double take when they land on me. I grin but I know she knows I just ran here. No rule against that, though, is there? I swear I see her suppress a small smile through sheer force of will, but that can't be right. She doesn't seem like the kind of person who would find me amusing.

Mrs. Garcia is a staple of the school. She's been here forever, no one knows for sure how long. She's not exactly known for being the most personable teacher at Oak Ridge High. Every year there's a rumor that *next* year will be her last, but she still hasn't announced plans to retire.

"Before you hand in your homework from last night, we're going to start today by doing some of those problems on the board," she says, sounding rather unimpressed with her class. A couple hands shoot up, begging to be called on to show off their skills. "Camilla, would you like to come up and do number twenty-four?"

"Um... okay," Camilla says, turning red and slowly walking to the board.

"Logan, you come up and do number twenty-five."

After a groan of disgust, Logan, the class president, rises to his feet and drags his homework off of his desk. He has such a thin, lanky body and he sulks from his seat to the blackboard.

Logan isn't happy, but at least he's re-writing his work on the board for everyone to see. Camilla isn't doing anything. She took a derivative and rearranged some terms with her first couple lines of math, but now she's staring down at her paper, as if trying to figure it out for the first time. I look back at Brody and we share a concerned look. We both feel awful for Camilla.

After a few minutes of humiliating agony, Mrs. Garcia notices that Logan is done and says, "You can both take your seats."

Camilla looks down at her feet as she shuffles back to her desk. As she sits down next to me, I can sense that she's on the verge of tears.

Mrs. Garcia walks to the front of the room and briefly inspects the work like she's hoping to gleam some useful information from it. Then she faces the class and says, "I think we've all learned something today," picks up the eraser and wipes the handwriting from the board.

"I can't believe her," Camilla says to me in French class an hour later. "The first time she asks me to do something at the board in two weeks and she tells me to do the *one* question I skipped."

"Yep, she's a bitch," I chime in, only half paying attention. Madame Miller told us to partner up and practice the new vocabulary words, but Camilla just wants to complain.

"Are you even listening to me?"

"Not at all."

"*Derek!*"

I lean back in my chair and put my hands behind my head, giving Camilla my characteristic smug grin. "Maybe one day she won't do *her* homework and then you can embarrass *her* in front of the class."

Camilla brushed her hair back behind her shoulder.

"That'd be great."

Camilla and I have known each other since second grade when her family moved to Oak Ridge. My parents made me go over to her house and play as a way of welcoming her to the town. I was dreading it as I walked the two blocks from my house to hers, but once I knocked on the door and her father invited me inside, I was so glad I went. Camilla's parents are Mexican and even though Camilla has spent her entire life in the States, her house is a window to a completely different culture. Camilla was my guide through that world and I was her guide through the world of Oak Ridge. She showed me the traditional Mexican cuisine, I showed her how to make friends on the playground. She taught me basic Spanish phrases that I could use with her parents, I taught her how to not get made fun of at school. That lesson was only mildly successful.

"Anyways, I want to forget about Mrs. Garcia for now," she says before moving her eyes up to meet mine with a puppy dog stare. "I have a really big favor to ask you."

"Can I just say no now?" I retort.

"There's this guy," she begins, ignoring my sarcasm as usual. "I really like him but I don't even think he knows I exist."

I suppress a sigh. This happens to Camilla a lot. She's nice and all, and plenty smart, but not exactly what guys in high school go after. She's a little on the bigger side and her quiet, reserved nature doesn't do her any favors - most guys think she's a nerd who'd rather spend an evening with a book than on a date. If only they knew how funny she could be when you really get to know her, when she finally risks vulnerability on the rare occasion that she tries to make a new friend.

"I was wondering if you could talk to him for me."

"Well, who is he?"

She lowers her voice to a whisper and gives a nervous look around the room. There's a hum of noise as the others pretend to practice their vocab, horrendous attempts at a French accent. "Brody," she breathes, leaning in so I and only I can hear.

I freeze and give Camilla a thoroughly unimpressed look. "No, really, who is it?"

She glances from side to side, leans in and repeats, "Brody."

My best friend, Brody? The guy I lift with and play baseball with, Brody? Why would she like Brody?

Well, I guess I could see it. He's six-foot-two and most of his body weight is muscle. I always feel like I'm playing catch-up with him in the weight room. He can bench ten more pounds than me and do one more rep of bicep curls than I can. You probably wouldn't notice the difference in our physiques unless you were as obsessed as we are, but I can see the appeal. I guess I never sat down to think about it before now—now that Camilla is begging me with those pleading eyes.

"What do you want me to do?" I ask her at last.

"Just talk to him."

"Why don't you talk to him?"

"Because he doesn't know I exist!"

"You sit in front of him in Calculus. He spends an hour a day staring at you."

Her face lights up and I can tell her heart does a somersault in her chest. "He's always staring at *me*?"

"Well, no. I mean he's literally looking at the back of your head. Not that he's staring *at* you specifically. Anyways, how do you expect him to know you exist if you never talk to him?"

"I'd get my friend to talk to him for me." She mocks me by shooting me a smug grin. Before I can reply, Madame Miller calls our attention.

I sit next to Brody in Ms. Cooper's English class. It's Brody's favorite and not because of Ms. Cooper. It's his favorite because he actually likes to read. In the past, he's brought copies of Shakespeare to practices to read while waiting for his turn in the batting cage. I asked him if I somehow didn't hear Ms. Cooper assign some reading, a nervous sweat forming on my brow. He chuckled and shook his head. "I'm just reading it for me."

I look over at Brody while Ms. Cooper talks in front of the class. Now that Camilla has told me about her crush, I can see Brody in a different light. His t-shirt fits him really well. Like, *really* well. His blonde hair is clipped close on the sides of his head and it looks sharp. There's something sort of enticing about his eyes too. How have I never noticed this before?

I actually know the answer to that. I've never wanted to notice it before. It would make everything so... complicated. It's easier to just ignore it for now.

Brody gives me a sideways glance and a confused look. I realize I've been staring for a little too long and, embarrassed, face the front of the room again. Ms. Cooper is wrapping up her thoughts on her spring break trip. "So, after the reflection that I did last night, I realized that what was so great about my volunteer trip to Peru was that it opened up my eyes to the privilege that we have and don't even notice. I had no idea how hard life was in other countries and that makes me more grateful for living in a house with air conditioning and clean, running water. Those aren't guaranteed in other countries like they are here, you know?

"Okay, enough about that. I just wanted to share some final thoughts on my service trip. For our next unit, we're going to read *The Great Gatsby*."

I sit up with interest, as does Brody. I'm familiar with this book, by which I mean I've seen the movie. *The Great Gatsby* sounds less painful than staying up late at night trying to make sense of last semester's *The Scarlet Letter*.

Ms. Cooper continues, "I didn't choose this book for us to read. It's on the school board's list of books that juniors are supposed to read in English class, and since we started the semester by reading *Breakfast of Champions*, now we have to read this."

I pick up on Ms. Cooper's subtle tone of frustration buried underneath her bubbly outward performance and I wonder if anyone else does too. Brody and I exchange a look and I know he caught it. I look around the room to see if anyone else is reacting. No one has. Now I look for the hundredth time at the posters and pictures Ms. Cooper has plastered haphazardly to her walls. Pictures of her on volunteer trips all over the country (and now the world), a photo of her with her parents on her desk, and some of the cliche, generic school posters they must hand out to everyone who graduates college with a teaching degree. *The difference between ordinary and extraordinary is that little extra… Diversity creates dimension in our world... No two people think alike. Study your way...*

There's a rainbow flag on her desk. I gaze at it for a few seconds, unsure how to feel about it. Was it there for me? It didn't feel like it.

My thoughts get interrupted when Ms. Cooper calls on Brody, who has enthusiastically raised his hand. "I have my own copy," he says. "Can I use that?"

I'm a little confused and then I notice the blonde girl in front of me (I think her name is Kelly) is handing me a stack of Gatsbies. I take the one on top and pass the rest of the stack to the girl behind me (Bridgette, I think; I know she's friends with Kelly. I always get them mixed up).

"That's fine with me," Ms. Cooper says. "Just bring it to class because we're going to be reading through some of it together."

I look over at Brody again. He carefully pens a note to himself in his neat and orderly notebook before carefully sliding it into his backpack. It sits next to mine, which is a disorganized and jumbled mess of papers, books, and pencils. I wonder how closely Brody's mind resembles his backpack, methodical and calculating; pure order producing pure genius, or maybe it's the other way around. Nothing makes me want to get my act together like observing Brody in his natural environment. Clean and organized, he saves time on decluttering his mind so he can think more clearly. Even now I can see his eyes are lost in a moment of intense thought before fixating back on the front of the classroom.

I return my gaze to Ms. Cooper before Brody notices that I'm staring again.

I have Ms. Cooper again for fourth period—creative writing. Brody tells me goodbye as he heads out to his German class and passes Logan in the doorway. "Hey, Brody," Logan says with a smile that's too big for comfort. "Congrats on the win yesterday," he adds as he and Brody try to squeeze through the door at the same time.

"Thanks, Logan," Brody says. "I'll catch you later." He slips through the door and Logan walks into the room with a grin.

"Hi, Ms. Cooper," he says before standing to hug Kelly and Bridgette. They squeal like they haven't seen each other in years even though they're all in the same first period class as me. After the mini reunion, Logan sits down at the desk next to me, where Brody was sitting just a minute ago. "Morning," he says to me.

"Is it?" I retort. When I don't want to talk to someone, I just say weird things to stifle the conversation. Sometimes people give up. Sometimes they don't.

"It is!"

"How do you know?"

"Because it's only eleven."

"Well it's 10 p.m. in Mumbai right now, and to that I say good night!"

That shuts him up. I lean back in my seat with my smug grin as Ms. Cooper summarizes her final thoughts on her trip to Peru for a second time.

"Okay, now to get started with our next unit," she says. "So far we've written some poetry and some short essays, but our next unit is going to be about short stories. We'll go over story structure, plotting, and how to introduce and develop characters. To end the unit, you're all going to write a short story. You'll have to turn in two rough drafts before the final draft and we'll do some peer reviews and edits with each of the rough drafts."

Kelly raises her hand in front of me. No wait, I think *she's* Bridgette and Kelly is the name of the girl behind me. Anyways, Kelly asks,"How long does it have to be?"

"However long you think it should be…"

Ms. Cooper's answer is met with confused silence.

"Two thousand words minimum. Ten thousand words max."

"Thank you."

It's the final push for the end of the school year and the assignments are starting to pile up. I already need to read *The Great Gatsby* and write a story of my own. How am I supposed to enjoy the end of my junior year with all of these annoying distractions?

I find Brody in the hallway on my way to lunch. We move with the crowd as it flows towards the cafeteria and as we're about to turn the corner and join the rest of the team at our table, a loud metallic crash echoes from a small corridor across the hall. "What was that?" Brody asks.

I shrug, hoping he'll forget it, but Brody can't resist his sense of curiosity sometimes. If I'm being honest, he likes being the hero too. I know as well as he does that what we heard was probably someone getting shoved against a wall of lockers.

Brody breaks away from the stream of students heading for lunch and I follow. We go down the narrow hallway, passing the history classrooms and a small bathroom, then round a corner to find three lacrosse players have got Logan cornered and are closing in on him.

"HEY!!" Brody roars. "The hell do you think you're doing?"

"Get lost, Hernandez," one of them shouts back, turning his back on us. Gavin Murphy. The best lacrosse player and the biggest douche in our school. His two henchmen scowl at us then go back to holding Logan against the wall.

"Fuck you, Murphy!" I shout. I don't know why guys who hate each other always refer to one another by their last names. "I heard your girlfriend dumped you the same day you were gonna ask her to prom! Hoping to take Logan instead?"

"Fuck you, Milligan!"

"Fuck Milligan? Fuck you, Murphy!" Brody chimes in. "I hear you had your heart set on being prom king! Can't be the belle of the ball without a beau, can we?"

"Fuck you, Hernandez!" Murphy and his teammates shout in unison.

"Fuck Hernandez? Fuck you, Murphy and your lacrosse lackeys whose names escape me at the moment! I find your temper to be quite incorrigible!"

"Incorrigible indeed!" Brody shouts, picking up where I left off and donning a hint of a bad British accent. "And I would be well-advised not to mention your dreadfully diminishing bench press performance!"

"Or your team's lamentable losing streak!" I shout, copying Brody's accent.

"Oh, come now, Derek, this situation doesn't need exacerbating!"

"No, I hear Gavin does that three times a day!"

"Fuck you, Milligan! Fuck you, Hernandez!"

"FUCK YOU, MURPHY!!" We shout in unison.

The history teacher whose classroom we were yelling outside of walks into the hall. "What's going on out here?" She's a short, thin woman standing with her legs shoulder width apart and her hands on her hips.

Next thing I know, we're all in the front office waiting for the principal.

We occupy six chairs lined up against the wall, all facing out the windows and towards the hallway outside. The occasional student or teacher walks by and gives us a curious look, wondering how half a dozen students and a teacher could have wound up in the office all at once. The young secretary speaks with the history teacher and then gets on her phone to call Principal Sampson. Five minutes later, a short black woman emerges from down the narrow hallway behind the front desk. Principal Sampson has always been articulate with her body language. She leans back on the secretary's desk and crosses her arms.

"So... what happened?" she asks the teacher, clearly disappointed in her students.

"I was eating lunch and doing some grading in my classroom when I heard a bang followed by a lot of yelling and swearing from out in the hall. I went out to investigate and I see *those* three have *that* one cornered," she points at Gavin, his teammates, then Logan, "and are engaged in a shouting match with *those* two," she finishes, pointing at me and Brody.

"In our defense," I explain, "we just wanted to practice our British accents."

"They were bullying Logan. We had to help." Brody adds.

"So we made fun of him for getting dumped and dissed his bench," I say.

"They're telling the truth," Logan says, his tone sounding a little bored, like this kind of thing happens to him all the time.

Principal Sampson gives a nod. "You three," she says, indicating Gavin and his buddies. "In my office. *You* three," meaning Brody, Logan, and me. "Go to lunch."

We stand from our seats and before we leave the office, I give a wave to the secretary. "Bye… Linda!" I have to stand on my toes to catch a glimpse of her nametag. "Have a great day!"

She looks confused as to why I'm wishing her a good day, but gives me a polite smile as we leave.

Brody and I proudly march next to each other on our way to the cafeteria, only a few minutes late to lunch. I didn't want him to drag me into the confrontation just a few minutes ago, but now I can't deny the warmth in my chest. My face forces itself into a grin against my will. "Well that was a fine performance, if I do say so myself," I announce to an empty hallway, bringing back the British accent.

"I concur, good sir," Brody replies.

We bump fists when a small voice speaks up from behind us.

"Um… thanks."

We spin to find that Logan has been following us the entire time. He's speaking to us, but his eyes are pointed more at our knees. "That was really nice what you did back there and I'm really grateful."

Brody and I give each other a surprised look, then look back at Logan. "Don't mention it," Brody says before turning around and walking back to the cafeteria to join the team. I follow shortly behind, throwing Logan a glance over my shoulder. He rubs his eyes and gives a quiet sniffle before raising his chin and walking to lunch himself.

After lunch, Brody and I go to the weightroom. Coach Cole gives all the players permission slips to go to lift weights during study hall, and none of us can really complain about it. The weightroom is the size of two classrooms and has half a dozen squat racks and deadlift platforms. The wall in front of the squat racks is lined with mirrors and there's a light dusting of chalk covering almost all of the equipment. Brody and I drop our backpacks next to a squat rack and stack a plate on each side of the bar for our warm-up set. Brody fishes a pair of gym shorts out of his backpack before dropping his light grey sweatpants to the floor. While they lie around his ankles, he stupidly gives a quick glance around the room.

"Probably should have checked to make sure there weren't any girls here first," he laughs. The male athletes often treat the weightroom like an extension of the locker room across the hall, but Coach Cole will yell at us when we take our pants or shirts off in front of the rare girl who decides to do squats in the rack at the far end of the room. "She didn't come here to see that!"

Luckily for Brody, it's just us and a couple other guys who have study hall this period. As I get ready for my first set, I can't help but glance at Brody in the mirror. He's wearing red boxer briefs that are pulled tight across his thighs. His quads look so muscular and sinewy. I hope mine look like that.

That wasn't what you thought it was. I was just doing a size comparison. I need to know how I rank with the rest of the team.

I turn my attention to my own reflection to make sure I'm centered on the bar, then glance down at Brody again as he slips his shorts over himself. That's the end of that.

After our warm-up sets, I remember what I told Camilla I'd do for her. I breathe a heavy sigh to myself and then turn to Brody.

I can't stand taking anything seriously. Whenever I have to do something I don't want to do, I try to get it done in the most ridiculous way possible.

"Hey, so you won't believe this," I begin to tell Brody. "I heard that Blake's cousin's best friend sits next to Camilla in chemistry and that two weeks before this upcoming Thursday she saw Camilla writing 'Mrs. Camilla Hernandez' in her notebook in class. I think she's into you, you should go talk to her."

Brody shook his head as he tried to untie the knot of connections I had woven in my story. "Wait... what?"

"Camilla likes you, go talk to her."

"Doesn't Blake's family live in Jamaica?"

Whoops. I forgot that detail. "Well... you don't know. His cousin might have a best friend in Oak Ridge."

Brody tried to hide a shy smile. It was... really cute, actually. I guess I could see what Camilla saw in him. "Okay, okay, Camilla told you to tell me. I'll think about it," he laughed.

Okay. He said he'd think about it. That's not exactly a yes. It's not a no either. At least I did what Camilla wanted.

Relief fills my chest and I smile as Brody gets ready for his next set, but for some reason it doesn't sit right. It's a lopsided satisfaction and even though I can't quite put my finger on it, I know something is out of place.

CHAPTER 3

The day ends with chemistry, which is taught by Mr. Holtz. Of course, the baseball team knows Mr. Holtz better as Kev, our announcer for all of our home and away games. None of us have a problem calling him Mr. Holtz in the classroom, but our real trouble is remembering to call him Kev on the ball-field. He's very adamant about it. I think he thinks it makes him a cool teacher. It does... kind of... it's also a little weird. Plus sometimes the lines get a little blurred. If you ask him a question about chemistry in passing before a game starts, he'll insist that you call him Mr. Holtz, but if you swing by his office to tell him what you want your walk-up song to be, he'll ask you to call him Kev.

Chemistry with Mr. Holtz almost passes without incident, but five minutes before the bell rings to end the school day, Logan and Bridgette walk in and Mr. Holtz says they have an announcement. It's kind of weird seeing Logan act so cheery only a couple hours after theismorning's incident. He makes eye contact with me for a split second before desperately averting his gaze to look at someone else.

"Hey, everyone. You know me. I'm Logan Burnett, class president." He just has to brag about it, doesn't he? "We're here to let you all know that the prom decorating committee's first meeting is this week. If you want to join, feel free to show up. We still haven't chosen a theme for this year's prom, so we're going to brainstorm some ideas and then let the juniors and seniors vote on which they like the best."

"If you want to come, we'll meet in Ms. Cooper's room this Friday after school," Bridgette adds. No wait. *She* was Kelly.

Before Logan and Kelly leave to go to the next classroom, Logan says, "It's gonna be a lot of fun and it looks good on a college application, so feel free to join if you're interested!"

I can't help but scoff.

"How could that look good on a college application?" I ask at practice, letting out another loud scoff. I have my sunglasses on so I don't have to squint on this bright afternoon. It's late March, but in Oak Ridge, that means clear skies and plenty of sunshine. It doesn't take much to work up a sweat.

The red dirt on the diamond seems to lightly powder everything on the field, from bat bags to leather gloves, to the old batting cage that now finds itself covering home plate. The netting is torn and fraying, and right now Parker Rodriguez, our first baseman, is taking swings underneath it. Coach Grady, who's also the algebra teacher, is pitching to us from behind an L-screen while us infielders are lined up outside the dugout.

Our shortstop Randy Fischer, Brody, and I are all leaning against the dugout railing while our catcher, a black senior named Austin Golfe, takes practice swings.

Coach Cole is sitting behind home plate in a purple camping chair, watching every one of Parker's swings intensely, but he overhears me and says, "You might be surprised, Derek. Colleges like to see involvement. It shows initiative and leadership."

I think he's joking but he has his standard, slightly grumpy face on, meaning he's focusing on something hard. A couple more *cracks!* of Parker hitting Coach Grady's pitches go by, and I say, "Coach, it's picking a theme and painting banners."

"I hear they already have a theme picked, they just pretend to let people vote so it looks like we have a say," Randy says.

"I'd buy it," Brody joins in. "Especially with Ms. Cooper running it."

I look at him with some surprise. "I thought you liked her."

He gives a subtle shake of his head, all without taking his eyes off of Parker. "I like English. I like reading. Not *her*."

Austin steps up to home plate and Brody begins his practice swings. I begin to think the conversation is over when Coach Cole chimes in again. "What makes you two think that you're above decorating for prom?" His tone is a little combative and I'm taken aback.

"Coach. The banners they paint get thrown away the day after prom."

"Maybe the same night," Brody adds, backing me up. "Besides, only weird artsy people are gonna be on that committee anyways."

"I think you should do it," he says, watching Austin hit a grounder to second base.

I shake my head in confusion. "Why?"

He shrugs. "It'd look good on a college app. You need some more rounding out."

"Coach, you don't think I'm gonna get a scholarship?" I ask playfully.

He turns his head, stares straight at me, then turns his head back to watch Austin. "You're going to do it."

I notice that this time it isn't a suggestion.

"Coach, we have practice after school." I can't help but chuckle when I say it, hoping Coach Cole picked up a sense of humor in the last five minutes.

"I bet the committee doesn't meet for that long, you can join practice a little late. You should go to the planning committee instead."

"Coach, you can't be serious."

"I am. I'll ask Ms. Cooper too to make sure you actually showed up."

My gut sinks. Now I've done it. Running my mouth got me in trouble. Not the first time. Definitely won't be the last.

Brody flashes me an evil smile and laughs. "Ha ha! Loser!"

"You're going too, Brody," Coach adds.

"*What?* But my GPA is *fine!*"

Coach shrugs again. "I know, but I just like telling you what to do."

Parker gets back to the dugout and notices something's wrong. "What's going on?"

Brody and I both shoot him glares.

"Nevermind," he says, raising his hands in surrender. "I don't want to know."

I know what you're thinking, and no. I'm not taking a guy to prom. I don't have any plans on coming out in high school and that means going to a school dance with a guy is out of the question. Like I said, it isn't anyone's business. So if you think you know where this whole thing is going and how it ends, I can promise you you're wrong. I'm letting you know now.

Three days later, Brody and I find ourselves sitting next to each other in Ms. Cooper's room when we would both prefer to be on the baseball field. We arrive early and Ms. Cooper asks us to help rearrange the desks into a circle, guessing that about twenty people will show up. Now that we both sit side-by-side, staring at the door, we count a grand total of seven: Logan, Kelly or Bridgette, the other one, Ms. Cooper, a girl who I recognize from my art class in freshman year, and ourselves. Our circle is way too big for the job at hand and Brody and I can't help but laugh quietly with each other.

"Thanks for coming, everyone!" Ms. Cooper says, sitting down at one of the desks in the circle. I have to admit that I do like it when teachers do that instead of sitting behind their desks at the front of the room. It makes it feel like they want us to be their peers. That said, I'm a little suspicious now. Either she's going to ask us for a huge favor and she's prepping us by pretending she's our friend, or she honestly wants us to be her peers. It's that second option that scares me the most. How can you trust anyone who's honest?

"Attendance is a little lower than we were expecting,

but that's okay!" she continues. "Logan, you're running the show here. I'm just the faculty sponsor, so do you want to explain what's going on?"

Logan flashes a borad smile. "Yeah! So, prom is going to be in the gym like always. Tickets are going on sale next Monday, but we need a theme first."

Oak Ridge is a pretty small school, so prom doesn't need much planning outside of picking a theme and making some decorations for it. Still, the pressure's already on to prepare for the night. Guys started asking girls to prom in February once the date was announced. Anyone who currently doesn't have a date still has time to ask a girl and line up a tux rental. Now that I think about it, you could probably be completely unprepared for prom until the day before and still go, as long as you bought a ticket on Friday afternoon and found a tux by Saturday night. You'd also have to find a date in under thirty-six hours, but plenty of girls go to prom in groups. Anyone of them would leave their friends in a heartbeat if it meant having a boy to herself.

I chuckle to myself as Logan talks about choosing a theme. "What we need to do today is brainstorm some theme ideas. Once we have four good ones, we'll make a little flyer that people can vote on and then hold an election next week. Whichever one wins will be the theme we go with.

"So, without further ado, let's get to brainstorming! Who has a good theme idea?"

I raise my hand. "Space. Something with space. And lasers."

Brody joins in. "Out of this world! That can be the theme!"

"We can have an area where people fight with

lightsabers!"

"And we can make a little flying saucer for people to take pictures in!"

We start laughing with each other. No one else is. Once our laughter dies down, I turn my head to face Logan, who's giving us an unimpressed look. He takes this so seriously.

"Well, write it down," I say indignantly.

He writes something down, but I don't think it's our theme idea. I'm also pretty sure he doesn't write down our ideas about an Indiana Jones theme or a powerlifting theme. There's a brief silence after that, then Kelly raises her hand.

"Go ahead," Ms. Cooper says.

"What about under the sea?"

"Classic, love it," says Logan, who immediately jots down a note. "Gabby?" he asks, pointing to the girl from my freshman art class.

"Midnight in Paris."

"Masquerade ball!" Bridgette calls out with excitement. Logan takes special note of that one.

"I have an idea," Logan says. "I want to make sure that prom is inclusive and accepting for all of Oak Ridges's students, so what about a pride-themed prom?"

"I love that idea!" Ms. Cooper exclaims. Kelly and Bridgette join in her adoration.

It doesn't sit super well with me. Gay pride in general rubs me the wrong way. It seems so... brash.

I'm afraid to speak up, but I do feel the need to make a point. "Doesn't that kind of imply that it's only for gay students?" I ask. "People might get confused and think that there are going to be two proms or something."

Logan pauses for a second and smirks. "No, I think people will understand."

But Ms. Cooper has something to say. "I think Derek makes a good point. Is there a way we can tweak the theme so that it's still inclusive but doesn't give the impression that it's *only* for the LGBTQ+ students?"

There's a brief silence as Brody and I watch all the minds in the room think...

"Over the rainbow!" Gabby shouts at last. "It can be sort of like *The Wizard of Oz*, but there's still the pride flag incorporated into it."

Logan is overjoyed. "Yes! That's *perfect!* I'll write that down right now." He scribbles on his sheet of paper and then holds it up to read. "Okay, so the four themes that people will vote on will be under the sea, midnight in Paris, masquerade ball, and over the rainbow."

"What about space?" Brody asks, using a playful tone of sarcasm to hide his true frustration. We're more alike than I realized.

"No space," Logan says flatly.

Brody and I look at each other. Well then. That's that.

Ms. Cooper grins and walks over to her computer, her fingers flying over the keyboard and clacking away. "I'll make a small flyer now and print off a bunch on Monday morning."

"So..." I begin. "Can we... go...?"

"There's no way over the rainbow wins," Brody says as we walk to our cars. "Smart money's on Paris. Girls love Paris."

"I think masquerade takes it," I say.

"Sucks that Coach made us do this. The C-man did us dirty."

"Why'd he do that anyways?" I ask. "It was so out-of-the-blue. Did he just not like the fact that I was making fun of it?"

Brody shrugs. "He just likes making people do things just because he can. I like the guy, but sometimes he has petty power trips."

Brody opens his car's rear door and tosses his backpack on the backseat. I drop mine in the bed of my truck and then look over at the baseball field. "No one's over there right now," I note.

Brody glances towards the field, then at me. There's a game tomorrow morning so Coach Cole and Coach Grady probably held a short practice while we were in the prom decorating meeting.

"I bet the equipment shed isn't locked. Wanna do a quick batting practice?" There's an obvious enthusiasm in my voice as I beam at Brody.

"Yes!"

We grab our bats out of our cars and hurry over to the field. Sure enough, the equipment shed is open and we pull out a bucket of balls. I sit on the bucket opposite home plate from Brody. He hits the balls as I toss them over the plate and we watch them go sailing into the outfield with a beautiful arc. Every ball lands in vibrant green grass with a barely audible thud. I watch his technique with each swing.

"That one was good… drive through a bit more… you swung a little late… that one was good…"

With every swing Brody twists his back foot and throws little plumes of dry, red dirt into the air around my knees.

"Boom!" Brody yells as his last swing sends the ball into center field. It taps the fence on its way down, only a few feet short of a homerun. "That seems like a good note to end on. Your turn!"

He hands me the bat and I pass him the bucket. He bats with his right hand but I bat with my left, even though I'm right handed. When I was learning in little league I just wanted to be different from everyone else. I sometimes go out of my way to be cheeky.

Brody tosses the pitches from across home plate and I swing at them ferociously, correcting my stance and technique with his feedback. He throws the last ball in the air and I nail with the bat, a beautiful metallic *ding!* echoes throughout the diamond as we watch the ball go sailing further and further until... Yes! Over the right field fence! Brody jumps up with excitement and I let out a triumphant howl.

I hate doing homework on Saturdays. I hate doing anything on Saturdays that's not baseball, but during the week, I'm so busy with practice and other assignments that I know if I don't work on my short story today, I won't get it done at all.

Why did I even bother signing up for creative writing? I should've taken German with Brody. Sure, taking two foreign languages at the same time might be a little confusing, but at least I could've spent more time with Brody than with Ms. Cooper. She was happy, though. She's written notes on my assignments complimenting my word choice and vivid imagery. She once told me after class that she thinks I'm one of her best students. I really wasn't expecting to hear that. Of course, she probably wasn't expecting creative talent from me, a baseball player who googles summaries for half of the reading assignments in her English class. But she said she was impressed with what she'd seen so far. "I think you're genuinely really talented," she said, her eyes glistening as she smiled. "I can't wait to see what you write next for this class." The compliment came out of nowhere. I thanked her, and I knew for the rest of the semester that I'd have to do my best. She was expecting it and she wouldn't accept anything less.

I tear a piece of paper out of my notebook and drop it onto my desk next to a pencil. I stare out the window at my front yard, hoping a story idea might hit me out of the blue... Is this what writer's block feels like? What is it Ms. Cooper says to do when this happens? "Write honestly, write bravely, and write truthfully."

Should I write about...?

No. That's a dumb idea. First of all, that's a pretty short story.

SHORT STORY

By Derek Milligan

I'm gay.

THE END

Ms. Cooper would probably give me an A for it. Still I'm not going to use it for an easy grade. That's a cheap trick and it feels disrespectful. To whom, I'm not sure. Myself, I guess.

I don't have a date to prom. I could write about that. Maybe I could write about a baseball player who doesn't have a date to prom. Okay... this has potential. Why doesn't he have a date? Because... his best friend asked out his crush!

All right, all right. This is a stroke of genius. I remember the basic plot outline that Ms. Cooper explained in class. Introduction, inciting incident, three attempts to resolve the issue, a final climax. I jot down notes and ideas for each plot point and before I know it, I have the structure of a short story.

I flip open my laptop on my desk, and while I'm on a roll, playing with creative fire, I begin to type up my story. My fingers fly over the keyboard with fervent inspiration, beautiful word choice and striking imagery burst forth in my mind like a lightning strike. I type it all down as fast as I can before the moment parts, before this creative spring comes crashing to a halt. With deep characters who feel as real as I am and the best plot I've ever written, I can tell Ms. Cooper is going to be impressed. I really outdid myself. This is going to be gold.

A couple hours later, I'm pulling on my uniform and getting all of my gear together. Bat bag? Check. Sunglasses? Check. Truck keys? Um...

They aren't on my desk. I find the shorts I wore yesterday and check the pockets. Not there either. After I get done checking all the pockets of my backpack and bat bag, I walk downstairs to find my parents hunched over a book, both wearing strained expressions and mouthing words I can't hear. "Are you two all right?" I ask.

They turn their heads towards me with a bit of a jump. "Morning, Derek!" My mom says. "About to go to your game?"

"Yeah, I just can't find the keys to the truck. What are you two doing?"

"Your mom has a book of crossword puzzles and she

got stuck. Then she asked me for help and now I'm invested in this too. By the way, would you happen to know a seven-letter word for disguise?"

"I would not. Would you happen to know where I put my keys?"

"I would not."

My mom looks up from the book, brushes her hair out of the brown eyes that she passed down to me, then she gives the kitchen one sweep of her gaze. "Did you leave them by the sink?"

My eyes dart to the sink to see my keys curiously sitting on the counter by the dishes that had been washed and left on the drying mat. Why on earth had I put them there?

My mom gives me a proud, slightly smug smile. "We need to get a key bowl," she says, returning her attention to the book of crossword puzzles.

I quickly throw together a peanut butter and jelly sandwich and toss it in a plastic bag. "Okay, I'm gonna go then," I announce when I'm done.

"We'll see you there," my dad says, not lifting his eyes from the page. "We might be late if we spend too much time on this crossword, though."

I chuckle to myself and head out the door.

Once at the baseball field, I drop my bag into the dugout before doing some warm-up stretches. The sun is already heating up the diamond for this morning's game as more and more of the Oak Ridge Trojans pull into the parking lot and begin their pre-game rituals with me. Blake is in the bullpen with Austin, whispering prayers to a cross on a gold chain between pitches. Ryan Tanaka, our left fielder, appears to be meditating in the dugout. Brody is doing cartwheels on the sideline and I'm leaning against the dugout railing, watching Brody spin while I eat my peanut butter and jelly sandwich.

The bus from the visiting team pulls up to the field. The Denton Dragons. They would be about as intimidating as they sound if their bus wasn't painted purple. The players hurry into the visiting dugout and begin their own warm-up and pre-game rituals. As I'm about halfway through my sandwich and Brody is about halfway through his obligatory cartwheels, a tall player from the Dragons jogs up to me. He's got a thick red beard, a wide frame, and a small, round button nose. I stop paying attention to my sandwich when I realize he's talking to me.

"Do you guys have any extra athletic tape?" he asks politely.

I stop chewing and look at his beard. I swear I can make out a chiseled jawline beneath that red scruff. I feel myself heat up and turn red as I meet his green eyes.

"...Yes!" I shout at last. "Yes! Just one second." I stuff the rest of my sandwich into my mouth and run into the dugout. I kneel on the concrete floor that's sprinkled with dirt and begin digging through the team's small cardboard box filled with miscellaneous athletic gear. I shove sports wrap and muscle rollers from side to side of the beat up box until I find the last roll of red athletic tape lying at the very bottom of the box. I fish it out and take a deep breath to calm myself.

I stand up straight, puff out my chest a little, then walk back to the bearded player who is watching Brody do another cartwheel. I hand him the tape.

"Here you go." I've unintentionally dropped my voice a full octave to sound manlier. "Just bring the roll back when you're done."

He smiles at me and I feel butterflies in my stomach. "Thanks! I shouldn't need too much."

I stand by Brody finishing his cartwheels as the player goes back to the visitors' dugout. He hands the roll of tape to his coach, a burly man with a beer gut. The player gestures to me and the coach gives me a smile and a wave to say thank you. I return the gesture. I'm about to look away when the player unbuttons his jersey and turns his back to his coach so he can apply the tape to his shoulder.

My eyes go from his beard to his arms to his bare chest. His prominent pecs draw my attention immediately, before it's snatched away by his bicep as he raises his left arm to scratch his right cheek. Then he looks at me.

Fuck!

I immediately turn to Brody, who has just finished his twelfth cartwheel. "All done?"

"Yep! Those were some pretty good cartwheels if I do say so myself."

My heart is racing. I need to sit down for a minute to catch my breath. That kind of thing has never happened to me. I'm an athlete; I'm around hot guys all day, but I've never been completely enamored by one before. It's scary.

A car pulls into the parking lot by the diamond and Blake's parents get out. They're both wearing Trojans t-shirts and ball caps. They drop a pair of seat cushions on the bleachers behind home plate and begin watching Blake in the bullpen as more and more parents arrive. My parents sit next to Brody's and Blake's as Kev begins testing the microphone.

"Testing, testing, one, two, three. It's a beautiful day for baseball! This is Kev Holtz signing on as the commentator for this Trojans ballgame against the Denton Dragons."

Before we know it, Kev is playing a recording of the national anthem and it's time to play ball.

The top of the first is over in a heartbeat. The first batter strikes out looking. The second hits a grounder straight to me, which I promptly pick up and throw to Parker on first base. The third hits a fly ball to center field, where Josh catches it and ends the first half inning.

We hustle back to the dugout and I'm about to sit down when Coach Cole points at me. "Derek, you're batting first."

"*What?* I thought I was batting fourth like always."

Coach shakes his head. "Nope, you're batting now."

I throw on my helmet and squeeze my hands into my batting gloves. Brody tosses me my bat and says, "Break a leg!" as I climb out of the dugout.

I take a couple practice swings before I notice who's jogging from the Dragons' dugout to the pitcher's mound—it's the bearded player.

"Batting first for the Trojans, third baseman, Derek Milligan!" Kev calls over the speakers.

There is a modest cheer from the audience, my parents being the most audible. "Let's go Derek!" my mom shouts.

As I walk up to home plate, I'm immediately aware of every movement of my body. Do my hands look stupid the way I have them on the bat? Are my elbows flared out too much? My steps are too small. People are going to think I'm scared!

I square up at home plate and the catcher shuffles into place behind me.

I look the pitcher right in the eye. Even from sixty feet

away, his stare feels like a punch to the chest.

He gives the catcher a nod, then winds up the pitch, his left leg rising until his knee is level with his left elbow, then in the blink of an eye, he widens his stance, twists his body, and the fastest pitch I've ever seen comes flying at me, straight into the catcher's glove.

"Holy shit!" I whisper in disbelief. I had no idea a high schooler could pitch that fast.

The catcher laughs. "Yeah, he's pretty good."

I square up again and try to calm myself. There's no way he can keep up that velocity all day. He's gotta save it, which means slower pitches are gonna be coming my way soon.

Sure enough, the next pitch is a slower one. I swing and manage a glancing blow, but it flies towards first base and on the wrong side of the foul line.

Kev leans into his microphone and his voice blares through the speakers. "Foul ball, which means a second strike for Milligan."

"Thank you, Kev," I growl. The catcher gives another chuckle.

The pitcher looks at me, then his catcher, then back at me with an evil smile. The admiration I felt earlier is quickly turning into rage. I feel used and toyed with. Well if he wants to play hard ball, we'll play hard ball. I'll knock his next pitch straight to the fucking moon!

He winds it up, twists, and the pitch comes in and I swing!

"Swing and a miss, and that's one out for the Trojans."

"Fuck!"

Randy is up at bat next and as I walk back down into

the dugout, Brody has his helmet on to start his warm-up swings. "That fast ball was scary," he says to me.

"It's scarier from home plate," I tell him as he shuffles past me to get outside.

We end up losing to the Dragons, 5–2. In the bottom of the seventh, Ryan hit a double, which put Austin on third base, but then that bearded pitcher threw Brody a couple of his fast balls and he ended up striking out.

Both teams line up on the field after the final inning and begin bumping fists to congratulate each other for a good game. I'm last in the line of the Trojans, absent-mindedly knocking knuckles with the Dragons, first with the catcher, then the first baseman, then the left fielder, and I think I somehow missed him when I see the pitcher staring straight into me, the very last player in his team's line.

"Thanks for the tape," he says, handing me back the roll I gave him just a few hours earlier.

Something in my chest dances when our eyes meet. He's a talented pitcher, but it sucks that he's on the other team. God, I want him to like me. I'm not sure I've ever wanted anything more in my life, but I can't let him know that. My heart is doing backflips just standing this close to him. I dig deep and seize the brazen discipline to look bored.

"No problem," I say nonchalantly, bumping his fist. "Good game. You're really good."

"Thank you," he says, flashing me what looks like a genuine grin. "You guys played really well too."

We awkwardly stand next to each other for a few seconds and just as I'm about to mumble a goodbye, Coach Cole taps the pitcher on the shoulder. "Can I borrow you for a minute?"

He obliges and before he steps out of earshot for a mysterious conversation with *my* coach, he shoots me one last quick smile. "I'll see you around."

I nod and watch as Coach pats him on the back as they talk near home plate.

CHAPTER 4

My mind drifts back to that pitcher the next day. Over and over and over again. It starts getting annoying, really. I only keep thinking about him because I really admire his athletic ability. Honestly. He's a great pitcher. Part of me is actually excited to play Denton again because I know I'll get to see him. Get to see him pitch, I mean.

Who do I think I'm fooling? Besides myself.

I step out of the shower on Sunday morning and as I inspect my face in the mirror, I decide I need a shave. My facial hair is pretty wispy and it makes me jealous of people like Brody who can already grow a full beard. That pitcher can grow a full beard too. And it looked good. I wonder if I'll get there someday. I wonder how often he has to trim it. Could I somehow nonchalantly ask him that next time we play each other?

Dammit. I'm doing it again.

A quick shave leaves my face silky smooth, just the way I like it. I leave the bathroom and head downstairs to find my mom standing in the kitchen. She's wearing her gardening gloves, a straw hat, and her face is glistening with sweat. "Gardening?" I ask her with a playful tone of voice.

"Damn deer," she says. "They got into my lettuce

again. How am I supposed to make our family salads with home-grown ingredients if the deer keep eating my lettuce?"

"Have you considered a shotgun?"

"Yes," she says curtly as she pours herself a glass of water. "Your father won't let me."

"I don't trust her not to use it on me!" my dad calls from the living room.

My mom rolls her eyes but she can't hide her smile.

I really envy my parents' relationship. They're always joking with and making fun of each other. I guess that's where I get my sense of humor. I get nervous when I think about finding someone who could not only handle the constant barrage of humor, but join in with it too. Brody is good at it, which is one reason my parents love having him over so much, but he also isn't gay. I wonder what that Denton pitcher's sense of humor is like. Would he be awkward and just smile politely? Or would he play along? I bet he'd play along. I bet he's really funny once you get to know him.

Ugh. Again? Stop!

I try to distract myself with television for the rest of the day, lying to myself by pretending I'm not fantasizing that the redhead is sitting next to me on the couch. I keep picturing his smile. Were there dimples beneath that beard? It was a little hard to tell.

Shit.

I manage to block him from my mind after dinner and by the time I pull into the school parking lot the next morning, I'm lost in the minutia of my own life again. I'm ready for another boring Monday as I settle into my seat in calculus.

43

"Derek!"

I turn to face Camilla in the seat next to me. She's shaking and breaking out in a nervous sweat. I give her a look up and down. "Sup?"

"I need your help. *Bad!*" she whispers so Mrs. Garcia doesn't overhear. "I had no idea how to do the homework that was due today and I had to copy it from Logan."

"Okay."

"You get this stuff way better than I do. I need you to help me with the homework tonight. *Please!*"

I shrug my shoulders. "Okay."

"*Really?*"

"Sure."

She gives me a sideways glance. "I can't tell if you're being serious or not."

"Yes."

"*Derek!*"

"I'll swing by after practice," I say, waving her off so I can listen to Mrs. Garcia talk about integrating by parts.

"There's one more favor I need to ask you for," Camilla says on our way to French class.

I know what this one's about. I fight the urge to roll my eyes. I like Camilla, but sometimes she can nag.

"Brody still hasn't texted me or anything," she says. "Do you think you could talk to him again?"

"Sure."

"Really?"

"Mhmm."

Another pause where she gives me a discerning look.

"Derek, I still don't know if you're being serious."

"When have I ever been serious?"

After lunch, Brody and I change shirts and then walk across the hall to the weight room. He makes comment about how hard it was to hit the Denton pitcher's fastball and I get a little annoyed that Brody has brought him up. I just know he's going to keep popping up in my mind.

I remember Camilla while Brody and I are setting up the weights on the squat rack. I suppress a groan as I prepare for this one small annoying task, because, after all, Camilla is my friend.

"How are things going between you and Camilla?"

"Oh yeah, I still haven't texted her," he says, a sudden light of recollection coming to his eyes. He shrugs it off. "Not sure I really want to, honestly."

"Not your type?" I ask as I lift a plate onto the barbell for the next set of squats.

"She might be, might not be. Just not super interested." Brody stands in front of the bar.

I decide to give it one last try for Camilla. "I was thinking about asking her to prom," I say casually. "She said she wanted to go with a friend, and that her dad would pay for a limo. If you aren't interested, I guess I'll ask her."

I look over at Brody to see a glimmer of jealousy fly across his face. "Well, hang on a minute…" he begins. "Just because I haven't texted her yet doesn't mean I wasn't planning on going to prom."

"Well you better get on it because there aren't many girls who haven't been asked yet and Camilla won't be available forever." That's a lie. Camilla's my friend but Brody and I are her last two valid pathways to prom. If one of us doesn't ask her, she isn't going.

"I'll get on it," Brody says, waving a hand at me and starting his next set of squats.

After practice, I hurry home to shower and eat dinner before I get back in my truck and drive to Camilla's. Her dad answers the door and and greets me with a smile. "*Hola* Derek! Good to see you again!"

"Hi, Mr. Sarsoza!"

"Come in, please! Camilla is in the kitchen."

I walk through the small foyer to find Camilla hunched over the dinner table. She's only marginally less distressed than she was this morning, an impression that isn't aided by the sloppy chaos of math notes scattered around her. "Derek!" she shouts as she looks up from her mostly blank homework assignment. "I'm so happy you're here!"

"Happy to help." I drop my own math notes onto the table and leaf through my textbook to the problems that were assigned for tonight. Before I sit down to dive into the work, I glance around her home and the memories of this house come flooding back. On that couch was where Camilla and I would hang out with the other bored kids from the neighborhood during her parents' Christmas party, stuffed into dress clothes just so our parents could ignore us and drink. The coat rack by the door was where you had to count when you were "it" in hide-and-go-seek, counting all the way to one hundred. On that patio was where Camilla held her birthday parties every June since she moved to Oak

Ridge in second grade. Loads of children used to go when we were younger—parents made them show up because it was polite. But from the summer after freshman year attendance started to dwindle. Last year there had only been five people, including Camilla, and I was the only boy. I felt incredibly out of place, although when Camilla and her girl friends started talking about which boys at school were the cutest, I can't deny that I was taking mental notes.

I could never tell Camilla though, and I hope she never guesses. She would only feel betrayed that I had kept it from her for so long.

Over the next thirty minutes, I patiently and repeatedly walk Camilla through integration by parts. She has to repeat the formula to herself over and over again, and then a few more times as she's working through each problem. "The integral of U D-V equals U-V minus the integral of V D-U."

I have to jump in for each question because she keeps making small mistakes that I know will carry through the problem and give her a completely different answer than the one in the textbook. "This is a definite integral, you have to add the constant... It's *minus* the V D-U, not plus." Mrs. Garcia knows how to spot those little mistakes from a mile away, and knows when someone just copied their work from someone else.

When we've done about half of the homework, Camilla glances at her phone and sighs.

Oh boy, here we go, I think. "What's wrong?"

"Nothing," she says, exasperated.

"Okay, then let's get back to the math homewo-"

"It's just that Brody still hasn't texted me or anything."

"Then why don't you text him?"

"I can't do *that!*"

I give her a confused look. "Why not? You want to talk to him, don't you?"

She doesn't know how to respond to that.

"You're friends with him on facebook, aren't you? Just send him a message saying that you're stuck on the math homework and you want his help."

She picks up her phone, opens the messenger app, then types a quick text. I see her take a few deep breaths, reading and rereading and proofreading the message, making sure it's absolutely perfect. Finally, she holds her breath and taps the send button, then lets out a sigh of relief. "Okay, that wasn't so bad," she breathes.

We get back to the homework and a couple minutes later her phone lights up. "It's Brody!" she announces as she looks at it, her face lighting up with excitement. "He wants to know what problem! Number... seven....teen..." she says slowly as she types it.

As I watch Camilla beam at me and bounce in her seat with unbridled enthusiasm, I can't help but feel a weight lifted off my shoulders. My responsibility in the whole situation has been completely absolved and now I can get back to not worrying about Camilla's love life.

"What should I say to this?" Camilla asks, holding her phone up to me.

Okay, maybe I'm not quite off the hook yet. I read Brody's message.

Lol integration by
parts isn't exactly

my forte either

I stare at it again. Am I missing something? What's so tricky about responding to that? "Um… maybe tell him he's hot?"

"*Derek!* Can you please be serious for once?"

"No."

"Wait, he just sent another text. Oh, it's a picture of his work."

We look at the picture together. His work looks right to me.

"What should I say back?" she asks me.

I think there's no way Camilla can be this inept at talking to boys, although it would explain more than a little about her social life. "Camilla, I can't hold your hand through this entire process," I say. "You have to figure some of it out yourself."

"But I've never liked a boy this much before!" she exclaims. "What if I say something wrong and he's not interested in me anymore?"

"If you think his interest in you is that fragile, then you really don't stand a chance anyways," I say with a smile.

She stares at me for a moment. "Was that supposed to make me feel better?"

"Yeah."

She scoffs and looks at her phone again, the glow from the screen making her eyes look wider and her expression more desperate.

"Just tell him thank you," I say. I rack my brain trying to think of what she should say next, then I think of that red-headed pitcher from yesterday. What would *he* do to tease me if he ever got my number, and, of course, if he were actually interested in me. "No wait, say this... 'Thank you so much! I'll have to find a way to repay you.' No emojis."

"That's good," Camilla says as she types it out. "Okay, just sent it."

"Don't text him again for the rest of the night."

"But what if he texts me?"

I shake my head. "Don't respond, wait until the morning. If you text too much he's gonna think you're clingy."

She nods with understanding. "Okay, that makes sense."

She puts her phone down and we work through the last few homework problems of the night.

CHAPTER 5

I'm walking to calculus class the next morning when some-one calls my name. "Derek! Wait up!" I turn around in the hall to see Logan scurrying towards me, his backpack fly-ing around wildly as he runs. His two friends, Kelly and Bridgette, follow behind him at a much slower pace.

"What's up, Logan?" I ask when he finally reaches me.

"We're going to have another prom decorating meet-ing this afternoon," he says, out of breath. "The vote for themes is happening today in first period and so we have to count them after school."

"Oh, okay. I'll let Brody know."

We walk side-by-side, with the girls behind us and I suddenly feel like I've been unwittingly inducted into some sort of social group.

"Kelly, Bridgette," I say to break the awkward, linger-ing silence. "What do you have for first period?"

"*I'm* Kelly."

"And *I'm* Bridgette."

"And we have math with you in Mrs. Garcia's class."

"You *do?*" I ask, surprised.

"We sit right next to Logan, didn't you notice?"

I'm about to tell them no because I only see the back of their heads—if I can't tell them apart when I'm looking them in the face, then I don't stand a chance when they're on the other side of the room.

"Are you excited for prom?" Logan asks in his sort of bubbly way.

"I'm not going," I tell him.

"*What?* But it's *prom!*"

"Oh well in that case, let me buy a ticket!"

Logan gives a little laugh. "Why aren't you going? Can't find a date?"

I shake my head. "Actually I can't find a *tux!* All the tailors in town are booked up. Couldn't get one for your life."

"I bet you'd have a hard time finding one that fits an athletic body type," Logan says casually.

"Well, actually, yes. That is a constant struggle of mine. That's why I always wear shorts." There's another awkward silence and I ask Logan, "Who are you going with?"

"Us!" Bridgette announces from behind me. "The three of us are going together!"

"That'll be fun," I reply.

"Yeah, but if I find a date, I'm kicking you two to the curb," Logan says.

The girls fake shock and tease him until we get to Mrs. Garcia's classroom. I sit down in the seat in front of Brody and tell him, "The school is voting on prom themes today, which means that the prom committee is meeting after school to count the votes. That's all we have to do; it should be a quick meeting."

He gives me a nod and I almost thank him for his help with the math homework last night, then I remember that he isn't supposed to know that I was there. I don't want him to think that I'm pulling all of the strings, or any of them for that matter.

Mrs. Garcia starts speaking and I turn around to face her at the front of the room. "Hey, everyone. Before we get started with class today there's something we need to do quickly. Logan, would you like to tell everyone what this is?" Mrs. Garcia starts walking along the side of the room, passing quarter sheets of paper along the rows of desks.

Logan stands up from his seat and addresses the class. "We are trying to decide what the theme for this year's prom is going to be, so Mrs. Garcia is handing out ballots right now. This afternoon, the prom decorating committee is going to count the votes and we'll announce the theme tomorrow morning."

Mrs. Garcia hands Camilla a stack of ballots. She takes one and hands the rest to me. I look down at the small sheet of paper as I absentmindedly hand the rest to the girl on my right.

Prom Theme Election!

Please vote for your favorite theme

- ❑ Masquerade Ball
- ❑ Midnight in Paris
- ❑ Over the Rainbow
- ❑ Under the Sea

"Too bad space didn't make it on the ballot," I murmur to Brody.

"That's a good point. Can we do a write in?" he asks. He

looks at Logan and raises his hand. "Can we write in a theme if we don't like any of the themes here?"

"No." Logan's response is firm and contains a not-so-subtle note of frustration. "You have to vote for one of the four themes on the sheet."

"But I really like the idea of a space-themed prom."

A few of the guys in the class agree with Brody and begin pounding on their desks as they chant, "OUTER SPACE! OUTER SPACE! OUTER SPACE!"

"QUIET!" Mrs. Garcia shouts. She says nothing more, filling the room with an uncomfortable silence for Logan to deal with.

He clears his throat. "I don't make the rules."

"You actually do," I retort.

Logan's face turns red. "I'm the class president and the president of the prom decorating committee!"

"I rest my case."

"Derek," Mrs. Garcia interrupts, clearly annoyed. "Just check a box. Stop being a smart ass."

I look over my shoulder at Brody and he's also laughing. I look at the list of themes again.

These are all just awful, I think to myself. I'm not even sure why I'm allowed to vote in the first place considering I'm not even going. Over the Rainbow is out. I don't know if it's just because I don't like Logan or because I don't like the idea of making it seem like prom is only for the LGBTQ+ club, but I'm not voting for it. I cross it out.

Under the sea sounds like it would be awful to make decorations for, so I cross that one out too. That leaves Midnight in Paris and Masquerade Ball. I won't lie, Midnight in Paris could be a lot of fun, but knowing that a bunch of girls are going to go crazy for it makes me want to vote for it less—I just don't like doing what people want me to do. If I have no choice, I turn it into a joke.

Masquerade Ball it is! That could actually be a lot of fun, now that I think about it. An air of mystery around the entire night, I might not even have to bring a date. No one would know from a distance who I was, and only my friends would know it was me when they were up close. I don't know why the idea of hiding in plain sight is so appealing to me.

I check the top box on the sheet of paper and walk up to the front of the room, placing it on Mrs. Garcia's desk. I turn around and give Logan an innocent smile as I walk back to my desk. He does not look happy with me.

"Which one did you vote for?" Camilla asks Brody when the bell rings, ending first period.

"I wrote in outer space," he says. "Sue me. I want to take a lightsaber to prom. What about you?"

"Midnight in Paris," Camilla says with a breathy, dreamy voice. "Paris is so *beautiful*."

"You've been there?" Brody asks.

"No… but, I mean, I've seen pictures."

I try to suppress a laugh and Camilla shoots me a dirty look.

She and Brody say goodbye and then Camilla walks next to me down the hall to French class.

"Derek, can you do something for me?" she asks after a few moments of silence. "I overslept this morning and as I was rushing out the door, I forgot my phone. I didn't text Brody last night, like you said, but I want to send him something today. Could I log onto my Facebook messenger account on your phone to check if he sent me anything?"

I roll my eyes as we sit down in Madame Miller's room. I doubt Brody has said anything to her since last night, but I oblige and hand her my phone. She quickly types in her username and password and then reads. "He saw my last text and said, 'Sounds good to me.' That's good, right?"

"No, that means he hates you."

Camilla gasps. "Really?"

I stare at her for a moment. "Yes."

She suddenly realizes I'm being sarcastic again and she's about to berate me when Madame Miller starts speaking. "Phones away, *tout le monde!* We're going to practice verb conjugations today!"

Camilla quickly hands me back my phone and I drop it into my backpack.

Brody and I walk into Ms. Cooper's room at the same time after school. She's stacked all of the ballots into a cardboard box. "Grab a couple handfuls and start counting!" she says. "We've got two hundred and sixteen votes to count."

She designates different desks for each of the four themes, then Brody and I begin to walk around the room, placing the ballots on the corresponding desks. We're about a quarter of the way through when Gabby and Logan walk in. Kelly and Bridgette show up shortly after and a few minutes later, all of the ballots have been separated.

"Okay, now let's start counting," Logan says. "I'll take Over the Rainbow with Bridgette. Derek and Brody, you take Midnight in Paris. Gabby and Kelly, you take Masquerade Ball.

Ms. Cooper, it doesn't look like there are many in Under the Sea. You can count those."

We all begin counting and before long, everyone is ready to announce the counts for their themes.

"Ms. Cooper, how many for Under the Sea?"

"Nineteen, and one write-in for Outer Space."

"Forty-one for Masquerade Ball," Gabby says.

"Seventy-seven for Over the Rainbow," Bridgette adds.

Logan looks at Brody and me. He's leaning on his desk, bouncing in the seat as he awaits the good news. "Seventy-eight for Midnight in Paris," Brody says.

Logan's jaw hits the floor. His bubbly smile from a second ago is gone and his eyebrows start to turn upwards with heartache. I definitely didn't want Over the Rainbow to win, but now that I see how upset Logan is, I can't help but feel kinda sorry for him.

Gabby gasps with excitement, but I glance over at Logan and he forces a smile to hide his obvious disappointment. Really, he looks deflated.

"Sounds like the theme is going to be Midnight in Paris!" I shout, feigning excitement.

"I guess," Logan says. "I was really hoping Over the Rainbow would win, just because it's more inclusive."

"So was I," Ms. Cooper adds. Kelly and Bridgette agree, although I think it's probably just because Logan is their friend.

"Well, maybe you miscounted," Bridgette suggests.

"They didn't miscount," Ms. Cooper begins, "but I didn't vote. I *am* the faculty sponsor of this committee and I think I should get to vote."

Brody and I watch as everyone else in the room nods

along in agreement.

"I vote for Over the Rainbow," she says, "which means that we have a tie."

"Well if there's a tie," Logan says, "then we in this room should vote to break the tie."

Brody and I give each other a sideways glance.

"Wait, hold on a second," I jump in. "Where does it say that Ms. Cooper gets to vote? I thought only the students get to vote since it's *their* prom."

"Well there were plenty of people who voted for the theme today who aren't planning on going to prom," Logan says pointedly, as if trying to make everyone in the room know he was talking about me. "So I think it's only fair that Ms. Cooper gets to vote since she's the faculty sponsor."

"It's just *one* vote," Kelly adds, giving me a look as if to say get over it.

"Now that there's a tie, the seven of us have to vote between Midnight in Paris and Over the Rainbow." He gives a quick glance around the room, almost glaring at Kelly and Bridgette. "All in favor of Midnight in Paris…"

Brody and I raise our hands, as does Gabby, though her hand is low and I can tell she's embarrassed.

"All in favor of Over the Rainbow…"

Logan, Kelly, Bridgette, and Ms. Cooper raise their hands.

"Looks like the prom theme is Over the Rainbow!" Logan shouts. Kelly and Bridgette clap with excitement and Ms. Cooper grins and pounds her desk. I can hear her whisper, "*Yes!*"

"All right. I'll tell Principal Sampson so she can make the announcement tomorrow morning," Ms. Cooper says as she stands from her seat. "Thanks for your help, everyone! I'll see you all later!"

Brody and I walk from Ms. Cooper's room to our cars to grab our equipment for baseball practice. "They'll have their inclusive prom, but... I don't know," Brody says as we walk out the school's front doors.

I shrug. "I guess if that's how people voted."

"Well, it was... kinda," he corrects me. "But still... I don't know."

We deposit our backpacks into our respective vehicles and retrieve our gear, then hurry across the street.

When we get to the field, we see that the batting cage is up around home plate and the other infielders are taking warm-up swings. Brody and I rush over to join Parker, Randy, and Austin.

"Sorry, we were at the prom decorating committee," I say, then stop myself. "Whoa, that felt weird to say out loud. What's going on?"

"We're a little late getting started today." Randy says.

"Coach Grady is in the bullpen with the new guy," Parker adds.

"New guy? What new guy?"

Before either Randy or Parker can answer, Coach Cole calls to us and jogs over to home plate. "Derek, Brody, glad you two are here now. A new player just transferred here; he's gonna be a pitcher for us. I thought today we could kill two birds with one stone by getting some pitching practice for him and some batting practice for you. Oh, here he is. Guys, this is Alex." Coach gestures behind us to someone running over from the bullpen behind the dugout. We turn around and my eyes fall on a tall, bearded redhead with jade green eyes and a button nose.

My heart catches in my throat and my face swells with heat as I start to blush. It's the pitcher from Denton.

"Hi, everyone," he says with a smile. His eyes land on me and he does a double take. "Long time, no see."

"As you all probably remember," Coach continues, "Alex has a wicked fast ball and one hell of a changeup. Who wants to bat first?"

Parker starts off the practice's batting line-up and we watch the first fast ball fly by him. "Jesus," he breathes. "How the hell am I gonna get used to this?"

Don't ask me how, but he nails some hits on the last two pitches, although they were both foul balls. Randy's up next and he sends a couple of Alex's pitches flying into the outfield. It's Brody's turn and he struggles at first, then makes contact with a couple fast balls, but misses the last slider.

Now it's my turn. I can feel those fucking butterflies again as I walk up to the plate. I square up, dig my feet into the dirt, and lock eyes with Alex. I can feel him staring straight back at me. He winds up the first pitch... *thump!* It hits the padding on the back of the cage. I almost didn't even see it. I curse to myself. This is not going to go well.

Alex winds up the next pitch, then flings it at me. I see it coming and swing, but I know I'm way too early. "Fuck!" I shout.

The next four pitches are no better. I can't hit a single thing Alex throws my way. Coach tells me when it's Austin's turn, and I walk back to the others by the dugout, my tail between my legs. "I haven't had a practice this shitty since freshman year," I say. "And I'm including the time I showed up with stomach flu."

"Looks like you were swinging too early," Randy says.

"I know, but for the life of me, I couldn't *slow down*."

Everyone takes three turns at bat. I only manage to hit two of Alex's pitches the entire practice. This is not a good start to his time on the team. I was hoping to impress him in some small way. All those feelings I thought would be gone when the Dragons climbed back on their purple bus and drove home have all come flooding back to me. I want nothing more than for Alex to watch me do something great and think to himself, *Damn, that guy is based as fuck.*

As I sulk back into the dugout after practice, I remind myself that self pity isn't attractive. I stand up straight, breathe in deep, and force a smile on my face, even though it's the last thing I want to do right now. "I'll do better tomorrow," I tell Brody. "Today must have just been an off day for me."

Brody shrugs. "It happens. We've all been there."

I notice Alex is a little slower packing his things up. I decide to hang back and talk to him. Brody slings his bat bag over his shoulder and looks at me.

"I'll see you tomorrow," I say, purposefully taking longer to put my own bat and glove away so that I can get a moment with Alex.

"Okay," Brody says, without giving it a second thought. "See ya!"

Once he leaves, I turn to face Alex. He's looking down at his feet as he ties his tennis shoes, his cleats tucked away in his duffel bag. My shadow covers his shoes as he's tying them and he looks up at me. A glimmer of recognition shines in his eyes. "So, you just moved to Oak Ridge from Denton?" I ask.

"Yeah, we were all packed up on Saturday, but I still had the game. I officially registered for Oak Ridge this afternoon."

A light bulb goes off in my head as I remember his conversation with Coach after the game. "Cool. Why'd you move?"

"My dad works for American National Bank and they transferred him from Denton to here." He stood up, finally ready to go.

There's a moment when neither of us know what to say. His eyes fall on me and I'm afraid to look back until he says, "I didn't catch your name, by the way."

"Derek. Derek Milligan."

I see his open hand swing out towards me and instinctively I reach out and shake it. His grip is firm and I squeeze back, but it feels more like he's testing me. I can't help but meet his gaze and his eyes bore into me, even though it looks like he's giving me a casual glance.

"Nice to meet you. I'm Alex Clark."

We release each other from our grips and I get the feeling that Alex and I are going to be competitors on the same team. I can't help but give him a bit of a sideways glance as we start to walk back towards the student parking lot.

"So, what classes are you in?" I ask.

He lists some of them off. I tell him we'll have the same teacher for history, but at different times. The rest of our schedule sounds different than mine. He hasn't made it to calculus yet. At least I'm ahead of him academically.

At my truck, Alex says, "Well, it's nice to meet you. I guess I'll see you at practice tomorrow." As I wave goodbye, he sits down behind the wheel of a little red ten-year-old stick shift. It's a convertible, which is nice, but it also looks like if he put the roof down, it wouldn't come back up. The paint's clear coat is chipping off in a few places and the front bumper has seen better days. My truck isn't exactly brand new, but it isn't in such a sad state as Alex's tiny car. When he starts it, it sounds like a weed wacker.

I don't mean to judge other people by what they can afford, but I'd think the son of a banker would have a little bit of a nicer car. He didn't need a BMW while he was in high school, but maybe something that didn't look like it was gonna fall apart if it hit a speed bump too fast.

Alex shifts the car into reverse, and gives me a cheery grin as he speeds out of the parking lot. I watch him disappear down the road before I start up my truck.

That night I'm sitting in my room giving my short story a final proofread before I print it out for Ms. Cooper's class tomorrow. I feel really good about the plot and the characters and the word choice. I think Ms. Cooper is going to be really impressed. Still, I can't help but feel a little nervous as I read it through one more time. What if she doesn't like it? What if she thinks it isn't my best work or isn't personal or isn't honest? I guess this is a chance that every artist has to take.

I can't help but allow myself a small smile. *I'm right*, I think. *I am an artist.*

My phone vibrates and the buzz fills my room. I try to

ignore it, but my curiosity gets the better of me. I push myself away from my laptop and fish my phone out of my backpack.

It's a text from Brody.

**By the way, we counted
the votes and the Over
the Rainbow theme won.**

"Yeah… I know… I was there," I say to myself. I'm about to type it out when I realize the message wasn't meant for me. Camilla forgot to log herself out of messenger! Brody just sent that to her!

I breathe a sigh of relief. At least Brody is reaching out to Camilla without my prodding. I set my phone down then immediately wonder if Camilla knows how to respond to that. Considering she needed advice before responding to a thank you last night, I can't pretend I have great confidence in her.

I consider something I know I shouldn't do. I reach out for my phone… and stop.

No, I already helped Camilla. She has to learn to do some of it for herself.

I stare blankly at my computer screen… and begin to move my hand towards my phone again….

No. I should respect their privacy. I should log out of Camilla's account right now.

I should.

I open my phone, and hover my thumb over Camilla's profile picture in the corner…

And then I tap the response bar, and…

I'm sorry. I know I shouldn't have.

**Dang! I wanted Midnight
in Paris to win!**

That was so stupid! Why did I do that? Oh shit, Camilla is going to be so mad at me! Of all the stupid and wreckless things I've ever done in my life, this tops the list! I just jeopardized my friendship with Camilla, my friendship with Brody, and Camilla's chance with Brody! I start shaking my head so fast and hitting my fist against my temple so hard that I hardly notice when my phone lights up again.

I steal another glance at the luminescent screen...

**Yeah, I didn't vote for
Over the Rainbow either.
It was super close, though!
There was actually a tie
between the two themes
and we held a tie-breaker
vote in the room.**

Okay, quick, Derek. How would Camilla respond? She's learning this for the first time.

**NOOOO!!!
SO CLOSE!!**

**Lol, well I bet prom
will still be fun!**

No one really cares

**about the theme
anyways.**

**That's true. Everyone's
too busy dancing to care
about the decor haha**

Okay. That was my last one. I've had my fun for the night, I did a quick favor for Camilla. It's time to stop and put my phone away.

Hit with a sudden burst of inspiration, which I know is really a desire to be distracted from the texting conversation that's making me uncomfortable, I begin retyping a few sentences of my short story. I've revised about a paragraph and a half when my phone vibrates again. I ignore it. No reason that I can't just sit here and type. No reason I need to get involved in someone else's business more than I already have. No reason whatsoever.

None.

I stop writing. I need to think about how to wrap up my story. As I do, my eyes gravitate towards the stupid black brick on the edge of my desk, watching it vibrate again to remind me that I have an unread text message.

Brody's probably just saying goodbye, ending the conversation. That's all. I tap my phone screen.

**So what are you
up to tonight?**

Well that was unexpected. For some reason, Camilla still hasn't responded or sent me a text to ask what the hell

I'm doing. That means that she's probably busy. I think I
know what she's doing right now.

**Just working on
my math homework.**

**Nice. How is inte-
gration by parts going?**

**A lot better now
that you've helped!**

Great! Happy to help!

**Thank you so much :)
What are you
doing tonight?**

**I'm just doing some
reading for Ms. Cooper's
English class.
We're reading The Great
Gatsby.**

I've never read it.

**It's one of my favorites!
I read it for the first
time last summer.**

There's a lull in the conversation. I don't know how

Camilla would respond to that and I don't want to drag it on for too long. This whole thing feels wrong. Luckily, I get one more text from Brody.

Well, anyways. I'll let you get back to your math homework. Have a good night!

You too!

I lock my phone and throw it into my backpack. I try to block out of my mind what I've just done as I stare blankly at my laptop screen. I finally decide that my story can't get any better than it already is. I send it to the printer downstairs, retrieve it, and staple the pages together. When I return to my bedroom, I drop the short story into my backpack, then collapse onto my bed.

As I try to fall asleep, I can't help but think about what I've just done. I lied to my best friend by pretending to be my other friend, and... and... I shouldn't ever do that again because it was dishonest and I got involved in other people's business, and... and...

I can't lie to myself. It felt really good.

CHAPTER 6

Brody and Camilla can't stop smiling at each other in Mrs. Garcia's room the next morning. Brody keeps whispering jokes to Camilla who giggles, but doesn't really respond. I thought that might be an issue—if Camilla can't be as talkative as I am when pretending to be her via text, Brody might figure out something isn't right.

God, why did I think it was a good idea to text Brody last night?

A few minutes before the first period bell, Principal Sampson begins to speak over the intercom. "Good morning, Trojans! We have a couple announcements before we begin class today. First, don't forget that prom tickets are on sale now! You can purchase them in the front office at any time. Second, the prom decorating committee counted your votes for the prom theme yesterday. You all voted for the theme Over the Rainbow!"

Logan raises a celebratory fist over his head and Bridgette pats him on the back.

"This prom theme isn't just about the classic film *The Wizard of Oz*, but it's also about acceptance and inclusivity. On behalf of the prom decorating committee, I want to invite not only all heteronormative couples, but also same-sex, queer, and trasngender couples to Oak Ridge's first inclusive prom as well."

Brody and I glance at each other, and I notice a couple other students sharing confused looks.   "Since when were they *not* allowed?" someone asks her friend quietly from the back of the room.

"Well, I guess they were kind of ignored until now," her friend suggests.

When the announcements are done, Mrs. Garcia stands up from behind her desk. "Okay, let's go ahead and do some problems from last night's homework before you turn it in. Kelly, why don't you do number eight, and Camilla can do number twelve."

Brody's help with the math homework the other day paid off. Camilla quickly solves the problem on the board and sits down. Mrs. Garcia gives her a nod of approval as the class waits for Kelly to finish her problem and take a seat.

When the bell rings to end first period, I sneak out of the room as quickly and surreptitiously as possible—I know that when Camilla gets time alone with me, she's gonna chew me out for texting Brody. The longer I can put that off, the better. So I slip out the door when she and Brody are still talking and I casually walk to French class.

Once in Madame Miller's room, I take my seat, pull out my French notes, and pretend to study. I know this isn't going to fool Camilla for a second, but maybe it will stall her.

Out of the corner of my eye, I see Camilla enter the room, creep past me, and take her seat next to me. "Hey..." she leans towards me. "Can we talk super quick?"

"Sure," I say, my eyes lingering on my notes, pretending like I just want to remember one... last... word... "What's up?"

"Why did you text Brody last night?"

I give a shrug as if I were genuinely confused. "You said that you wanted my help with Brody. I was only trying to do what you asked."

"I meant I needed help *in that moment*," she clarified.

"Oh sorry, ha ha. Guess I went a little too far. I'll leave it to you now."

"No, wait, actually..." she leans in more. "Could you do that again?"

My heart drops into my gut and I narrow my eyes at her. "What?"

She lowers her voice to the point I can barely hear her. "Can you text Brody from my account again?"

I don't even know how to respond. If I say yes, I'll be lying to Brody more and Camilla might suspect I've got an ulterior motive. If I say no, I'll be abandoning Camilla when she needs me the most and... well...

I'm not going to pretend that I wasn't secretly hoping there would be another excuse to text Brody like that again.

I open my mouth to respond when Madame Miller says, "*Bonjour, tout le monde!* Go ahead and put your notes away for a vocab quiz!"

Camilla can't find an opportunity to talk to me during the first half of French—Madame Miller would think she's trying to cheat on the quiz. In the second half of class, she can't get a word in edgewise around Madame Miller talking about grammar using the subjunctive tense.

When the bell rings, I bolt out of the room and hurry to Ms. Cooper's English class before Camilla gets the chance to say anything. When Brody sits down next to me, I have to remind myself that he hasn't told me anything about him and Camilla, so I shouldn't ask how things are going. I should wait for him to bring it up.

"Hey, you wanna bench in the weight room today instead of squats?" he asks. "I hear we're playing a scrimmage game with the JV after school and I wanna look more intimidating."

I laugh, a little too loud. "*Yes!* Let's do that!"

He gives me a bit of an awkward smile. "Ooookay!"

Ms. Cooper begins talking about the last chapter we were assigned to read from *The Great Gatsby* and for once I feel relieved to be in her class.

After English, I wave goodbye to Brody and stretch my legs. I'm staying here for creative writing and I'm already getting restless with anxiety. We're about to do the in-class peer review of our short stories, and I had no idea it would be so nerve-racking. My legs are wobbly and I have butterflies again, just like when I was batting in front of Alex. Putting myself on the line creatively doesn't feel any better than doing it athletically. I wish someone I don't know would read my story. That way if they don't like it, I won't be shattering some grand illusion that an admirer might have of me.

Ms. Cooper begins to speak at the front of the room and I take my seat, still shaking a little bit as I glance around, guessing who would be the best person. God, is this what coming out feels like? I never want to do that.

"You're going to partner up and peer review each other's stories. You're not only going to keep an eye out for grammar and phrasing mistakes, but I want you to also think about story structure. How could your partner change certain aspects of his or her story to improve it?

"Okay, go ahead and pull out your first drafts, something to write with, and find a partner."

There's a moment of silence before the first person dares to creep out of her seat and look around the room for someone to partner with. At least I'm not the only person who's apprehensive.

"Don't be shy!" Ms. Cooper shouts. "Be brave! Put yourself out there!"

This motivates a few more people to stand up and wander around the room for a suitable peer. I rise from my seat and hang towards the back of the room, looking at other people who seem shy, but before I know it, they've all found a partner for the class and I'm left by myself.

"Does anyone *not* have a partner?" Ms. Cooper asks.

I think about not letting her know, but I know that a peer review is part of my grade, so I reluctantly put my hand in the air. A second hand across the room catches my eye, and I follow it down to its skinny arm to see whose body it's attached to and...

Fuck. It's Logan.

"Logan and Derek, you two can partner up!"

"Great!" Logan shouts.

"Yay..."

I sheepishly hand over the first draft of my story, my arm trembling as I extend it. I try to disguise my anxious body language with my I-don't-care face, but any discerning eye can tell it's just for show.

Logan doesn't seem to pay that much attention because he snatches the bundle of paper out of my hand and flings his own story at me without so much as a glance.

I sit down at the desk next to him, and as his eyes dance over the lines on the page, in my own self-absorbed paranoia, I can't help but re-read my own story over his shoulder as Logan experiences it for the first time now...

DILLIAN'S BIG KERFUFFLE
By Derek Milligan

There was once a boy who played baseball in high school. He was really good at it. He was a pitcher for his team, which wore purple and green jerseys and was called The Velociraptors. The boy's name was Dillian.

One day in the spring, after a home game where Dillian hit a homerun, he heard the principal announce on the school's intercom that tickets for prom were on sale. "Great!" Dillian thought. "Now I can ask my best friend Sarah to prom!"

Dillian had always had a crush on Sarah. She was pretty and had blonde hair and green eyes. She always liked to draw in class and often got in trouble for it because teachers thought she wasn't paying attention. Really, she was listening. She was just drawing too.

Dillian got very excited that he could finally ask Sarah to prom and find out if they could be more than friends. Dillian looked for Sarah at school that day, but couldn't find her. Whenever he saw her in class, she was on the opposite side of the room. In first period, he tried to talk to her after class, but she ran away too fast and he couldn't catch her. In second period, he tried to pass her a note asking if she would go to prom with him, but the note got passed to the wrong person. It was passed to an ugly girl named Gretchen and she thought that he was asking her! Dillian had to kindly explain afterwards that the note was meant for someone else. She ran into the bathroom crying and didn't come out for the rest of the day.

Dillian didn't have a class with Sara again until the end of the day. Finally, in last period, Dillian decided to ask to go to the bathroom five minutes before the end of the class. So he went to the bathroom (because he really did have to pee) and then waited outside the room for Sarah when the bell rang. That way, when class ended and she ran out of the room, he was already ahead of her and could talk to her.

When the bell rang, Sarah came running out of the room and Dillian stopped her and said "Do you want to go to prom with me?" He grinned widely because he knew that Sarah would say yes because they were good friends and had been good friends since they were in first grade.

Sarah looked down at her feet and said "No." and Dillian was confused.

"Why not? I only meant as friends." That was a lie. He meant as more, but he was afraid that he scared her off by not saying that first.

"I'm already going with someone." Sarah said.

"Who?" Dillian asked. He was getting angry because he wanted to go with Sarah and somehow someone had asked her before he had the chance.

"Brian."

"Brian!?" Dillian shouted. "My best friend?"

"Yes." Sarah replied. "I'm sorry, Dillian."

Dillian was shocked. His best friend had asked his good girl firend to prom before he did! How could Brian have asked Sarah? Brian was his best friend, he knew that Dillian wanted to ask Sarah. They had talked about it before. Dillian felt like he had just been stabbed in the back.

Dillian decided that he had to change Sarah's mind so that she would go to prom with him to prom. He went home and he stayed up very late thinking and writing and making notes until he had a plan. It was Monday and starting on Tuesday, he would put his plan into action.

The next day, he went to school and he found Becky, who was a very popular girl who knew everyone and talked to everyone and always knew the school gossip. Dillian walked up to Becky and said, "Becky, you'll never guess what I heard about Sarah."

Becky looked excited to hear a new piece of school gossip and said "What!?"

"I heard that she sneaks into the boys' lockerroom and smells their underwear."

Becky was shocked. "No way!"

"Yes! I saw her do it!"

Becky pulled out her phone and started typing. "I'm going to tell everyone!" she said and ran off to go tell all her friends.

Then Dillian began wandering around the school until he saw Sarah and he walked up to her and he said "Sarah do you want to go to prom with me?"

Sarah said "Dillian, I already told you that I'm going with Brian."

To hear her say that again made Dillian's heart hurt again. But he held his chin up high and said "But Brian is mean. He called spread a rumor about you that you go into the boys' lockerroom and smell their underwear."

Sarah was shocked. "What?"

"He did! I just heard it from Becky!"

Sarah began to cry and Dillian knew that his plan was working. "Do you really want to go to prom with someone like that?"

"I guess not." Sarah said. Dillian was about to hug her when Brian ran up and said "Sarah! I just heard the worst rumor about you!"

"Stop pretending!" Sarah shouted, her green eyes wet with tears. "You spread that rumor about me!"

Dillian thought his plan was perfect, but then Brian took Sarah's hands in his and said "I didn't spread that rumor about you. I would never say something like that about you." They looked into each other's eyes and Sarah smiled.

"I believe you" she said and she smiled at him and then they hugged.

"Dang it!" Dillian said to himself. "My plan is ruined."

That night he went home and began working on a different plan that he would start to put into motion on Wednesday.

The next day he went to school and he carried with him a bucket of water. Dillian waited by the front doors of the school and he kept looking out the window trying to see who was coming. When he saw that Brian was coming, Dillian poured the bucket of water all over the floor and then ran around the corner and hid. When Brian walked in, he was looking down at his phone and didn't see that there was water all over the floor, so he slipped and fell. Dillian ran to Sarah, who was waiting in their first period class and talking with her friends. When he found her, he said "Sarah, Brian just fell and sprained his ankle!"

"Oh my gosh!" Sarah shouted in shock.

"I guess that means he can't go to prom!" Dillian said.

"I guess not!" Sarah said.

"In that case, will you go with me?" Dillian asked.

"Yes!" Sarah said.

They held hands and Dilian was really happy! Then Brian walked into the room. "Hi, guys" he said, nonchalantly.

"Brian!" Sarah shouted. "I thought you broke your ankle!"

"No, I just fell. I'm okay. But why is there water all over the floor?"

Brian didn't know that Dillian poured the water out, but Sarah ran over and hugged him. A few minutes later, Sarah walked up to Dillian and said "Sorry, Dillian but Brian isn't hurt, so I guess I'm going with him."

Dillian was really upset. He had been so close! She said she would go with him! If only Brian had actually broken his ankle! Dillian went home that night and worked on a new plan.

The next day, Dillian went to school and it was Friday, the day of prom. So he had to make Sarah want to go with him that day or he wouldn't get to go to prom at all. Dillian brought his bat with him to school that day and went to the history teacher's classroom. The history teacher, Mr. Smith, stepped out to go to the bathroom, and Dillian took out his bat and smashed everything on Mr. Smith's desk. He broke his computer and monitor, his pencil sharpener, his computer mouse, his class notes, and his desk chair. Mr. Smith was very surpised when he came back and saw that his desk was completely destroyed. "Who did this?" he shouted with anger.

Dillian was happy because he was mad and said "Brian did it! I saw him!"

Mr. Smith walked to the principal's office and Dillian knew he was going to tell the principal what Brian did. So he ran to Sarah and said "Sarah, I just saw Brian take a baseball bat and smash everything in Mr. Smith's room."

Once again Sarah was shocked. "Oh no! Will he get in trouble?"

"Yes!" Dillian said. "Mr. Smith is going to tell the principal now. He's going to get expelled!"

"That means he won't be able to go to prom!" Sarah said.

"Well, you can still go to prom with me, if you want," Dillain said.

"Okay! That sounds like a plan!"

Then Brian walked in the room again and said "Hi, guys."

"Brian! How could you smash everything in Mr. Smith's room?" Sarah said.

"I didn't!" Brian replied. "I just explained to the principal that it wasn't me."

"Oh good! Sarah shouted. "So we can still go to prom together!"

Dillian was sad. He had tried his best but it was not enough and Sarah was not going to prom with him. Just when he thought he would have to go home and sulk for the night, Brian turned to him and said "Hey, you!"

"Me?" Dillian asked.

"Yeah, you! You tried to take Sarah away from me! You tried to break my ankle by making me slip in that water you poured out! You tried to get me expelled by breaking everything in Mr. Smith's room! Sarah is going to prom with me and that's final!"

Dillian was angry now and he jumped to his feet. "No! She is going to prom with me! You knew I wanted to aks her but you asked her anyways! You're my best friend! Why would you do that?"

"Boys, please don't fight over me!" Sarah shouted, but no one heard.

"We may be boys, but we will settle this like men" Brian said. He held up his hands in fists and stared at Dillian angrily.

Dillian, caught up in the heat of the moment, decided to fight with his best friend, so he held up his fists too. Dillian threw the first punch, but missed. He was aiming for Brian's eye, but his fist went past his ear instead. Then Brian threw a punch, and he hit Dillian in the cheek. Dillian fell down, but before Brian could hit him again, he stood up and jumped out of the way. Then Dillian pretended like he was going to move left, so Brian moved to his left, but then Dillian actually moved right and he hit Brian in the nose and he could feel it crack under his fist. Brian fell down to the ground and his nose was bleeding. There was blood everywhere and Dillian knew that Brody's nose was broken. It was purple and at a weird angle and it was bleeding.

"You're right" Brian said as he sat on the ground in a pool of his own blood. "I should not have asked Sarah to prom without asking you first."

"Now you know why I was mad" Dillian said

"You had every right to be" Brian said.

Dillian helps him to his feet and they shake hands and hug and Dillian knew that they would be best friends forever.

THE END

I find a couple grammar mistakes in Logan's story, at least what I think are grammar mistakes. His story is about a kid climbing a mountain who begins to miss his mom and wonders if he can make it without her. I think I'm supposed to cry when I read it because his mom had just died of cancer, but I'm too focused on what Logan thinks of my story to give a shit about his.

When Logan's finally done reading, he glances at me, then back at the story, then back at me.

"What do you think?" I ask, doing my best to pretend like it was just something I threw together.

"Is this really two thousand words?" he asks with a raised eyebrow. "Seems a little light."

"It's about a hundred words short but Ms. Cooper's not gonna count them all."

Logan shrugs. "I think it... has potential."

"Really?" I ask. A wave of relief washes over me and I feel like I can breathe for the first time all day. "What would you do differently?"

He rocks his head from side to side as he thinks. "Well, there seems to be an interesting dynamic between Dillian and Brian. Dillian keeps saying that Brian is his best friend, but they don't really act like it. That suggests to me that there's some underlying tension between them."

I give Logan a blank stare. What did he just say? In all of the hours that I spent taking notes and outlining the plot and the characters, never did I once intend for there to be an "underlying tension" between the two characters.

Logan continues. "Plus, the bit at the end. They fight, Dillian breaks Brian's nose, and they make up, they hug it out, but then no one goes to prom. The story just kind of ends. It seems more like Dillian wanted Brian's attention more than he really wanted Sarah as a date, which is certainly interesting, but... actually... yeah I think that's a change you should make."

"What is?" I ask, unable to follow his thought process.

Logan leans in and lowers his voice. "Dillian wants Brian's attention more..." He raises his eyebrows at me and suddenly we're on the same page. "Dillian should realize he wants to go to prom with Brian and he's pissed that Brian asked Sarah instead."

I shake my head wildly. Where the hell was this coming from? "No no no, Dillian wants to go with Sarah."

"Well maybe he does at first, but what if at the end when his third attempt to ask Sarah fails, he realizes he wanted Brian as a date all along?"

"Dillian isn't gay."

"Well we could change that."

I'm about to argue back with him when Ms. Cooper puts her hand on my shoulder. "How's it going over here?" she asks with a grin.

"Good! I think I have an idea to help Dill- sorry, Derek improve his story, but he isn't so sure." Logan briefly explains my story—for some reason his synopsis makes it sound so stupid—and he concludes by saying, "It just seems like Derek isn't super open to the idea."

"I didn't write the character to be gay, is all," I rebut, hoping it will help me even though some part of me knows it won't.

Ms. Cooper gives me a playfully castigating look over the rim of her glasses. "Derek, your characters can have whatever sexual orientation you want. Have an open mind. Making your main character gay could really make him jump off of the page."

I open my mouth to debate, but she holds a hand up and hushes me.

"Derek. Don't argue with me."

She moves on to the next pair of students and I know her decision is final.

"So..." Logan says after an awkward moment of silence. "Do you have anything to say about my story?"

"What? Oh... yeah... it was fine. Good, actually. Don't change anything about it."

84

Practice is a scrimmage game with the JV baseball team. Usually they play on the smaller field that's over by the middle school, but for today they walked the extra half mile to our neck of the woods.

For some reason freshmen seem so much smaller now, especially as they sling bat bags larger than they are over their shoulders, or don ball caps two sizes too big for their heads. I hope they feel nervous as they walk onto our turf—or, well, it's real grass but I hope they feel nervous just the same.

Brody and I climb down into the dugout and begin to change into our uniforms. I take off my shirt just as Alex walks in. I turn away quickly so he doesn't see me blush, but I get the distinct feeling of someone watching me as I drop my shorts and step into my white pants. As I button up my jersey, Coach Cole sticks his head over the railing and looks down at me. He scans the dugout until he finds…. "Alex! Can you come up here for a minute please?"

Alex zips up his pants and hurries out with his t-shirt still on. I can't hear what he and Coach Grady are talking about, but it's a pretty short conversation. Alex gives a curt nod of his head and a brief "Okay" before he hustles over to the JV coach and begins talking to him.

"Man, that Alex guy is a great pitcher. I'm glad we finally have him on our side," Brody says to no one in particular. "The JV don't stand a chance against his fast ball."

Then Coach Cole comes down into the dugout and breathes a heavy sigh. "Okay, guys. So a little bit of a snag. The JV team's pitcher is sick today, so they need a replacement. Alex is gonna be pitching for them and Blake will be pitching for us."

Before anyone can react, Coach turns around and hops up the stairs into the sunlight.

"God *dammit*, Brody!" Austin yells.

"You jinxed us, you fucking idiot!" Josh shouts from across the dugout.

Brody hung his head and stretched his face into a visual apology. I groan because I know I'm going to strike out at least twice today. And in front of the JV. Shit.

At the very least I can say that my field work was good. I caught one ball as it tried to zip past my head, I tagged a couple players, I was in the zone. But just as I predicted, my batting game was in the gutter. I struck out twice with Alex. I hit one of his pitches, but it went sailing over the visitors' dugout, straight into foul territory. I could even hear some of the JV benchwarmers mocking me from the visitors' dugout. I didn't think I could sink this low as an athlete.

"I can't figure it out," I say to Brody as we take off our cleats in the dugout after the game. "Why do I keep striking out against that guy?"

"He's got a wicked arm!" Brody shoots back at me. "Lots of guys on the team don't do as well when Alex pitches."

"But it's not the *same*. My batting has really tanked since Alex joined."

"Is there something about him that makes you nervous?" Brody asks.

Yes. Fuck yes.

"Not really."

"Maybe you could practice with him one-on-one if you don't improve after a while?"

We walk out of the dugout and back towards our cars.

"At least we still won," I say.

Brody bumps my fist and we both laugh. We walk in silence for a moment and I suddenly remember my secret. Brody still hasn't said anything to me about Camilla. Does he know it was really me he was talking to last night? Has Camilla come clean? Is he planning on texting her more tonight?

Brody notices I'm staring and raises his eyebrows. "Huh?"

"Nothing," I say quickly before deciding to mask my guilt with a dumb joke. "Or everything. Who knows?"

Later that night, I'm sitting at my desk as I read the next assigned chapter out of *The Great Gatsby*. I've only been reading for about thirty minutes, but after the exhausting day I've had, I begin to nod off. I'm completely drained and I didn't even realize it until after I came home, showered, and ate dinner with my parents. I check my watch, and realize that I either need to make myself a cup of coffee to stay up for another hour and a half, or accept that I'm not going to get anything else done and go to bed now.

I could go downstairs and watch TV with Mom and Dad, I think to myself. But they're probably watching something educational. I breathe a heavy, frustrated sigh as I stand to walk over to my bed. I drop onto it face-first and let out a groan. My chest is already sore from the workout I did with Brody today. I know I'm gonna feel it tomorrow.

I curl up on top of the sheets when I hear a buzzing

sound. I almost ignore it until I remember who it could be. I open my eyes just a crack, barely enough to see my phone sitting on the edge of my desk... all the way... over there...

Then my phone buzzes again. "Okay, okay," I say to it as I roll out of bed. "I'm coming."

I tap the lock button and look at the screen.

How's your night going?

It's from Brody. I can feel my mouth curling into a smile. I try to force it down until I remember that I'm alone in my room and no one can see me. I let it spread over my face as I unlock my phone to respond.

Okay, just feeling tired. You?

Same. I had a rough day.

Oh no! What happened?

I accidentally jinxed my team and we almost lost our game.

Yikes.

Yeah...

There's a lull in the conversation and my mind begins to race. I really want to take the conversation further, but I don't want to push him, especially since he thinks I'm someone else. As I write and rewrite drafts of texts in my head, my phone lights up and buzzes again.

**So... When am I gonna
take you on a date?**

I freeze. I can hear my heart start to pound in my ears and my face flushes with heat.

You wanna go on a date?

**Of course! How can I not?
You're so cute and I
wanna get to know
you more!**

Even though I know he's talking to Camilla, I can't help but feel flattered myself.

**That's so sweet!
I think you're
really handsome**

Oh you do?

**Yes! I stare at you
all the time in class!**

I never noticed lol

Sometimes when I get

bored, I'll just look over
at your arms and dream
about them haha

Oh shit. I went too far. That was way too much. I
immediately start thinking about how I could reel that back.
Act like it was a joke!

That's honestly really sweet

Was he just saying that or did he mean it?

Really?

Yes! I never knew you
were so into me haha

I feel embarrassed
for saying that haha

Don't! I look at you a
lot in class too

You do?

Yeah, I try to be really
subtle about it haha

So when are we going out?

Let me talk to my parents,

I know they were planning on doing something this weekend, so it may have to wait until next Friday.

But I really wanna go out with you! I'm not making excuses!

Okay cool :)

I put my phone down and breathe a sigh of relief. I just bought Camilla some time to read those messages and figure out when she's free for a date with Brody.

But holy shit! What a rush! To open up like that—and to my best friend, no less! Maybe I do stare at Brody more than I let on. Maybe sometimes I catch a glimpse of his biceps when he's wearing a t-shirt with his sleeves rolled up and all I can think about is how they might feel if he wrapped them around me.

To allow myself to dream about it for just one night without an ounce of shame... I don't know if I've ever felt anything so wonderful.

I think about sending Camilla a message to apologize for texting Brody again. I think about coming up with another excuse until I finally stop arguing with myself and I whisper, "That was really fun. I'm gonna do that again tomorrow."

CHAPTER 7

I wake up the next morning wondering if I dreamt my conversation with Brody last night. When I scroll through Camilla's messages and confirm that it was real, another rush of energy crashes into me. It was real! It was real! I got to talk to someone about being gay! Kind of. Close enough!

I can't hide my grin as I start my truck and drive to school. I roll down the windows and breathe in the fresh air. It's that part of spring when even the mornings are getting warm. I turn on the radio and sing along to every song as loud as I can. My spirit feels so big today. Nothing can bring me down.

I stroll through the front doors of the school and I wave to everyone I recognize. "Hey, Austin!" "What's up, Josh?" As I approach Mrs. Garcia's room, I see Logan down the hall. Something about the way I carry myself catches his attention and he does a double take.

"Hey, Derek," he says. "You seem different today."

"Woke up on the right side of the bed," I reply, beaming.

"Well the right side of the bed looks good on you."

"I think it looks good on everyone!"

God, I sound like a fucking Hallmark card, but I don't care. I genuinely could not be happier.

I sit down in Mrs. Garcia's room and Brody walks in a minute later. My heart flutters and my eyes dance from his face to his arms to his chest and back to his face.

"You seem happy today," he says to me as he takes a seat.

I'm about to respond when his eyes dart over my shoulder towards the door and linger. Camilla just walked in. They grin at each other, lost in puppy love, and Camilla takes her seat in front of Brody.

"Hey," she says shyly.

"Hi," he says as he rests his head on his fist.

"I talked to my folks and I'm free next Friday."

"Awesome, I'll think of something for us to do."

I can feel my heart sink. This isn't right. Brody is supposed to be falling for me. He was talking to me just last night. Why is he giving Camilla that flirtatious look, his eyelids drooping a fraction of an inch as he ever so lightly tilts his head back? That isn't right. That's for me.

I shake my head. That's a stupid idea. I know what I'm doing. I am aware of the reality I exist in. I always have been. Besides, thirty minutes ago I said nothing was gonna get me down today. Nothing will. I'm sure of it.

I force myself to hold my chin high in French class as I wait for Camilla to confront me about texting Brody last night. Every time there's a pause in Madame Miller's lecture, I expect a dirty look and threat to get hissed my way. But it never comes. At the end of class, she waves to me and smiles. "See you later!"

I wave back, relieved but somewhat let down. I was

hoping to give her a smug smile while she chewed me out. Damn. Maybe next time.

Ms. Cooper's English class can't last long enough. She keeps asking questions to the class about the symbolism in *The Great Gatsby* and every time Brody answers one, I get an excuse to stare.

After lunch we go to the weight room and do a back/bicep workout. Brody's biceps pump and flex with every rep, it looks like his vein is going to pop right through his skin, and for the first time I can look at it without getting jealous. I don't feel the immediate and urgent desire to outperform him. I can for once just look at it and admire, and be grateful to recognize something beautiful in the world.

After our workout, we quickly change in the locker room and Brody scoots out the door before me so he isn't late to his civics class. I take my time because I'm not worried about being late to history. I would actually prefer it.

As I walk from the locker room to Mr. Thomas' class, the only sound echoing through the deserted hallway is the soft scuffing of my shoes on the tile. I'm about to round a corner when I pass a corkboard filled with announcements and flyers. One in particular catches my eye and I stop to read it.

LGBTQ+ Club!
Embrace yourself! Be proud! Be an ally!
Meetings on Wednesdays after school
in Ms. Cooper's room

The text of the flyer is over a rainbow background and the paper is crisp, as if it's just been printed. I'm studying it when a thought pops into my head. A scary thought that I didn't know I'd ever intentionally think.

I should go.

No, that's crazy. I have practice after school every day, so logistically it just wouldn't work out. Not to mention I wouldn't want people who see me there to tell their friends they saw me there. I shrug the idea off, hoping that it never surfaces again. As I'm about to turn towards Mr. Thomas' class, I hear papers shuffling, shortly followed by scuffing shoes and a thump. I retrace my steps and peer down a hallway to find a pile of flyers for the LGBTQ+ club scattered on the floor and Gavin Murphy pinning Logan against the wall. Gavin has his forearm across Logan's throat, and Logan's face is growing a sickening hue of purple as he struggles to breathe.

For a second, a split second, I think about walking away—about turning around and pretending I saw nothing. Then I remember how Brody did the right thing just last week. Brody always does the right thing.

I let out a roar. "HEY!! LET HIM GO!!"

"Fuck off, Milligan!"

Logan's eyes find me and linger. Sheer terror has taken over his face as his eyelids begin to droop with the onset of unconsciousness.

I drop my backpack, take a step back, then build up as much speed as I can in ten feet and slam into Gavin. We crash onto the floor and in the brief struggle, I climb on top of him. He swings a punch that comes within an inch of my face. I land a fist squarely on the bridge of his nose. His head whips back and hits the tile floor. He slows down for a moment and I know he's seeing stars. I jump to my feet, and run to Logan, who's sitting with his back to the wall, coughing and wheezing as his face slowly returns to a normal color. I grab his tiny wrist and pull him to his feet. "We gotta run. Now!"

He gives me a confused look before the door across the hall begins to open. I pull him around the corner, grab my backpack, and we disappear down the hall. We hide in a small alcove as the teacher sticks her head down the main hallway, trying to figure out where those two other boys ran off to.

"Thank you," Logan whispers. "That's the second time you've gotten me out of a sticky situation."

"Yeah, well… whatever."

"It's not whatever! It's a big deal!" His voice is hoarse as he talks.

"If you tell anyone about this, leave me out of it. I'm not your bodyguard, you got lucky. Twice."

"Okay," he says with a nod of understanding.

"And maybe carry pepper spray or something."

"You can't have pepper spray in school," he replies.

"You can't choke people out in school either. You can't tackle and punch people, but you just thanked me for it. Remember that the next time you're pinned against a wall."

He lowers his head in shame and I can't help but feel guilty. Logan is openly gay, relentlessly bullied for it, and helpless to prevent it or fight back. Now the guy who saved him twice is yelling at him for being such an unbearable burden.

"Look…" I say with a kinder tone. "Do you know how to stop a bully?"

He gives a little shake of his head.

"You punch him *once*." I hold up a single finger as I say it. "You punch him once and he never picks on you again. The next time Gavin tries to pull some shit on you, punch him one time. Hard. He'll leave you alone forever. It's not good enough to get outside help because as soon as I'm gone or the teachers are busy, you're on your own."

He sniffs. "Okay, I can do that."

"I bet there's a youtube video on how to throw a punch," I joke.

He gives a little laugh and raises his eyes to meet mine. "Thank you, Derek. Seriously."

"No problem. Now get to class before that teacher shows up again."

I'm more than a little late to history, but I come in quietly and I don't think Mr. Thomas even notices, much less cares. I sit in the back of the room and try to take notes, but it's hard to focus. I just saved Logan. I'm kind of a hero. I told Logan not to tell anyone, so that kind of makes me a super-hero with a secret identity and everything. I don't actually have a super power, so I guess that makes me Batman.

That's fine. I can be Batman.

It's especially warm and breezy at practice, and as we run through our fielding drills, I can't help but feel slap happy as the wind flutters the shirt over my chest. The outfielders are at bat as Coach Grady pitches to them. Us infielders are trying to catch every ball they hit our way. I can tell my energy is rubbing off on everyone else. Even Randy and Parker are getting louder and louder, poking fun at each other, and laughing between pitches.

Ryan hits a ball and Brody jumps up to catch it as

it goes zooming over his head. "BOOM!" he shouts. "YOU'RE OUT!!"

Randy picks up a grounder and throws it to Parker before Tony Gunderson can make it to first base. "*YEE-EET!!*"

"What is *wrong* with you guys today?" Coach Cole asks as he watches us from the dugout. "You're acting like dumbasses."

"C-bear, don't be like that," I call back to him from third base. "You're invited to this party too!"

He shakes his head and tries to hide his smile, to no avail of course.

About halfway through practice, the infielders and the outfielders switch. Alex, who had been batting with the outfielders, walks to the pitcher's mound as we put our helmets and batting gloves on and take some practice swings. "Derek, you go first," Coach tells me.

I know I should feel nervous—I've barely hit anything that Alex has thrown my way—but there's something different about today. I just know it. I'm the hero. I'm Batman.

I look at Brody one last time as I walk to home plate. "Here goes nothing," I say with a smirk. *What's the worst that could happen?* I think to myself. *I strike out... again. It isn't exactly new territory.*

I square up at the plate, swing my bat in an arc and raise it to its ready position. I lock eyes with Alex... but... it's not the same. I don't feel the butterflies or a random wave of heat crashing over me. I don't feel anything. He winds up the pitch and I know it's going to be a fast ball. He twists his body and releases the pitch. I see it, step with my right foot, rotate my left leg, and bring the bat down to meet the ball with a loud metallic *ding!* The bat vibrates in my hands as the ball goes flying over the outfield.

Brody and the other infielders cheer as it crashes into the right field fence. Alex follows it with his eyes from the pitcher's mound, then when it finally hits the ground, he spins to look at me.

I look right back at him as if to say, "What up, bitch? This is *my* field."

I hit the next five of Alex's pitches, except for one ball that almost grazes my crotch. I can't help but think that was on purpose, even as Alex lifts his hand to his mouth and shouts, "Sorry!"

After practice, Brody and I are walking back to our cars and he says, "Dude! You totally *killed* it today!"

"Thanks! I don't know what came over me. I was on my A-game!"

"Something about you seems different today," Brody says.

"You're actually not the first person to tell me that today."

The sound of soft footsteps reaches my ear and I turn around to see Alex walking behind us. He's wearing a pair of sunglasses and I can't tell where exactly he's looking. More importantly, I don't care. Maybe he and I can actually be friends now that I've defeated him on the field of battle— now that I've proven I'm better than him in this small way.

I hold my chin up high and walk alongside Brody, excited that I get to text him again later tonight.

How's the French

homework going?

I'm working on the changes Ms. Cooper suggested—well, really demanded—of my short story when my phone lights up. Brody remembered that Camilla is in French class with me. That was sweet of him.

Sacre bleu! It's the worst!
How has your day been?

Hahaha!!

I made him laugh. The edges of my mouth curl up.

It was really good!
I was thinking about
you a lot

My mouth drops open. It hangs there as I read and re-read his text in a futile attempt to react. I'm nervous and scared, but I carefully type out my response with my trembling fingers and send it before I second guess myself.

I thought about
you a lot too

And it was true! I thought about Brody all day! Every free minute in class (when I knew I could get away with it) was spent focusing on his arms as he reached behind his head to stretch, on his thighs when his shorts rode up the side of his leg, on his amber eyes when he gave Camilla that look in first period that made me so jealous. He's giving me that look now. Well, he's giving it to his phone screen, on the other side of which he thinks is Camilla, but he isn't crushing on Camilla because I am Camilla and Camilla is me and for once I finally have control over my love life and I never knew it would feel this good!

Oh you did?
What were you
thinking about?

I was thinking
about your arms

My arms?

They're really big,
they drive me crazy

Oh really...
I was thinking about
your pretty eyes

No one has ever complimented my eyes before. Were my eyes actually worth looking at? Were they really pretty? As a guy, something about thinking of my eyes as pretty feels off to me. The word pretty is just too feminine for my liking.

I was thinking
about your muscles

I was thinking

about your hair

> I was thinking
> about your butt

I was thinking
about YOUR butt

I laugh at that and somehow I know Brody's laughing
too.

I was thinking
about your hands

> My hands?

And what they feel
like to hold

> I was thinking
> about your lips

What about my lips?

I can't stop myself. I'm high on whatever endorphin
this conversation is sending through my veins.

> Yeah, your lips.
> I was wondering what
> they feel like

**I wanna know what
your lips feel like too**

                                    **I wanna know what
                                    it's like to kiss you**

I wanna kiss you too

I want to kiss Brody too. I've never wanted anything so bad. I'm pumped full of so much energy right now that I'm hopping up and down between texts. I want to run to Brody's house down the street, knock down the front door, run up to his room and kiss him. God, what would that feel like? I bet his lips feel kinda rough but in a good way. I bet it would feel intoxicating. I can imagine grabbing his face in my hands and pressing his lips against mine. I would kiss him and he would kiss me back and then I'd rest my forehead against his and I'd feel the heat radiating off from him and I'd see the nervous sweat on his face and he'd ask me to kiss him again.

Then I realize I haven't responded to him yet.

                                    **Then we should do that
                                    on our date next week**

I agree

I let out a nervous laugh and once again, I know Brody is laughing too

Well, it's getting late.
I should go to bed.

Okay. Good night, Brody

Good night :)

    I was afraid he'd say the name. The wrong name. I know he doesn't really feel this way about me. I know this is all a charade, but for just a few minutes I want to get lost in this fantasy where Brody and I are planning an evening together and neither of us can wait. The last thing I want is to come crashing back to reality when Brody says the wrong name.The last thing I want is to be reminded that none of this is real.

CHAPTER 8

The prom decorating committee meets again the next afternoon and when Brody and I walk into Ms. Cooper's room, she tells us to go to the cafeteria where Logan promptly hands us paintbrushes and says to start painting. On a giant sheet of craft paper on the cafeteria floor is a rough pencil sketch of the yellow brick road leading to the Emerald City from *The Wizard of Oz*. "Derek, you start painting the outlines of the bricks," Logan instructs me.

"I'll help!" Brody says, holding up his paintbrush. I feel a rush of excitement at the idea of spending some one-on-one time with Brody, but Logan shakes his head.

"No, that's okay. I'll help Derek. Brody, you wait a few minutes for the black paint to dry and then you can fill in the brick with yellow."

"Okay," Brody says with a shrug. I know he doesn't care, but I can't help but feel a little disappointed.

I walk over to the bottom of the backdrop and I kneel down on the cold tile floor. I wish I had Austin's catcher padding right now. I can already tell this isn't going to be fun. A moment later Gabby walks into the cafeteria, pushing a cart with one-gallon jugs of paint, small plastic mixing cups, and paper towels. Logan pumps some black paint into two plastic cups and hands one to me, then sits across the backdrop from me on the hard floor. "Okay, so let's start at the bottom where the bricks are large and then work our way up to where they get smaller," he says as he dips his brush into his cup and then leans forwards to cover the first pencil mark with black paint.

I do the same, working on the edge of the yellow brick road closest to me. It's a little weird working so closely with Logan after I rescued him from Gavin yesterday, especially since neither of us acknowledges it. Still, the tense silence gets to be a little much and I decide to break it with a question. "So...where is this going to go, exactly?"

"By the entrance," he says. "We're gonna have a little red carpet area where people can get pictures taken and this is gonna be the backdrop for that."

"Why not a yellow carpet?"

Logan laughs. Really loud. I stare at him.

"That's a *great* idea! I'll have to see if we have room in the budget for that!"

I give a little nod and go back to painting. A few minutes after we paint the first lines, Brody decides they're dry enough for him to come in and start painting the bricks a vibrant yellow.

"Have you made up your mind about prom yet?" Logan asks me after a few minutes of concentrated silence.

"What do you mean?" I ask without looking up.

"Are you going?"

I raise my head to find him looking at me from the other side of the yellow brick road. I swear that out of the corner of my eye, I can see Brody looking my way too. "I don't see that happening," I say. Telling him no flatly seems a little mean, considering his close involvement with the event.

106

"What would it take to get you to go?" he asks.

I shrug. "A date, really. If I had someone to bring with me, it wouldn't even be a question."

"Well… who *would* you bring if you could?"

I shrug again.

"No special someone?" he prods.

"Nope," I say, but I give myself away as my mouth curls uncontrollably into a little smile.

"Yes there is!" he teases. "Who is it?"

He's beaming at me and all of a sudden I find the will-power to force my smile into a frown. "There isn't anyone," I insist. I wish he'd drop it.

I can feel the weight of his gaze on me as I go back to painting the brick lines. A moment later he goes back to painting his side of the road.

Since the backdrop shows the yellow brick road shrinking into the distance as it approaches the Emerald City, as Logan and I paint, the bricks get smaller and smaller and our two sides of the path get closer and closer. As we near the end point where the road disappears over a hill, Logan says, "I just ran out of paint."

"Here, we can share mine," I say, putting my cup of paint between us. "We only have a little bit left to go."

Logan and I continue painting, our hands accidentally bumping when we dip our brushes at the same time. "Oh sorry," I say, looking up at him after I bump his arm. I look back down at the paper and go back to painting. After a moment, I realize Logan has stopped painting, and I look up at him. "Is something wrong?"

"You have really pretty eyes," he says.

"What?"

"I've never noticed before. I guess I wasn't looking for it."

"Um... okay... thanks..." And it was the weirdest thing. Even though I don't like Logan, even though he's annoying and kind of full of himself, the compliment seems genuine and my heart warms to him just a little bit. Maybe he isn't so bad after all.

Then Brody shifts uncomfortably at the other end of the backdrop.

"Is it me, or was Logan acting weird today?" Brody asks me as we walk towards the baseball field. Once the yellow brick road was painted, Brody and I felt like it was acceptable to leave so that we could still make the end of practice. Being on the baseball team has its advantages.

"I think he was being a little more friendly than usual," I say.

"At least towards you... I don't know. Something about it rubbed me the wrong way."

"You said the same thing when they chose the prom theme," I point out to him.

"Yeah... But would you really go to prom if you had a date?" he asks.

"Probably."

"Do you want to take Camilla?"

That catches me by surprise. "What are you talking about?"

"You just mentioned it the other day, and if you really want to go with her, then you can. I don't want to get in anyone's way."

I shake my head. "No no no, she really wants to go with you. She's crazy about you! Besides, I thought you wanted to go with her."

Brody shrugs. This is unexpected. "I thought I did too, but I'm having second thoughts."

What? The conversation I had with Brody last night did not suggest second thoughts. Not in the least. "What's wrong?" I ask casually, doing my best to hide the fact that I'm freaking out.

"It just... doesn't feel right... I don't know. Hard to explain."

I know I shouldn't, I know it's probably unrelated, but I can't help but think—hope, really—that Brody's reluctance at taking Camilla has something to do with how Logan was talking to me just a few minutes ago.

"Gotta be honest, dude, I didn't see this coming," I say to Brody as we start to do our warm-up stretches by the dugout while the rest of the team is in the middle of practice. "Just by looking at you and Camilla in class, I thought everything was going well between you two."

"I don't know. It just kinda came out of nowhere." He shakes his head as he switches legs and begins to work on stretching his right hamstring. "That's not true," he corrects himself. "Honestly, it's something I've kinda been feeling for a while, it was just kinda subtle?" He phrases it like a question, like he's not entirely sure he's describing it well. "I tried to ignore it but... I know I can't keep doing that..." He shakes his head again. "Ah... I hate myself. I feel like a dumbass. And a jackass. I'm a dumb jackass." He says it like a joke and flashes me a toothy grin, but I can tell that it's just to hide his disappointment in himself.

"I need to think through it some more," he says. "But I don't think I can take Camilla to prom. I don't want to lead her on."

I know exactly what Brody was talking about. I think over it some more as I'm in the shower after practice. That's exactly how I felt a long time ago, when I first realized that my friends seemed to get a lot more excited about girls than I did. How they would ogle at them when they walked by, or take off their shirts whenever the girls started watching them play outside. *I'll feel that way too*, I would think. *I'm just a late bloomer. But I'll feel that way too.* Then my muscles started coming in and a faint mustache started growing on my upper lip, foreshadowing manhood. I grew six inches in seventh grade alone and I was stronger and faster than almost everyone else on the team, except Brody. But still. I waited. I waited and waited and fucking begged the universe or whatever powers that might give me their ears to let me feel the same thing my friends felt—to feel the same excitement that filled their eyes when they saw a woman at the local pool strip down to her bikini and still, *fucking still* I felt nothing.

Wait a minute.

What is it that Brody's feeling now?

It hits me like a lightning bolt as I change into dry clothes and suddenly my mind is racing. A tsunami of thoughts flood my mind and all of a sudden I'm excited. My heart is racing and my breathing gets faster and faster as I start to consider what Brody might have been trying to tell me.

I'm waiting for it later that night. I know it's coming, I can feel it. And even though I should feel sorry for Camilla, I can't help but feel excited. It's an apprehensive excitement. I don't want to get my hopes up and at the same time I do, because after what feels like an entire lifetime of romantic failure, I need one win—just a single, solitary win. For once. Why don't I deserve it when all of my other friends do?

My phone buzzes and from my bed, I can see the blue glow emanating from the little rectangle on my desk. With a sense of finality I sit up from the bed, walk over to my desk, and look down at the illuminated screen. A new message from Brody to Camilla.

Hey
I have some bad news

I pick it up, and take it back to my bed. As I lie back down again, I unlock it and type my reply.

Oh no. What's up?

I have to cancel our
 date next weekend

Crap. Do you want
to reschedule?

No, I don't think
that's a good idea

What's wrong?

I don't want to lead you on.
I thought I knew what I
was looking for, but
honestly I'm not sure what
it is I want.

It's nothing to do with you.
I think you're very pretty
and super sweet

I just can't figure out what
it is I'm looking for and
I don't want to lead you on
while I figure it out

I just wanted to be honest
with you and I'm sorry

I know I should be mad—well, I know Camilla should
be mad—but I'm not. I'm delighted, but I'm careful. If my response is too positive, he'll know something's up.

Well, it sucks to hear,
but I actually do want
to say thank you

Other guys would've led
me on for a few weeks

Thank you for being

straightforward with me

**Of course. You've been
so sweet to me, you
deserve the truth**

Well, I guess I'll see
you in class tomorrow

**Yeah
See you in class**

And the conversation ends. I lock my phone and breathe a sigh of relief. As I lie on my back, I stare up at my ceiling and take a moment to be grateful for the last couple of days. Even though it was short-lived, it's been thrilling to get a glimpse into Brody's romantic side; to express my attraction to another guy and have him express his own attraction towards me, even if our conversations were based on somewhat asymmetric information. I relive one more time how it felt to tell Brody I want to kiss him and read him tell me that he wants to kiss me back, and then I finally log out of Camilla's account.

I'm expecting Brody to be down in the dumps the next day. He just had to tell Camilla—or, well, me—that he's cancelling their date because he's having second thoughts about a relationship with her. Prom is right around the corner and he basically just ended all prospects of going via text last night. That's enough to upset anyone for a day or so. But when I show up to Mrs. Garcia's room on Friday morning, he is oddly energetic.

"Morning!" he calls to me as I walk in, grinning and stretching his arms out wide, as if inviting me for a hug.

"Good morning..." I say as I give him a sideways glance.

"It's Friday!"

I nod in agreement. "Yes it is."

"We play Brackettville tomorrow."

I nod again. "We do."

"Are you still good to hang tomorrow after the game?"

"Yes I am!"

He beams at me. "Great! Wanna do triceps and shoulders in the weight room today?"

"Yes!"

I feel like the old Brody is back. He's energetic and whispers jokes to me in class and he doesn't have a girl to distract him or bring him down. That other form of Brody was only around for a few days, and he was fun for a while, but in retrospect he made my days at school a little lonelier, even if I was too high on life to notice.

Camilla, on the other hand, looks pretty bummed. Bummed isn't the right word exactly. She looks bummed when she glances at Brody, but when she turns her attention to me, she looks furious. At first I'm afraid of the wrath she's going to unleash on me when we're alone after class, then I ask myself what's the worst she can do? She can't tell anyone what a jerk I am or how dishonest I am because she was in on the whole thing, and all too willing to let me do the heavy lifting in her relationship with Brody as long as she got to enjoy the payoff. Any accusation she could possibly lob at me could just as easily get turned around and thrown right back at her.

Bring it on, Camilla. I'm looking forward to it.

I decide to toy with her, so when calculus ends, I take my time packing up my notebook, dropping my pencil into my backpack, saying goodbye to Brody and finalizing our workout plan for the afternoon, even though I'm going to see him later, and finally I take a big, long stretch and tell Mrs. Garcia to have a great weekend. She gives me a suspicious look in return. "You too, Derek," she says as she stares at me with narrow eyes, wondering why I'm wishing her a good weekend now when I never have before.

I casually walk out of the room, Camilla tapping her foot impatiently as she waits by the door. I look at her as I pass. "Oh, hey, Camilla! How's it going?"

"*Derek!*" she hisses through gritted teeth.

"What?" I ask innocently.

"You *know* what!"

"No I don't…"

"Why the *fuck* did you do that!? I wanted to go to *prom* with him!"

"Why are you talking to me about it? Bring it up with him!"

Before she can retort, the bell rings and we turn into Madame Miller's class. That silences Camilla's rage until Madame is distracted enough so she can whisper threats and insults to me without her noticing. My attempt to hide my smug grin throughout the entire ordeal is met with little success.

Brody and I meet up in the weight room and I expect him to have calmed down a bit from his high earlier this morning, but to my surprise he's just as ecstatic as he was a few hours ago. "Wanna start with military press?" he asks. "Then we can do some skull crushers and... what else?"

"We can do reverse flies and some kickbacks too."

Brody likes the suggestion and agrees to it, setting up the barbell to the right height on the squat rack for military press.

"I was thinking last night..." he says between reps, "... that it really has been a while... since you and I hung out.... Just us."

"I was thinking the same thing too," I say, unable to hide the charmed tone in my voice.

He finishes his set and steps out of the squat rack, allowing me to step in.

"My parents are going to a college reunion this weekend in Ohio, so we won't have to worry about them. We can go in the pool for a bit, and my dad just restocked the minibar."

"Won't they notice... that there's booze missing...?"

Brody shakes his head. "If my dad does notice, he hasn't said anything to me about it. It's sort of a don't-ask-don't-tell policy."

I can feel my body warming up and my shoulders starting to burn as I push to straighten my arms for the last warm-up set. I slowly lower the bar to my upper chest and leave it to rest on the rack support. I add five pounds to one side as Brody adds five pounds to the other, then Brody steps up to the bar for his second set.

"So..." and I'm afraid to ask, but I need to know. I have to risk Brody guessing everything to satiate this small desire of my curiosity. "How's it going with Camilla? Did you talk to her about your... apprehension?"

Brody finishes his last rep, then panting, looks at my reflection in the mirror, and shakes his head. He then turns to face me. "Just didn't work out."

I notice he's using the past tense. "Damn, sorry to hear that. Have you been able to figure out what exactly you're going through?"

He shakes his head again as I step up to the rack for my set. "I thought I wanted something, and then I got it, and I realized it wasn't what I really wanted in the first place. You know what I mean?"

I do. I remember in eighth grade when the only thing I wanted was to kiss Ashley Donati, the pretty blonde girl in my math class, at the end-of-year dance in our middle school's gym. I slow danced with her as I glanced around the gym, I knew that in that moment I was the king of eighth grade—every other boy wanted to be me. When the song ended, I whispered to her, "Follow me." I led her behind the bleachers and she asked why we were there as she rubbed her arm and looked shyly down at her shoes. Just like I'd seen in the movies, I put a finger under her chin to raise her eyes to meet mine, then leaned forward for a kiss.

That's all it was. A quick smooch and then the awkward adolescent silence. She smiled and said, "C'mon, Derek. The teachers are going to be looking for us." I forced a smile as she took my hand and led me out onto the gym floor again. She insisted on holding my hand afterwards, but I refused, shaking my hand loose and making up some excuse about getting a snack.

That night I lay in bed thinking and overthinking and talking to myself incessantly, though quietly so my parents wouldn't hear. Why hadn't that been the thrill I was expecting? It was nice, but I wasn't blown away. At least I could brag about how I'd kissed a girl, but something still felt off. Somehow the reality of the experience had been lopsided next to my expectations. I didn't feel sparks, I didn't feel a gut-punch of excitement deep within my soul. I didn't even want to do it again. Did that mean that I was…?

No, no. That couldn't be it. I just didn't like Ashley as much as I thought I did. I was afraid she might overanalyze it like I had and then run to tell her friends about how I kissed her and ditched her, but much to my luck, she was moving that summer anyways and the word about my bewildering and erratic behavior never had the chance to make the rounds. The length of summer break saved me from the rumors born in the easily-distracted minds of fourteen-year-olds.

Now, as Brody explains his own disappointment at getting exactly what he wanted, I wonder how similar his experience is to my own from three years ago.

"I know what you mean, man," I say as I lower the weight to my shoulders to rack it. "I've been there myself once or twice." My shoulders are burning now and a sweat is breaking out on my forehead. I dab it away with the bottom of my shirt as Brody steps up to the rack again.

"Yeah, not fun because I thought I was gonna go to prom with her, and she thought she was gonna go to prom with me. But I knew I couldn't lead her on thinking that I wanted a relationship." He counts out six reps and racks the bar again, his face red. "So I guess I'm not going to prom now."

"Neither am I," I add.

"What are you talking about? You can go with Camilla."

I shake my head. "I somehow don't think she'd want to go with me. Plus I'd kinda feel like a rebound from you," I joke.

Brody laughs and shrugs. "There's something ironic about a third of the prom decorating committee not going to prom themselves."

Later at night in my room, I push my laptop shut after working on my short story for an hour. My mind turns again to Brody and what he said to me in the weight room. Was he trying to hint at something or am I overthinking this? He couldn't possibly have been telling me what I think he was telling me... right? I don't want to make the mistake of jumping to that conclusion.

CHAPTER 9

I pull my truck into the parking lot by the baseball field on Saturday morning. I walk into the dugout and ask Austin if I can borrow his eye black. He tosses me the stick and I smear it on without looking, then toss it back.

I take off my sneakers and slide my cleats onto my feet, then step out into the sunshine to do some warm-up exercises in left field. As I do my stretches, spreading my feet apart and bending forward to reach for the ground, the visiting team's bus pulls into the parking lot and the Brackettville Bandits unload. The Bandits are wearing dark green jerseys and grey pants, but as they climb off the bus, I notice they're wearing some accessories too. It looks like they're all wearing identical sunglasses and matching camouflage bandanas over their mouths and noses, like bank robbers trying to hide their faces. As they walk from the parking lot to the visitors' dugout, we can tell that they're glaring at us from behind those disguises. I stand up straight from my stretch to get a good look at them. I look at Brody, who's getting warmed up next to me, to make sure I'm actually seeing what I think I'm seeing. He looks about as confused as me, which confirms that yes, an entire baseball team of wannabe badasses just shuffled off of a school bus, giving us the evil eye as if they actually thought they looked intimidating.

"What the fuck was that?" Brody cries when the last one scurries into the dugout.

"I honestly have no idea."

"Brackettville think they're the shit," a voice I don't recognize says from behind me. I look over my shoulder to see Alex doing a pigeon stretch on the grass. *Oh, right*, I think to myself. *That's what he sounds like.*

Alex takes off his hat to scratch his head of wavy red hair. "I've played them enough to know they're more bark than bite."

"How much more?" Brody asks.

"Not a whole lot—they're still a strong team, but they talk a bigger game than they can play."

"Good to know," I say.

"Their pitcher kinda sucks. All over the place. Half the team's gonna get walked today."

Brody and I laugh at that, and we share a look that tells me we're both excited to kick the Bandits' asses.

Top of the first. Parents from Oak Ridge and Brackett-ville crowd the stands, I quickly eat my peanut butter and jelly sandwich, and Kev's booming voice fills the park. Alex strikes out the first batter, but the second hits a double, quickly followed by another Bandit who hits a single and sends the first runner to third base. "You guys ready to lose today?" he asks me as he takes a wide stance, prepared to run home.

"Those bandanas were cute," I say with a friendly tone to be as condescending as possible. "Where'd you get those? Walmart? I'd love to borrow one sometime."

"Shut up."

"And those *sunglasses!* Let me guess... Oakley knock-offs?"

He turns his head to glare at me and misses that the batter hit Alex's pitch into the outfield. The runner gets a late start towards home plate, but Tony catches the ball in right field and the runner hurries back to me at third when his coach signals him to stop and run back.

"Oops, better luck next time," I say casually.

The sun is beating down on us both, and the small cloud of dirt he's kicked up when he made the run for home lingers in the air, settling on our shoes and dusting our pants and jerseys. The runner resumes his wide stance, waiting for the exact right moment to sprint. The next batter comes up to home plate and we watch as Alex throws the first pitch... strike. He winds up the second pitch... strike again. He's about to throw the third pitch when the runner on first base tries to steal second. Alex spins and holds his arm up to throw, and my runner gives a little jolt, itching to dart to home plate. Alex turns again, an entire one hundred and eighty degrees, to face my runner and glares at him, his arm raised to throw the ball to me. Alex's threat is enough to scare the runner shitless. He immediately stops himself, falls on his ass, and scrambles back to third base. I lock eyes with Alex and give him a curt nod of approval. The other bandit is now on second base, but at least my runner didn't get to steal home. I look him up and down and see his jersey and pants are both now covered in dirt. All for nothing. I snicker and he glares at me again.

Regaining his focus, Alex takes a deep breath and looks at the batter. He winds up the third pitch, and... *ding!*

The batter hits the ball straight down the third baseline. I jump a foot in the air, stretch my arm towards the sky and feel it crash into my glove. I clench my hand around it, land on my feet, and then raise it in triumph. That's the third out, barely avoiding the Bandits scoring the first two runs of the game.

I jog back to the dugout and Coach Cole says, "Nice catch, Derek!"

"I just wish I could've tagged that douchebag out," I say as I take off my hat and put on a helmet.

Austin bats first, and after he ignores three balls pitched his way, he hits a grounder towards the Bandits' shortstop and makes it to first. Brody's up next and, and after a strike, he knocks the second pitch into foul territory. The third pitch he hits into the outfield, but the right fielder catches it and Brody has to return to the dugout. "Break a leg," he says to me as I walk up to home plate.

"Batting next for the Trojans, third baseman, Derek Milligan!!" Kev shouts into the microphone. I hear my mom and dad cheer with some of the other parents in the bleachers. As I get to the plate and look down at the catcher, I realize that he's the same asshole who was on third base with me a minute ago. "What's up?" he asks with a subtle middle finger hidden by his catcher's mitt so the umpire doesn't see.

"Beautiful day for a homerun, don't you think?"

I square up at the plate, and raise my bat, looking past my right shoulder at the pitcher. He raises his front leg and twists to throw the first pitch, but it comes in low and far away from me. The umpire calls it a ball and the catcher throws it back to the pitcher.

"Let's go, Derek!" my mom shouts.

A drop of sweat rolls over my left eyebrow and down the side of my face. Man, it got hot early. The pitcher raises his front foot again, takes a step, turns his body, and releases the pitch. I watch as the ball flies over the grass and right for me. I push back with my front foot, twisting my back towards the pitcher and I wince as I feel the ball slam into my back with an ugly *smack!* I let out a loud grunt as the pain screams for a second, then radiates from my right shoulder blade. I drop the bat and put a hand on the catcher's shoulder to stop from falling over. I regain my balance and take a few steps away from the plate. My face is screwed up in a tight wince as I take some shallow breaths and try to walk it off. The initial sharp pain of the impact wears off, but a dull, throbbing ache comes in waves. I give another grunt as Coach Cole hurries over to me. "Derek! Shit! Where'd it hit you?" he asks quickly, hesitating to lay a hand on me out of fear he'll touch the area of the impact.

"My right shoulder blade." I squeeze the words out of my mouth, my face still tense with agony.

"We'll put some ice on it when you get back to the dugout," he says.

"You okay?" the umpire asks a moment later.

"Yeah... Yeah, I'll be okay," I say, taking a deep breath, filling my lungs at last and letting my face relax from its pained grimace.

"You can take your base," the ump says. "When you're ready."

Coach picks up my bat and takes it to the dugout as I jog to first base. The crowd starts to clap now that they can see I'm going to be okay. I know the pitcher's following me with his gaze, trying to make eye contact with me so he can attempt a visual apology. I ignore him. I'm too pissed off to let him atone.

Even moving around, shifting my weight from one foot to the other, brings a swell of pain on my back. I doubt anything is broken, but I know I'm gonna have a wicked bruise for the next couple weeks. Fucking asshole.

Josh bats next, and I can tell from first base that he's a little nervous after the fiasco he just witnessed. He knocks a pitch into center field and I dart for second base. I grunt with each step, the pain building and building in my back. I wince again and I can barely see through the small slits my eyes have become; I don't even see second base when my foot touches it. I look over at third base, expecting to see Austin, but to my surprise, he's running for home. The centerfielder threw the ball to the third baseman a little late and Austin took his chances during the delay to turn on his heel and run for home. He drops to his butt and sticks out a leg, sending up a puff of dirt as he slides past the catcher. The umpire calls him safe and the crowd cheers wildly. "Austin Golfe earns the first run of the day for the Trojans!" Kev calls over the speakers.

Parker bats next, who strikes out, quickly followed by Ryan, who hits a flyball into the outfield, which is promptly caught by the left fielder. When the third out is called, I jog back to the dugout as quickly as I can without the pain becoming too intense. When I climb down the stairs, most of the team is staring at me. "Way to hang in there." "That looked like it hurt." "Do you want some ice?"

Coach Cole turns to Blake. "Your mom's a doctor, right?"

"That's right. Do you want me to get her?"

"Yes, and Derek's parents too."

This can't be good. "My parents?" I say as if the whole situation is a joke, hoping that if I act like it's getting blown out of proportion it will actually be true. "What do you need to get my parents for? I'm not dying."

"Derek, go ahead and take off your jersey and lie down on the bench. Alex, scoop some ice out of the cooler and put it in a plastic bag."

I hear Alex hurrying to the far corner of the dugout as I unbutton my jersey. My back stings as I try to let my right arm out of the sleeve. I can hear people suck their teeth as they see the site of the impact. Blake's mom hurries into the dugout, my parents close behind her. "Go ahead and lie down, sweetie," she says in her Jamaican accent. I notice her voice is a half octave higher than normal when she says it.

"How does it feel, right now?" my dad asks as I lie down on my stomach on the bench.

"I mean... it hurts."

"It is a sharp pain?" Mrs.—or, well, Dr. Robinson asks.

"No no, it's dull. It's over the whole area, not in one specific spot."

She pokes around the area a bit, I grunt as she does. "I don't think you fractured your scapula," she says at last. "But you need to ice that down and I think you need to sit out the rest of this game."

I give another grunt, this one out of frustration more than pain. "Crap."

"Sorry, bud," she says at last. "He'll want to take something for the pain when he gets home," she says to my parents. "It's not pretty but he'll be okay. Just a bad bruise."

"If it's just a bad bruise then I can keep playing."

Dr. Robinson shakes her head. "I wouldn't risk it."

"Risk *what?*" I ask angrily. Coach shushes me and I fume with my chin resting on the bench. *Hypochondriacs*, I think to myself. *All doctors are hypochondriacs. I'm fine. I can keep playing.*

Alex comes back with a bag of ice and Coach says, "Go ahead and put it on him."

Alex kneels down on the dugout floor to put his face close to mine. "One, two, three, cold!" He drops the bag on my shoulder blade and the instant shock of the cold makes me yelp again.

"A little more warning next time?" I say with a glower.

"Sorry."

A benchwarmer named Justin has to take over for me and I watch the rest of it from the dugout with a pack of ice strapped to my back. I feel like I'm watching Brody play for the first time now that I don't have to worry about playing myself. I never noticed how muscular he looks when he swings his bat, or how great his butt looks in those baseball pants. Shit. How the hell have I never noticed before?

While he's waiting to bat, he leans against the dugout railing next to me. "That's gonna be a wicked bruise," he says.

"No kidding. It's gonna be there for a while."

"Blake's mom said to take something for the pain..." he says, lowering his voice and moving in close. "We'll work on that tonight." He gives me a slightly mischievous smile and his amber eyes seem to glisten in the sunlight. For a brief moment, I can imagine Brody looking at me just like that in the dead of night, right before I place my hands on his face and kiss him.

I smile back, trying to hide how anxious that look made me. "Can't wait," I whisper back so Coach doesn't overhear. We bump fists before he walks up to home plate.

After the seventh inning, the Trojans win 4–2 and the bag of ice on my back has completely melted. I undo the sportswrap and drop the bag into a trashcan. Brody looks at my back and breathes an uneasy sigh. "How's it feel right now?"

I swing my right arm around a little bit. "It feels tender, but not bad. I know it's numb right now from the ice."

"I think you'll feel it more later," he says, unable to take his eyes off my shoulder blade.

"No, I'll feel it tomorrow," I joke.

He laughs. "That's right!"

I button up my jersey and we climb out of the dugout together. After my parents stop us and I tell them that yes, I feel okay for now but I just want to go home and shower, Brody and I walk to our cars in the parking lot behind the bleachers. I gingerly step up and slide behind the wheel, the dull pain on my back rising as I lean against the driver's seat. I wince again as I start the truck, then wave goodbye to Brody for a few hours as I pull out of the parking lot and head home.

CHAPTER 10

I take a long shower, hoping somehow the hot water will soothe the ache on my back. When the pain starts again, I decide I should take some tylenol. I get close to the mirror and try my best to look over my shoulder to see the damage. Sure enough, on my right shoulder blade, close to my spine, is a giant red splotch. The skin around it is swollen and it feels warm to the touch. I know that within a few hours, the whole thing will turn purple and it'll take at least a couple weeks to heal entirely.

Great, Brody said he wanted to go swimming tonight. Now he's going to think I look like a freak. He's gonna do what guys do and gawk at it every chance he gets, marvelling at how big it is, how inflated it looks, how red it is. I'll be like a kid who just broke his arm—Brody will want to sign my cast and talk about how sickening it is to look at my arm sticking out at an odd, unnatural angle. Am I just going to be a gross spectacle for him tonight?

Even though I've been looking forward to this night with Brody, now I can't help but feel a little anxious. I don't want him to think I'm entertaining in some disgusting way. I'll just try my best to avoid turning my back on him tonight, at least while we're in the pool. We'll probably go inside once it gets dark, then I can throw my shirt on and that'll be the end of it.

Once my mom makes me confirm with Brody that we'll be ordering pizza (she's always worried I'm gonna go hungry), I grab my swim trunks and head out the front door.

I walk down the sidewalk to Brody's house; we still have about two hours of daylight to burn before it gets too dark to stay outside. Today has been unusually warm for early April, which means we can spend longer in the pool before the cold sends us shivering back inside. When I reach the Hernandez house, I see the pizza girl handing two large cardboard boxes over to Brody. The girl walks back to her car and Brody holds the door open for me. "Long time, no see!" he calls to me as I walk across his lawn. "How's your back doing?"

And so it begins. "Okay. I took some tylenol. Still hurts to touch."

"Well, maybe I should get you a beer," he suggests playfully. "You know, to ice it down some more."

"Right right right," I say quickly, playing along. "Good idea."

I follow Brody downstairs to the walkout basement. He flips on the lights and I immediately see the minibar his dad has just recently finished installing. Black granite countertops and red-stained wood are accented beautifully by some recessed lights above the cabinets and hidden LEDs under the bartop. Four stools are tucked neatly underneath the bar and the back wall is adorned with a large mirror, in front of which sit several bottles of liquor. Brody steps behind the counter, sets the pizzas on the bar, and slides open the top of a deep freeze.

"There's a ton of beer in here," he says. "We can probably have a six pack if we want without my dad getting too suspicious." He pulls out six beers and sets them all on the counter next to the pizzas. "Three each should be enough to get us started." He closes the deep freeze and gestures towards the patio and the pool.

I hold the door open for him as he carries the pizzas and beer, then sets them down on a glass-topped patio table. The large pool sits just behind the house and just next to a gazebo with a bench swing that looks a little rusty and unstable. I'm about to say something about it when Brody says, "Dig in, I'm just gonna throw on my swim trunks." He hurries inside and runs up the stairs to his room. Brody's room. I've been there before often enough, as best friends tend to do, but tonight it seems a much more intimate space than usual. A place where anything we talk about stays between us; a place where anything that happens never leaves those four walls.

Stop.

I'm right. I hate to admit it, but I'm right. I don't want to be so focused on something else that I forget to enjoy where I am. I open the first box of pizza (pepperoni, bacon, and jalapenos), and take a bite while it's still hot. Bliss. Pure bliss. A slice of pizza, or seven, is exactly what I need after today—hell, after this week.

I take a second bite of the pizza when I realize I still have my swim trunks draped over my shoulder. I take another quick bite of pizza, then kick off my shoes and peel my socks off. I give a brief glance around to make sure none of the neighbors are watching, and I pull down my shorts and underwear, hastily stepping into my trunk's inner mesh and pulling them up to cover my manhood. I stuff the last bit of my first pizza slice into my mouth when I hear a booming voice echoing from inside the basement.

"ARE YOU READY TO RUMBLE!?!?" Brody rounds the corner by the bottom of the stairs, shirtless with a pair of red swim trunks cinched around his waist. Cannonball shoulders and bulky pecs distract me for a split second before Brody sets out on a charge straight for me.

I can't help it, my mouth curls uncontrollably into a smile, then a grin, even as I take a couple steps back. Brody bounds over the threshold of the open sliding door, and crashes into me, wrapping his arms around me as we both fall into the pool.

The sound of cicadas in the evening is cut short by the dull white noise of the pool's filter, like the hum of an electric current under the water. I let my body float towards the surface and gasp for air when I breach. My shirt is still on, and now it's completely soaked, but I'm laughing too much to care. I lift myself onto the patio and peel it off my drenched body, dropping the shirt in a sopping pile on the tiles.

Brody gasps and lifts himself onto the walkway beside me. "Your back! I totally forgot! Are you okay?"

I turn around to see his amber eyes, wide with fear, staring straight at me. "Yeah," I say, putting him at ease and hoping he drops the subject entirely. "It feels totally fine, actually."

He breathes a sigh of relief. "Okay, good." Then his expression turns mischievous again, and I get butterflies right before he puts his arms around my body, and once more wrestles me into the pool.

I've seen Brody shirtless plenty of times, and I'm sure his bare chest has touched mine before, but tonight feels different. Tonight he feels warm. Tonight when he wraps his arms around me, I feel a tingling sensation all over my body, like it's the first time we've ever touched. All I want is for it to last longer than the split second it takes for him to throw me into the water. I want to feel his skin on mine. Maybe if our arms can touch, if our chests can touch, and our hands can touch, it wouldn't be a big deal if our lips touched.

Stop it.

But maybe tonight is different. Maybe tonight I can make that happen.

That isn't what you're here for.

After about fifteen minutes of nonstop wrestling, jumping, and throwing, Brody and I stop horsing around in the water long enough to move the pizza boxes and the beer to the edge of the pool. We stand on the shallow side, elbows on the patio floor, eating our pizza and drinking our beer. After my fourth slice of the pepperoni-bacon-jalapeno masterpiece, Brody opens the second pizza box to reveal a beautiful Hawaiian pizza, topped with ham, pineapple, and cajun shrimp. "Oh my God," I say in absolute delight. "It's so beautiful."

Brody laughs and tears himself off a slice. "I'm getting pretty full," he says. "I'm probably gonna eat this slice and then just drink the rest of the night."

"I'll copy you," I say. I take a slice of the Hawaiian pizza and begin chomping away. By the time I fit the last bit of the crust in my mouth, I know I need to mellow out and digest. I grab my half-empty can of beer from the patio and lean back against the edge of the pool. I spread my arms out so that my elbows are resting on the poolside, keeping the pressure off the new bruise on my back.

Brody finishes his pizza and follows my lead. We face the trees that sit at the rear edge of his backyard, the beginning of the woods. The sinking sun has left it in obscure darkness; we can't see more than twenty feet past the first trees that delineate the barrier between Brody's domain and nature's.

"You know what I've noticed?" Brody says all of a sudden, sipping casually from his can of beer. "Something's different about you but I can't quite put my finger on it."

I blush. He noticed something different about me? What exactly does he mean? I need to know before I start running my mouth and get myself into trouble again. It probably wouldn't be best practice to start by saying, "Yeah, when you thought you were texting Camilla this past week, you were actually texting me and it felt really great to connect with you on a level other than our friendship and now I can't help but feel a romantic connection between us. What's new with you?"

I clear my throat to sound more casual. "Yeah, I don't know...." I realize that I might be able to subtly hint at something, if only I know how to word it just right. "I guess I... started seeing someone in a new light. Not in a bad way—in a good way! In a way that gave me an outlet to... I guess, express a part of myself that I... hadn't been able to express before... Does that make sense?"

Brody's eyes twinkle as his mouth slowly stretches into a broad grin. "No."

I chuckle.

Brody finishes his second can of beer and sets it down by the side of the pool, cracking open his third. "I'm kidding, I do kinda know what you mean."

My heart flutters and, dammit, those fucking butter-flies are back for a second.

"I've been feeling the same way this past week."

"You have?" I ask.

"Yeah," he says with a smile.

Was my hint strong enough? Was he picking up what I had put down? My mind is racing and I can't think of what to say, so to break the tension, I finished the last swig of my second beer and reached out for my third. "Cool."

The sun's getting low now, so we finish our beers and pull ourselves out of the pool and onto the patio. I take a step towards the table when I feel Brody's arms around me again. He squeezes from behind and for some reason, I can't help but feel like he holds on for a little too long before he turns on his back foot and falls into the pool, bringing me along with him.

We crash into the water, and I notice that this time Brody's arms are still around me, even as we start to head for the surface. He finally releases me as we reach the air again and take deep breaths. "Sorry, I just had to do it one more time," he laughs.

I smile as I heave myself onto the patio again, then realize that there isn't a towel in sight. "We forgot something."

"Oh shit…" Brody says. "I'm gonna have to run in and grab a couple." He opens the patio door and takes a deep breath. "I'll be super quick. Here I go!"

He dashes across the basement, leaving little damp footprints with each stride. He rounds the corner and I hear him darting up the stairs. Thirty seconds later, the thumping of footsteps grows louder and louder until he comes back across the basement and onto the patio, a purple towel in each hand and a pair of black gym shorts draped over his shoulder.

I thank him as I take one of the towels and pat my face dry. I run the towel down my body, and before I can ask Brody where I should change, he steps to the other side of the table and drops his trunks. I instinctively turn my back, then immediately wish I hadn't. My heart is pounding in my ears as I follow Brody's lead, dropping my swim trunks to the ground, and drying myself with the towel. I turn towards the table to retrieve the underwear and pants I've left hanging on the back of the chair. I point my face at the ground, but I can't help it. I glance over in Brody's direction. I only see his right butt cheek and the side of his thigh. Still, more than I'm used to seeing. I feel a thrilling whirl; I'm a little lightheaded, and it's probably the alcohol that keeps me from feeling ashamed from looking in the first place.

I grab my underwear and step into it, then do the same with my shorts. I pick up my cold, soaked T-shirt from the ground and wring it out over the water. The splashing catches Brody's attention. Now that he's got his ass covered, he steps out from behind the table and says, "Oh I've got another shirt for you. Follow me."

He picks up his own towel and heads inside, leading me up the stairs to the first floor, then turns a corner and up another set of stairs to the second floor. As we walk down the hall to Brody's bedroom, he stops, pushes open the door to a bathroom, and flicks on the light. "You can just hang your wet shirt and swim trunks on the edge of the tub for now."

I do so, then turn off the lights, following Brody down the hall to his room. He flips on the light switch and it's the same old room he's had for his entire life. A bed in the corner, a desk facing out a window, posters of baseball players on the walls, classic novels in a pile on the floor by his bed. I've seen it a thousand times, but it's not the same this time. This time we are both in here shirtless. This time I can't help but look at Brody in a completely different light. This time, I want nothing more than to stay here and reenact my fantasy.

Brody pulls open a dresser drawer and pulls out two shirts, one red, the other a faded green. He tosses me the green one and I can feel my heart sink as he slides the red one over his body, hiding from me his chiseled pecs, his cannonball shoulders, and his muscular arms. He gives me an askance look and I quickly pull the green shirt over my head, fitting my arms into the holes. Good thing we wear the same size.

Then Brody shouts, "All right! Let's get drunk!"

I've never been drunk before. In fact, the three beers that I've had tonight is already the most I've had in one sitting. It isn't uncommon for Brody and I to sneak a beer or two each when his parents are preoccupied with something else, but three in just a couple of hours is a new limit for me. Now Brody's walking behind the basement minibar again and grabbing a bottle of something off the wall. "Have you ever had vodka?" he asks.

I shake my head. "Only the beers you sneak me."

"Well... let's try it out! Let's see what mixers my dad has." He slides open the door to the fridge and peers inside. "I'm seeing root beer, Sprite, and orange juice. Which do you want?"

"I'll take the root beer," I say.

Brody agrees that that sounds good and lifts the two-liter bottle of root beer from the fridge. He fishes some ice cubes out of the freezer side and throws them into a pair of short whiskey glasses. "I don't think these are the right glasses for it, but it'll taste the same."

He pours in what he guesses is a little more than a shot of vodka into each glass and then fills them the rest of the way with root beer. We each grab a glass, and before I can drink, he raises his for a toast. "To a great baseball season!" he shouts.

"To a *great* season!"

We touch glasses, then our eyes meet, and without breaking our gaze, we each take a sip, tasting the cool root beer and the sharp, burning taste of the vodka.

"I think it's a little strong," I say, fighting back the urge to cough.

"That's okay," he squeezes out of a tight throat, and I know he's having trouble swallowing it too. "It means we'll get drunk faster."

After a couple more mouthfuls, we both give in and add more root beer. Then the concoction tastes way sweeter, and it goes down way smoother.

"God, I need to lose my virginity," Brody says after sinking onto the couch next to me with his second drink in hand. It's a mixture of vodka and orange juice, which I think is called a screwdriver. I watch him take a sip, then look at me with a frustrated expression.

"You probably would have if you didn't tell Camilla to take a hike," I say with a matter-of-fact tone. "You're shooting yourself in the foot here."

He chuckles then says, "That's true. She just didn't feel right, though. You know?"

"No."

"I mean, I just didn't really like her enough to date her and I know I can't lose my virginity to someone I don't really like."

"Well a second ago you were complaining about having it at all—that kinda gives me the impression you just want to get rid of it."

"Fair enough, fair enough," he says, taking a swig of the screwdriver. "Give it six months, I'll fuck a watermelon if it counts."

"What's the rush?" I ask, finishing my own drink and walking over to the bar, realizing that I'm a little off-balance as I go.

"I guess I just don't want to go to college a virgin... *If* I go to college, that is. I've been thinking a lot about it and I might not."

Caught completely by surprise, I take a step back from the bar. "*Really?* You know college recruiters are going to be paying attention these next few games, right?"

"I know, I know, but the more I've been thinking about it, I'd only go to college to play baseball, but I know I'm not going to the majors. I said that to Coach Cole and he was like, 'Oh, well you never know...' I told Grady too and he was on the same page as me.

"The way I see it, my baseball career is going to end after college. Best case scenario, I end up on a double-A team, I still need a day job, and I have a very slim chance of ever going to the majors...." He breathes a heavy sigh. "I'm not trying to be pessimistic, I'm trying to be realistic, and *real-*

istically it's just not smart for me to organize my whole life around getting into the majors when that probably won't happen."

"But if you get a baseball scholarship, at least you can get a college degree for free or pretty cheap," I counter.

"I know, but a degree for what? I've been doing a lot of thinking about it, not just the last few weeks, but the last few months, and I think I want to be an electrician. That means trade school. Going to college for a degree that won't be useful so that I can play a sport I don't have a future in isn't smart. It's spinning my wheels for four years."

"But,"—the words are beginning to jumble in my mouth—"you're so good at English and reading and all that artsy fartsy bullshit!"

"What does that have to do with anything?" he asks back. "I don't want to be an English teacher or a professor or any other career that would involve reading and writing every day. That's what I do for fun. You don't shit where you eat!"

"But-"

"But but but!" He shouts, spreading his arms wide. "Kiss my butt, lick my butt, Anything but butt! Why are you fighting me on this?"

"You're right," I say, taking a screwdriver of my own back to the couch to rejoin him. "You're right. I'm sorry. I just didn't see it coming. And I don't know if it's the alcohol or what, but everything you've said makes so much sense. Still, I know my parents want me to go to college. I don't think I could take your route."

"Do you want to be an accountant too?"

"I'd rather gouge out my eyes."

Brody laughs at that, so hard he loses his balance and almost falls off the couch.

"No, I don't want to be an accountant. I don't know what I want to do. I think I should probably just go to college and figure it out there."

"Well, if you get a scholarship, that's probably not a bad idea," Brody says. "If you have to pay for it, I think you need a plan."

I nod. "Yeah, you're right... but I also think college is the right path for me."

Brody and I lock eyes and for the first time I realize that our close friendship, our once-in-a-lifetime bond, is limited. Its days are numbered. Brody will stay in Oak Ridge, attend a trade school, learn to be an electrician and stay within our small area of the state. I'll go to college somewhere, wherever offers the best deal—it could be across the country for all I know—and then move somewhere completely different for work when I graduate. And just like that, this tight bond between us will gradually erode; slowly at first as we try to keep in touch over the several hundred miles that separate us, and then we'll grow apart entirely, hardly recognizing each other if our paths cross in a bar when I come home for Christmas. I'd look over at that man, at the face I'm staring at right now, and I'd say to myself, "I think I know that guy... or at least I used to."

"Are you okay?" Brody asks all of a sudden.

"Yeah..." I say. "I mean... no..."

"What's up?"

"I just realized that once we graduate next spring, I'll go to college, you'll stay here, and..."

"...Yeah."

"Yeah…" I quickly rub my face in my hands. "Well! No reason to get upset about it now! Let's make a memory worth missing!" I raise the screwdriver I just poured myself and shout, "To old friends!"

"To old friends!" he echoes, and we both take a sip. Then we look at each other before we set our glasses down, and I know immediately that this is a challenge. I quickly take one gulp after the other, the sweet orange juice leaving a tangy aftertaste as I swallow the last drop and set the empty glass back on the counter half a second before Brody.

"BOOM!" I shout. "Next round's on you!"

He laughs, gets up from the couch and makes his way to the bar. I follow him and watch as he pours us each a vodka Sprite, then comes around to my side of the bar, moving aside a stool to stand next to me.

"Your back doing okay?" he asks, leaning against the bar with an unsteady wobble.

"Yeah, I've barely noticed it all night."

"Is it sensitive to touch?"

"Not sure."

Brody raises his arm, reaches his hand around my right shoulder, and pokes a finger in the area of the impact. I feel the pressure of his fingertip, but only a small trickle of discomfort comes along with it. "Does that hurt?"

I shake my head. "No, notat- notat- not… at… all…"

He laughs, retracting his arm back to his side. "You're drunk!" he shouts.

"Nooooo!" I argue. "I'm just slurring my words and I can't balance, but I'm not drunk!"

"That's what being drunk is, genius!"

"Oh… well then I guess I'm drunk!" I announce.

"Good news! Me too!"

We cheer, finish our drinks, and Brody quickly pours us each another. I take a gulp and I get an idea. It's a great idea! It's foolproof! I blurt it out as soon as it comes to mind. "Let's wrestle!"

"What?"

"You and me! Right now! Bring it!" I move into the middle of the open area and take a wide, athletic stance. "I can pin you down in ten seconds!"

"Bullshit!" Brody yells, setting his drink down on the countertop with such force he's probably cracked it. He marches over and stands a couple feet away from me, just out of arm's reach. We give each other fake glares that thinly veil our drunken laughter. After a tense moment of silence, Brody lunges at me, grabbing my forearm. He quickly rushes around me and tries to grab me from behind, like he did by the pool. I kneel, grab his wrist that's now in the middle of my chest, and thrust my right shoulder to the ground, lifting Brody off of his feet and slamming him onto the carpeted floor.

He reels after landing with a loud thump on his back. "How... the *fuck* did you do that?" he asks.

"Not quite sure," I say, standing up to go back to the bar. I take a single stride, when I feel a tugging on my ankle. Brody, still lying on the ground, has taken hold of my foot and is trying to bring me back down to the ground. "Oh fuck!" I shout. Next thing I know, he's got an arm around my waist, and he rotates sharply to one side, bringing me back down to the floor with him.

"Gotcha!" he shouts as I try to crawl away from his grip, flailing around with my chest on the floor. He grabs one of my swinging arms and pins it to my body. He moves up my back to grab my other arm, but lets go of my legs in the process. I take the opportunity to forcefully sweep one of his legs, causing him to lose balance in his drunkenness and topple onto his back. I quickly and sloppily jump on top of him, pinning down both of his shoulders and giving him a triumphant, smug grin.

He struggles against me, then realizes I have him pinned down too well. He rests his head back on the soft carpet in defeat. "Damn, you got me," he accepts with a good-natured smile. A handsome smile that shows off his dimples. God he looks so cute. I'm only a few inches from his lips and I wonder again what they feel like, and in the haze of the alcohol and adrenaline I feel the room start to spin around me and it's like I'm back in the pool, underwater holding my breath with my head swimming and my balance coming and going, pitching and rolling from side to side and it's oddly freeing because I know the world is whirling around me and I don't even notice that I'm leaning forward until my lips touch Brody's and linger, the tension finally broken, and I notice how his lips feel rough, just like I thought and secretly hoped they would. And then I feel the struggle again.

Brody tries to buck me off, his hands finding my chest and giving a single, hard shove.

"*Dude!* What the *fuck!?*"

I roll off of him, recoiling and falling onto the carpet. My head still feels like it's floating, completely detached from my body and unable to control it. "I'm sorry," I blurt out.

Brody and I stare at each other for a moment, his eyes wide with shock, mine wide with fear and regret. Every hope I had for the night comes crashing down to reality. No making out, no feeling Brody's sweaty forehead on mine, no journey up to his room. Every other wish I had for the night collapses into a pile of revolting shame.

"I'm sorry," I say again stupidly, the words coming out in a single, unintelligible syllable. I scramble to my feet and hurry for the stairs, rounding the corner and crashing into the wall. I stumble up the stairs, falling to all fours because my feet alone are not enough to carry me. Once at the top, I speed as best I can through the kitchen to the front door. I mean to stop, but my momentum carries me and I slam into the door. I reel it open and stagger out of the house. As I walk down the sidewalk towards my house, I can feel the neighborhood moving around me, the houses and the trees ebbing and flowing and my feet slapping loudly against the concrete. I lose my balance and collide with a tree. I put a hand on its trunk to steady myself, the rough bark grounding me in reality, but only long enough for my stomach to protest against the flood of alcohol I've carelessly poured down my throat tonight. It spasms and I retch, leaving a mess on someone's lawn.

My main focus right now is getting home. I can think about how much I just fucked up in the morning, but for right now, I need to get home.

I stumble up the front steps of my house, unable to remember the last minute of how I got here. I try to quietly sneak through the kitchen, but I can't keep my feet from slapping against the hardwood floor so loudly that I must have woken my parents. I'll worry about that in the morning too.

I go to the kitchen sink and pour myself a glass of water, quickly downing it then immediately regretting my own haste. It feels like it's going to come back up. I take a couple deep breaths. No, no. I think it'll stay down for now.

I crawl up the stairs, embarrassed, exhausted, ashamed. I grab the small trash can from the bathroom in the upstairs hall and take it to my room, placing it on the floor next to my bed. I strip off my shirt and shorts, and I reposition the pillows so that I can't lie down flat—I'm afraid everything will come up again if I do that.

As I turn off the lamp on my nightstand, all I can think about is how badly I messed up. Would Brody hate me? Would he figure everything out? Am I a bad person?

Before I can spend too long thinking about it, my eyelids become too heavy to focus and I give up trying to work it all out.

CHAPTER 11

I wake up a few hours later, before sunrise. I feel a tingling in my stomach; I quickly grip the trash can next to my bed, puke into it, then set it down and fall back asleep.

I begin to stir again later in the morning. I can hear my parents downstairs. It sounds like they're making breakfast. I'd normally join them, but when I move, I feel an ache in my stomach, like it's tied in a knot. I have a headache too, a splitting one. I guess this is my first hangover. Fuck.

I gently swing my legs over the edge of the bed, and tiptoe down the hall to the bathroom, taking my empty water bottle with me. I rummage through the medicine cabinet until I find some aspirin. I take a double dose and then fill up my water bottle. When my parents aren't together in the kitchen, I'll have to sneak downstairs to throw away the trash bag of vomit that's currently sitting in my room. I know if I go down now, they're going to ask how last night was, what I'm doing with a trash can filled with vomit, and why I look hungover.

They're smart people. They'll do the math pretty quick, and then I'll be in deeper shit than I already am. Better to wait until the early afternoon when I feel a little better, then act like I slept in because Brody and I were up so late. Hopefully they didn't hear me come in—or at least they didn't check their watches. Otherwise my whole charade is gonna come crashing down pretty quick.

Just gotta lay low until this afternoon. Easy as that.

I open the bathroom door and find my mom staring straight at me. I freeze. Her eyes give a little flicker and I know she just processed something.

"Morning," I say, forcing a smile.

"Morning, sweetie." She's trying to hide the fact that she knows something and slaps on a superficial smile. I know that smile. That's not a good smile.

Double fuck.

"Feeling tired?" she asks.

If I say yes, she might ask why and then I'll have to lie to her, which will make things worse. If I say no, she'll tell me to go to some labor-intensive chore that'll make me throw up again.

I take my chances. "Yeah, the bruise on my back is really sore, and I have a bit of a stomach ache too."

"Too much junk food at Brody's last night?"

"...Yeah."

"Looks like it."

Triple fuck!

"I'm gonna go lie down, try to sleep it off."

"You go do that," she says. Her smile turns to an expression of disappointment as I walk back down the hall to my room.

I close the door behind myself and I hear my mom's faint footsteps as she walks down to the kitchen and talks to my dad. I can't hear the entire conversation, only bits and pieces. But I do make out "Derek.... Brody's place.... Feels tired.... Stomach ache..." Then my dad says, "Oh *really?*"

Quadruple fuck.

Well, I'm in deep shit. I'm in shit up to my fucking neck. Nothing I can do about it now, but at the very least I can sleep off my hangover. I sit down on my bed again and go back to sleep.

I'm in and out of consciousness for the next several hours, checking the time on my phone every time the sunlight or my headache or my stomach ache disturbs me enough to rouse me from my shallow slumber. Before I know it, it's noon and I still feel like crap. Then it's 1:30. Then finally a little before 3:00, I decide that my bodily discomfort has diminished enough. I feel a little hungry, but the thought of most food makes me want to throw up again. I need some plain bread. Or crackers. Not a lot. Just something to keep my stomach from growling. It's too tender to be growling right now. Every small vibration that calls out for food is a painful rattle that makes me groan.

I rise and nudge open my bedroom door, peering outside to make sure no one is waiting for me to come out, the way parents stay up late to wait for their kids when they're out past curfew. The coast is clear. I quietly walk down the stairs and into the kitchen. I don't see my parents at all. Did they go somewhere?

I gently open the cabinet door, retrieve the box of crackers, then move as quickly and as quietly as I can back up the stairs before either of my parents can confront me about last night.

Once I'm back in my room, I sit down on my bed, and check my phone. Nothing. No calls. No texts. Then a thought comes to mind.

Does Brody remember last night? We were pretty

drunk. Does he have any memory of me kissing him? Could I just play it off as a dumb thing I did while drunk? If I had laughed afterwards, he'd maybe believe the dumb-drunk-decision story. But I was embarrassed, humiliated, and then I went home. If he remembers it, he knows it was genuine. He knows I'm gay.

What should I do? How can I convince Brody that I was actually just drunk and didn't mean it? Could I tell him I thought it'd be a funny joke? Maybe I could convince him that actually he kissed *me*.

No.

It comes deep from within and reverberates around my mind. An echoing decree.

Brody's my best friend. I've lied to him so much these past two weeks. I've completely betrayed his trust, and now I need to earn it back. I can only do that with honesty. I'd have to look him in the eye and say, "Brody, I'm sorry I kissed you. I was drunk and I didn't mean to make you uncomfortable. The truth is that—"

I mean I guess I wouldn't have to *actually* say it, right? Maybe I could just say sorry?

No. Too late for that. You kissed him, you need to tell him the whole truth. No hand waving.

Fine, okay. I'll just say, "Sorry I kissed you, blah blah blah. Didn't mean to, yadda yadda yadda. The truth is that I'm... you know...."

What did I just say? No hand waving. Say it!

I can't really say it.

You must.

Why?

He's your best friend. You owe him that.

All   right.   All   right.   I'll   just   tell   him.
Straight   up.   "Brody...   SorryaboutlastnightI'mgaybutI-
hopeyou'recoolwiththat." See that wasn't so hard was it?

If you say it that fast he won't hear you. That's cheat-
ing.

Look, it's not like I'm coming out to him right now. I'll
just wing it.

I tell my inner voice to shut up as another thought
comes to mind. I'm going to have to tell Brody that I was
texting him from Camilla's account. Full honesty means full
honesty, and that's what scares me. Last night when Brody
and I were talking about the future, it was hard enough to
internalize the fact that our friendship would one day come
to an end. But when I was thinking about that, I knew it
wouldn't be for several years. Now I realize that our friendship is already on its last legs; tomorrow may very well be the
end.

I put down the box of crackers I'm nibbling on. I'm
so alone; in this bedroom, in this house, in this world. And

now my best friend might not talk to me anymore. I curl up on my bed, thinking about the incurable solitude I've created for myself and immense loneliness that lies before me, and I can't help but silently cry.

There's a knock on my bedroom door in the evening. My mom has made pasta with sausage for dinner and I can smell it wafting up through the house as she opens the door. "Derek, time for dinner," she says.

"Okay, be right down." I'm feeling quite a bit better now, at least physically. I'm not looking forward to the social and emotional train wreck that school is going to be tomorrow, but I can eat a small dinner without too many issues.

I walk down the stairs just as my mom is dishing out some of the pasta onto a plate for me. She hands it to me with a smile and I take it, sitting down at the table. My mom sits on my right, and my dad on my left. As we begin eating, I am suddenly aware of a tense silence in the room. Are they going to say anything? Are they going to tell me my punishment? Is *this* part of the punishment? Exactly how fucked am I?

My mind races with each passing minute of silence. Then finally, my dad opens his mouth to speak. "Good dinner, sweetie!"

Are they trying to torture me!?

My stomach protests with each bite, but I know I need the food. Starving myself will only make things worse. I eat slowly, my parents outpacing me, which is quite unheard of around here. When I finally finish, I pick up my parents' plates, offering to do the dishes. *Yes*, I think. *Suck up. Appease them. They don't have proof, so if I act good, maybe they'll just forget the whole thing.*

Pasta uses a lot of dishes. I start by washing the ones we ate off of, then the pot my mom boiled the pasta itself in, then the slow cooker that she used to make the sauce and sausages. That one was the hardest; there were bits of the sausage caked onto the sides of the heavy ceramic pot, but I don't complain. As I wash, I'm hoping that my parents will move into the living room, but they don't. They stay at the table, and I know my fate is sealed.

I wash the last of the serving spoons as my dad says to my mom, "I can't figure out where I put my car keys." I lay them all out to dry on a rack next to the sink, then wipe down the counter with a sponge as my mom responds with, "We need to get a keybowl." I try to surreptitiously sneak back through the kitchen to the stairs, but as soon as I start to walk away from the sink, clearly hoping to leave, my dad says, "Wait." I turn my head to look at him and he points to my seat at the table. "Sit." My heart sinks in my chest.

Oh shit. Here it comes.

I obey, pulling out the chair and taking a seat. My dad looks surly, frowning intensely. My mom has her arms crossed. Neither of them say anything for a moment. Then finally my dad speaks again. "We know you were hungover today."

No point in denying it. I remain silent and wait for him to say more.

"Weren't Brody's parents home?" he asks.

"No, they're out of town."

"We thought we could trust you and Brody to be more responsible than this. Apparently we were wrong."

He pauses again, as if he's waiting for me to say something. I don't. I just sit there and let their admonishing glares weigh me down.

"You're grounded," my mom says. "A week."

I want to know what being grounded entails—I get in trouble with them so rarely—but I don't want to ask. I'm afraid it'll make things worse.

"No phone. No TV. No computer," she continues. "You can use your truck only to go to school and practice and back. No going out after with your friends." She sticks out her hand on the table, palm up. I reach into my pocket, pull out my phone, and quickly turn it off before leaving it in her hand.

"Go get your computer," she says. "If you need to work on a homework assignment, you'll get it back, but you work on it *here*." She points a firm finger to the kitchen table. "If we see you doing anything other than homework on it, we'll add another week to your punishment."

"Okay," I say, somewhat relieved but still sullen. This punishment wasn't so bad. Nothing my parents could do to me was worse than the very-likely reality that my friendship with Brody was over.

I walk up the stairs to my bedroom, grab my laptop off of my desk, and bring it back down to deposit it on the kitchen table with my parents.

"We're *very* disappointed in you, Derek," my dad adds as I'm on my way out of the kitchen. Maybe he thinks I haven't figured that out.

I turn around to face him. "I know. So am I."

The rest of the night drags on. Without a phone to distract me, or a computer either, there's nothing to do but

154

sit around my room. I get caught up on my reading for Ms. Cooper's class, so there's a silver lining.

Even though I slept for most of the day, my body is begging for more rest by 10 p.m. I move the pillows on my bed so that I can completely lay down and my last thought of the night is a dreadful anxiety about the shit show that is sure to play out at school tomorrow.

CHAPTER 12

When I wake up on Monday morning, my stomach is still a little achy, but I know some food will fix that. I hurry downstairs for a bagel and it hits the spot just right. I reach into my pocket for my phone and remember that my parents have it. Shit.

I quickly dress for school and take a deep breath as I get in my truck and freeze behind the wheel. I sit in the driveway for a moment, just thinking... How will Brody look at me today? What will he say to me? Will he talk to me at all? What will Camilla do when she sees me? Can I avoid the disaster that today is bound to be if I just refuse to start my truck?

You can't stay here forever.

Finally, I start my truck, shift it into reverse, and back out onto the street.

I park in the back of the student lot, hoping to run into as few people as possible. I can feel butterflies in my stomach again, but not the same ones I felt at Brody's. Not the same ones I felt while I was staring Alex in the eye. This is a new breed, and I hate them.

I walk through the front doors and keep my head down. Even though I'm pretty tall, no one pays much attention to me since first period is about to start and most people are just hurrying to make it to class before the bell rings. Even though I'm power walking at a decent pace, I miss the bell and I walk into Mrs. Garcia's class about thirty seconds late. I push open the door and she stops mid-sentence to stare at me. A painful silence fills the classroom as every head turns in my direction. Mrs. Garcia gives me a slightly annoyed look, waiting for my smug excuse about why I didn't make it to class on time. Instead I just mutter, "Sorry, I'm late," and take a seat in the back of the room. I try to catch Brody's eye as I go, but he isn't paying me any attention. Camilla gives me a scowl. Mrs. Garcia is watching me with a slightly confused look, probably wondering why I'm not giving her the usual amount of shit, or why I'm not taking my seat next to Brody.

I don't know if it's just in my mind or if it's because other people notice I'm sitting at a new desk, but I can swear that a few people turn their heads towards me for a brief glimpse throughout the class. Not in an innocent way, to acknowledge a slight change from the daily routine, but in a curious way. I feel like I have something drawn on my forehead and no one told me. I'd pull out my phone just to check, but I don't have it.

An hour later, the bell rings and Mrs. Garcia's class ends. Before she excuses us, she calls from the front of the room, "Derek, can you stay for a moment, please?" More heads turn to face me before everyone exits the room. I watch Brody leave, followed by Camilla, then I walk to the front of the room.

"I'm sorry I was late today," I begin. "I just got a late start to the morning and... it won't happen again."

She waves her hand dismissively. "Yeah, I don't care about that." She leans against her desk and crosses her arms. "Are you feeling okay?" When she asks, she gives me a probing look.

I give my head a little shake of surprise. "Yeah, I'm fine. Why do you ask?"

"You were late and you weren't a smartass about it. That's not like you."

I pick up on the backhanded concern, but I know immediately she doesn't mean it as an insult. "It's fine. I'm fine."

She doesn't look satisfied, but I have to get to class. "I don't want to be late for second period too," I say as I begin to walk towards the door.

She doesn't stop me.

I have no choice but to sit next to Camilla in French, but luckily we don't do any partner activities. I still have to suffer Camilla's evil glares every other minute. It's fine. I deserve them and I know it.

Sitting next to Brody in English class is pure torture. Everyone around us can feel the animosity, the anger. I don't dare glance in his direction. I can't take the chance that he might glare at me, that he might stare at me with those amber eyes, and give me some gut-wrenching look of contempt. I can take Brody not talking to me, but I can't take him hating me. Please, anything but that.

Even though Ms. Cooper continues her lesson about *The Great Gatsby*, something about Brody's silence catches her attention and makes her narrow her eyes with suspicion. "So, who can tell me what the green light means?"

Crickets. Brody's hand stays on his desk. The rest of the class is completely silent.

"No one?" Ms. Cooper asks, her eyes flicking towards Brody. He doesn't look up from his notebook.

"Quiet today, aren't we?"

You don't know the half of it, I think.

I get a much needed break from Brody and Camillia in creative writing, but I can't seem to lose Logan's attention. His head turns in my direction every few minutes and I don't know if he's always done this or if it's a new habit of his, but either way it's getting on my nerves. I know he can tell something is wrong.

Maybe he would understand...

If I can find some time alone with him, I might just consider that.

Lunch with the team is awfully quiet. I get the feeling they can sense something is off between me and Brody. Instead of sitting next to him like I usually do, I sit a few seats down. I'm not much for conversation today, and neither is he. For some reason, though, I get more sideways glances than Brody. Way more. Something's off and I can't quite figure out what it is. I feel like I'm the butt of some elaborate joke and everyone keeps watching me, waiting for me to notice the kick me sign on my back, or the toilet paper on my shoes. As I walk through the halls, I catch more eyes than usual, and every giggle that a girl gives when she whispers something to her friends I swear has something to do with me. Maybe I'm just paranoid. Maybe I'm paranoid for a good reason.

After lunch is study hall, and even though Brody and I usually go to the weight room to workout together, I know I'm the last person he wants to spend time with right now. I decide to stay in the library instead to get a head start on my math homework. I take a seat at a table between the metal bookshelves and flip open my textbook. Someone comes around the corner just as I start to write out the first problem, and when I look up, I see Gabby from the prom decorating committee. "Is it okay if I sit here?" she asks in a low voice.

"Yeah, go ahead," I say, gesturing to the chair opposite me.

She sits down and retrieves a copy of *The Great Gatsby* out of her backpack. "Gotta get caught up on Ms. Cooper's reading assignment."

I nod to be polite, but then go back to ignoring her, focusing on my homework. That's when she taps on the table with her fingertip.

"Hey, Derek," she whispers.

I look up at her.

"Is it true?"

My stomach drops. What has she heard and who has she heard it from? "Is what true?"

"That you're gay."

What? No. Please, God, no.

I laugh, maybe a little too hard. "What? *No!* Of course not! Who told you that?"

She shrugs. "Just some rumor going around today. I

didn't mean any offense by it."

My face gets hot. Really hot. I can feel a sweat break out on my forehead. "Ha ha. Okay, but *who* told you?"

"It doesn't matter."

"It *does*." She can tell I'm angry and that I'm masking it with an unconvincing laugh.

"I heard it from Kelly."

"Great, sounds good, thank you," I say quickly, packing up my math book and grabbing my backpack, heading to a completely different part of the library.

"Wait, Derek! I'm sorry!"

I ignore her as I walk away. This explains everything. That's why everyone's been looking at me today. That's why the team was giving me sideways glances. That's why girls were whispering and giggling behind my back. Someone told Kelly and she started the rumor, and a rumor about a star athlete being a closeted gay guy was a pretty good one, definitely something that people would eat up and spread like wildfire. I've barely talked to Kelly, so there's no way she would have guessed that on her own. Someone had to have told her and I think I know who that someone is.

I storm out of the library and hurry down the hall to the weight room. If Brody felt like telling everyone about what happened at his place, then everyone could watch me beat the shit out of him. I throw open the weight room doors and my eyes dart around, searching for Brody by each squat rack... He's not here. He must be changing.

I go into the locker room across the hall, walk past the first row of lockers, past the second, and in the third alcove I find Brody sitting on a bench, tying his shoe. He's already in his gym shorts and a different T-shirt than what he wore to class. He and I stare at each other for a moment. He sees how furious I am and his stern expression gives way to confusion for an instant before he corrects it. "I'm not lifting with you," he says flatly.

"No shit, asshole!" I shout back.

"When were you planning on telling me that I was texting you the whole time?"

That stops me dead. My aggression drops like a stone into water and I don't know how to respond. I was hoping to break that news to him myself. Camilla must have told him.

"I didn't mean to."

"You didn't *mean* to?" he snaps back, marching around the bench to yell in my face. "I don't exactly see how it could've been an accident! I thought I was opening up to someone I really liked and instead my best friend was playing a prank on me!"

"It wasn't a prank! I—"

"SHUT THE FUCK UP!!" he roars. "I'm done with you, Derek! I can't trust you anymore."

He glares at me, his face only inches from mine. Wild with rage, his eyes are a knife to my heart. He walks past me, and as he does, he knocks my shoulder with his own. That does it. I drop my backpack, turn on my heel, and shove him into the wall. He wheels around and shoves me back. I stumble into the lockers with a metallic bang that echoes off the cinder block walls. The bruise on my right shoulder blade screams in pain. Brody charges at me to pin me, and I jump to the side, throwing a punch that hits him square in the face. There's a satisfying thud as my knuckles meet his cheek bone. It's a sickening feeling and it fuels my fury.

Brody recovers quickly and swipes at me with his

right hand, pushing me back into the lockers and landing a fist on my left eye. My head rocks back and bangs against the lockers. Before the pain sets in I raise my fist for another punch, but Brody grabs my wrist and pins it against my body, shoving me against the lockers for a third time, but this time holding me in place so I can't move.

I start to struggle, but now my head is ringing and a dull pain has begun to grow stronger and stronger on the left side of my face. I have no choice. I accept defeat.

I can feel Brody's grip on my wrist begin to hurt, but I'm more focused on his glare boring into me. "Don't talk to me," he growls. "Ever."

"Stop talking about me behind my back and I won't have to talk to you in-person."

He contorts his face in frustration. "What the fuck are you talking about?"

"I know you told Kelly that—about me. Now the whole school knows."

His grip loosens only a bit and his expression changes from white hot rage to... to... well, I'm not sure what. Bewilderment? Regret? I can't tell.

He pushes off against me, making sure to shove me into the lockers one final time before he storms out.

I walk up to the mirror on the wall and inspect my face. There's a red mark where my left eye meets the side of my nose and I know it's gonna be another nasty bruise. A teacher or someone is gonna ask how I got it. I'll play dumb and say I don't know or I fell or some shit. They can't make me say anything and I can't get in trouble for fighting if neither Brody nor I confess to it. Brody won't say shit about his shiner because I know he wants to stay out of trouble too.

I poke at the mark a couple times; it's already feeling tender. I give a final huff of anger before I turn around, pick my backpack up off the floor, and head for the door. I pass the second row of lockers, then the first, then I stop in my tracks as something catches my eye. Alex is standing there in the alcove, frozen. His green eyes staring right back into mine. Neither of us say anything, but I know he heard the whole thing. I was walking so fast when I entered the locker room just a minute ago, I didn't even see him.

He opens his mouth, as if he has something to say, and I give him the cold shoulder, walking back out into the hallway.

With nothing better to do, I slowly make my way back to the library. I keep my head down as I walk back in, hoping no one notices the darkening bruise on my face. I shuffle to the back corner of the reference section and sit down on the floor. I think about pulling my math book out of my backpack and working on my homework, or grabbing my copy of *Great Gatsby* and getting some more reading done. But I can't. I just can't. All I can do is sit down and fight back tears as I think about how much of my world has come crashing down around me.

Brody and I went from best friends to mortal enemies in a little over a day and a half, but not without me attempting to push our relationship in the romantic direction first. The bruise on my face is gonna raise some questions later today. I can lie to teachers and say I got it this weekend, but there are people in my history and chemistry classes who saw me earlier today. They'll know something's up.

And how can I forget that now there's a rumor going around about me that I'm gay? Worst of all is that it's true and there's nothing I can do to prove otherwise. I can tell people no if and when they ask, but why should they believe me? Why should anyone believe me? I can't help but wonder what else Brody told Kelly. Did he tell her about how I was texting him pretending to be Camilla? Did he tell her that I kissed him? Is there any way I can convince the rest of the school that it was a drunk mistake?

My private life has just been opened for the world to see. I didn't want to hide it forever. I hoped maybe when I went away to college on the other side of the country I could explore things a bit more—go on a date with a guy, kiss a guy... have sex with a guy... fall in love with a guy. Still, I want that part of my life to stay private, but that would be easier to do somewhere else, not here. Not in Oak Ridge where everyone knows everyone and the rumor mill is incessant and vicious. If I go to college on a baseball scholarship, I'd want to keep it secret from the team, at least for a while, until I knew I wouldn't get cut and maybe had a hot boyfriend to show off.

Now, who knows? There's no way the team here hasn't heard about this. They're gonna ask me at practice if it's true. They're gonna ask if I've been in love with Brody this whole time. What am I supposed to say? The truth? I don't know what the truth is anymore. I didn't *always* have a crush on Brody. Sure I noticed he was hot and handsome and cute, but it's not like I've wanted to fuck him since freshman year. I really didn't think of him in a romantic way until I started texting him and flirting with him. Maybe I flirted with him in-person without realizing it. Maybe other people noticed.

Maybe everyone just wrote it off as a bromance until they heard from a reliable source that I'm gay.

I'm going to confront Kelly next time I see her. That fucking bitch. What made it her business to tell other people? And why would Brody tell her in the first place? Was ignoring me not punishment enough? Was hating me not punishment enough? Was punching me in the face not punishment enough? Why did he have to tell my deepest, most personal secret to one of the school's designated gossips?

It feels like study hall will last forever, but the bell still rings too soon. I look at my feet as much as I can as I walk through the halls, hoping no one gets a good look at my eye. When I take my seat in the back of Mr. Thomas's class, I casually rest my head on my left hand as I look down at my notes from last week. Friday feels like a lifetime ago.

Mr. Thomas turns off the lights in the room for a short video he wants to show. He turns them back on for his lecture halfway through class, and even though the girl sitting next to me is staring at my eye, I'm sitting too far away from Mr. Thomas for him to see it. He's older and his eyesight isn't the best. I just avoid looking up from my notes as best I can.

After an hour, the bell rings again and I hurry out of the room. Unfortunately for me, I sit at the front in chemistry. Mr. Holtz is going to spot the shiner on my face. How could he not? I only have a couple minutes to come up with a convincing lie that someone in the room wouldn't immediately object to. I'll just say I did something stupid in the weight room. Let's see... I... dropped a weight on my face when I was doing some dumbbell bench press. It would cause the bruise on my eye and it sounds stupid enough that I wouldn't make it up. I can feel the edges of my mouth curling into a smile. It was dumb enough to work.

I sit down at my desk in the second row and Mr. Holtz begins to write on the board. Hopefully if he starts his lecture before he sees my face, he won't stop class to ask what happened. After writing COVALENT BONDS on the white board, he puts the marker down in the tray and begins talking. When he turns around to face the class, I lean over and dig my notebook out of my backpack, taking my sweet time. The longer I delay eye contact with him, the longer it'll take for him to notice, and the less likely it is that he'll ask what happened.

After rummaging around in my backpack for a whole minute, I finally dig out my notebook and a pencil. I sit up again, lean over a new blank page, and begin writing. Maybe I could just look down at my notes the entire class and he wouldn't even see the bruise to ask about it in the first place.

"So typically when we think of a covalent bond, we think of something like this." I hear him pick up a marker and begin to draw on the board. I have no choice. I have to look up. I watch him draw a carbon atom on the board and a ring of electrons around it. He adds four hydrogen atoms and with rings of their own, sharing electrons with the carbon atom. "So this would be a methane molecule."

Mr. Holtz turns around again and he sweeps his gaze across the classroom. His eyes land on my bruise, looks at someone else, then does a double take. His face contorts into an expression of concern and everyone turns their heads towards me. Fuck.

"Derek," he says. "Your eye."

"Can I go to the bathroom?"

A couple minutes later I'm in the boys' bathroom

down the hall. I wash my face, gently massaging the soap into the red mark. It's pretty sensitive now. What are my parents going to say? Shit, I didn't think about that until now. It feels good to escape for a few minutes and enjoy a brief moment of the privacy I used to take for granted. *I have to go back to class now*, I think with a heavy sigh. I push open the door and step out of the boys' room at the exact same time that a brunette comes out of the girls' bathroom. Kelly.

We see each other, she almost says hello, then reconsiders, and drops her hand to her side mid-wave. She looks at the floor as she tries to walk away.

"Hey!" I shout. Then I chase after her, stopping right in front of her and getting close so I can talk to her in a low voice. If I'm too loud a teacher will come out and ask what's going on.

"Hi, Derek," she says, trying to feign a happy face to hide her fear.

"So I saw Gabby today and she told me that you've been talking about me behind my back."

"Gabby? I haven't talked to Gabby."

"*Don't* fuck with me," I growl. "I know you've been going around telling everyone I'm gay. How could you do that to me, Kelly?"

Her face went from confusion to stone cold contempt. "I'm Bridgette."

"Fuck! Wait a minute, not so fast," I say, tugging at her wrist as she tries to walk away again. "You knew exactly what I was talking about, which means you've been talking behind my back too."

There's an overwhelming look of guilt in her eyes.

"Why do you do shit like this?"

"It's not as simple as you think."

"Yeah, I bet there's a real method to the madness."

"You think I like this?" she asks quickly before giving a cursory glance around the empty hallway, nervously adjusting her skirt. "Look, I won't tell anyone else, okay?"

"Thank you." I say it a little more like it's an insult than I intend. "Who'd you hear it from in the first place?"

"Kelly."

"And who'd she hear it from?"

"No idea."

I give her a skeptical look.

"No, really. I have no idea."

"Who did you tell?"

"Just some friends."

"And they told their friends and they told their friends and then Gabby asked me about it in study hall."

I can tell that she wants to apologize again, but I decide that I'm done looking at her. "Get the fuck out of here," I say pointing with my thumb over my shoulder to whatever class it is she came from.

She scurries around me like a mouse trying to avoid the gaze of a hungry lion. Her footsteps grow quieter as she scampers down the hall and I walk back to chemistry in the opposite direction.

Mr. Holtz tries to stop me after chemistry to ask about my eye. I explain I have to make it to practice and bolt out of the room before he can protest. Once outside, I retrieve my bat bag from my truck and walk to the baseball field across the street. I'm not looking forward to practice today.

I'm gonna be around Brody again and I'm sure the team has heard the rumors about me by now. I somehow know that I'll be the center of attention at practice, but no one will say anything about it. That makes it worse.

It looks like I'm the first one on the field and I breathe a sigh of relief because at least I can have another few minutes of privacy before the team shows up. I walk down into the dugout to change when I see Alex again, standing at the far end, staring at me.

I nod to him, as if to say hello, and drop my bags on the opposite side of the long bench. I face the wall and quickly change my shirt, put my ball cap on, and pull my glove out of my bat bag. When I turn around, Alex is standing just a few paces away from me. He runs a hand over his beard and casts his green eyes down at the floor. "I... uh..."

We hear voices outside the dugout and before I can ask Alex what he wants, he walks back to his things at the other end of the bench.

Austin and Parker come down the stairs and as soon as they see me, I can't help but think they get a little quiet, just for a second, before continuing their conversation. I don't know if it's because of my face or because of what they've heard.

I'm gonna overthink everyone's reaction to seeing me if I stay down here, so I go out onto the field and start doing some warm-ups. I just need someone to play catch with.

"You about to warm up?" someone asks from behind me. I spin to see Alex holding up a baseball and raising his eyebrows.

"Yeah, let's toss the ball a bit."

"Sure," he says. "Let's go to the outfield."

I don't protest, and as we begin walking, Alex gives a glance over his shoulder to make sure we're out of earshot. "You okay?" he asks.

I can feel his intense gaze like always. "Never better."

"Look, I'm sorry to bring this up, but I heard a rumor about you."

My blood boils and he instantly tries to calm me.

"Relax, relax. I'm not going to ask you about it." He breathes a heavy sigh and I can tell he's deciding whether or not to say something when he almost blurts out, "Look, I know I'm new on the team and I don't want to overstep some boundary, but if you did want to talk…" The words hang in the air until he decides not to finish the thought, and punctuates his sentence with an abrupt nod.

I give him a sideways look. Why would I want to talk to Alex? I don't know him.

Hang on. I don't know him… Someone I don't know, who doesn't have all the same friends as me, whose social group isn't completely intertwined with all of Oak Ridge. He could be the perfect person to vent to.

Still, can I really emotionally dump my entire life on the new guy? "I don't know, Alex. You probably don't want to hear everything I have to say."

He shrugs. "I really don't mind, and it looks like you could use someone right now."

I begin to weigh my options until I realize that I don't have many at the moment. I either have to talk to someone or bottle everything up until I explode.

Half convinced Alex is gonna back out anyways, I ask him, "Are you busy after practice?"

He shakes his head. "Nope. I can give you my number

before we go."

"No use. I'm grounded and my parents took my phone. Can you remember an address?"

"Sure."

"323 Auserre Drive. Come at 8 p.m. but park a couple houses down the street."

"I take it I shouldn't ring the doorbell?"

"No. There's a tree outside my bedroom."

CHAPTER 13

Alex and I toss the baseball back and forth a bit, then do our warm-up stretches and sprints. Once practice gets started and Coach Cole tells the outfielders to practice hitting and the infielders to practice grounding drills, Randy asks where Brody is. He still hasn't shown up. "He wasn't feeling well," Coach says a little dismissively. "He went home."

A couple people glance at me. Great.

Without Brody there, practice isn't nearly as bad as I thought it would be. Still, I know what everyone is thinking, what's on everyone's mind as they catch glimpses of my bruised eye.

When I get home, I quickly shower and hide from my parents in my room. I wait until my dad calls me down for dinner to show my face. I don't want to start a conversation about my eye earlier than I need to. It'll give us something to talk about at the dinner table.

I slowly walk down the stairs, and when I round the corner to the kitchen, my mom clasps her hands over her mouth and gasps. "*Derek!* What happened?"

"I was doing dumbbell bench press today and I dropped the weight on my face."

She gives me an incredulous look. "And what was this dumbbell named?"

"You think I would make up dropping a weight on my own face? If I was going to make something up, don't you think I'd invent a better story than that?"

"It looks like you got into a fight," my dad says.

"Did the school call you about a fight?"

"No," he admits reluctantly.

"There you go. Just a stupid mistake is all," I say definitively, ending the subject and taking a seat at the table. "Now, how was work?"

"It was good," my mom says absent mindedly.

I shake my head. "No no no. Don't just say it was good and wave your hand. You hate it when *I* do that to you, please don't do it to me. Tell me what happened at work."

I then pretend to listen as my parents fill me in on their office gossip all while managing to evade trouble for myself. I won't lie, sometimes I'm smart as fuck.

After dinner, I slip back upstairs and check my watch. Alex should be getting here soon. I keep an eye towards the road, twilight setting in as the sun vanishes behind the trees. I work on my math homework for thirty seconds at a time, expecting to see a crappy little red convertible come passing by the house at any minute. Finally, after laboring through three problems, I hear the familiar whine of an engine that sounds like it should belong to a moped, but I know it's actually Alex's car. I look down the darkened street to see a pair of headlights flick off. I hear the faint sound of a car door closing over the chatter of the living room TV downstairs. Hopefully my parents are distracted enough that they won't hear anything.

I open my window as Alex reaches the stretch of the sidewalk in front of the house, waving to get his attention. He nods at me and walks over to the oak tree and heaves himself onto the first branch that's a few feet off the ground. I remove the screen from the window and I keep an ear to the door as he climbs to make sure my parents are still watching TV. Before I know it, Alex is hanging from a branch just a couple inches below and a foot away from the bottom sill of my window. He reaches over, grabs the window sill, and heaves himself up. "Hi!" he announces when he sticks his head through the window.

"*Shhh!*" I scold him. "My parents aren't supposed to know you're here."

"Sorry," he says quietly as he swings a leg over the lip of the window.

I put the screen in my closet. That way if Alex needs to get out in a hurry, he doesn't have to fiddle with the stupid thing. Alex starts to push the window closed and I stop him. "Wait, leave it open. The crickets and the noise from the street'll hide our conversation—just in case one of my parents walks by the door."

"Good idea," he says.

Then we both just stand there.

"So...." he says.

"So...." I repeat.

"What's up?" He sits down on the bed, kicking off his shoes and pulling his feet up underneath him. I follow suit.

Before I explain everything to him, before I start at the beginning, I have to figure out where the beginning is. Was it when I got drunk and kissed Brody? No, it was when I started texting Brody from Camilla's account. No, it was when Alex showed up to practice. No, wait, maybe it was when Camilla told me she had a crush on Brody. Or maybe the beginning was all the way back in seventh grade when I kissed Ashley Donati behind the bleachers and didn't feel the immediate urge to do it again.

I take a deep breath and say, "Okay, maybe I should preface all of this with a confession."

"Okay...?"

"I'm... well... you know."

"No... I don't know."

When I first saw Alex on the baseball field, when he asked me for athletic tape and those green eyes met mine for the first time, I had no idea he would eventually be sneaking into my bedroom so that I could tell him about all of this.

"I'm..." The butterflies begin again and I feel like I'm gonna throw up. I have to say it fast or I just might. Deep breaths. Here we go, here we go.

Don't look him in the eye if that makes it easier.

"I'm gay."

And a weight is gone. I can breathe again. I can feel my blood pressure decreasing in real time and I'm overwhelmed with the simultaneous desire to laugh and cry. "I've never said that before," I add, risking a glance at Alex and fighting the urge to start hyperventilating. He doesn't seem to react at all. He's already heard the rumor. He's not surprised. That's the opposite of what I hoped for. I've always wanted people to be a little shocked when they heard, like I was the last person in the world they expected to be gay.

I look down in my lap, feeling somewhat defeated even though I just came out to someone for the first time. I'm thinking about what to say next when I feel Alex place a large, warm hand on my shoulder. It's nothing more than that, but somehow it's the most comforting gesture anyone has ever done for me in my entire life. I put my hand on top of his and look back at him. "Thanks," I whisper. Now his expression looks like he's watching an animal suffer. He looks so concerned, so sorry for me. Not exactly what I was expecting; I'm confused more than anything, but I can't deny the small satisfaction I get from this situation.

"Okay..." I breathe at last. "Now you know. Let me start at the beginning..."

I tell Alex everything. How Camilla told me she liked Brody, and asked for my help at first, then things spiraled out of control and I went along with it because I secretly enjoyed it even though I was being dishonest to my best friend, and Camilla went along with it because she got to free ride off of my hard work. I tell him about how I thought, really hoped, that Brody was gay and I fantasized about kissing him, and how Camilla thought I had done something or persuaded him to break things off with her. I leave out the part about me drooling over Alex when I first saw him—he's straight, I don't want to creep him out—but I explain how Brody invited me over for a night of drinking and shooting the shit and then we got too drunk and I ruined everything by kissing him and now the whole school knows I'm gay.

Alex just listens and reacts. He furrows his brow, scratches his beard, asks questions when something's confusing—which I understand, it's a confusing story—and when I'm finally done I exhale a heavy sigh and wait for him to say something. Anything.

"I don't know Brody very well," he begins. "I don't know anyone at the school very well. I'm too shy." He chuckles to himself. "But Brody doesn't strike me as the type of person who would backstab a friend like that."

"Well, he didn't strike me that way either but here we are."

"I'm sorry, Derek," he says, putting an arm around me and pulling me in for a hug. He's warm and it feels good to have his arms around me, rubbing my back. I hardly notice when his hand runs over the bruise on my right shoulder blade. He holds me for at least a whole minute and I try to hide the fact that I squeeze a couple tears out of my eye and onto his shoulder. I sniffle quietly, but I know he still hears me.

I smell the faintest hint of a cologne as I pull away and say, "What do I do, Alex?"

He leans back on his hands. "What do you want?"

"I want Brody to be my friend again. He's my best friend and I don't want to lose that. I want to go back to being gay in secret, and if it's not too much to ask, I wouldn't mind a boyfriend too so I could enjoy being gay for once instead of putting it off until college."

Alex laughs and I can't help but crack a smile too.

"Well that second thing—about being gay in secret," he says. "That's gone. You can't get that back. The rumor's out there, you can refute it, but no one will believe you. Not because of how you act or anything, people just believe what they want to believe. I'm sorry. I really am. But the sooner you come to terms with that, the better you can plan for the obstacles in front of you.

"That first thing about getting Brody's friendship back —do you really want that?"

"Yes!" I say back.

He holds up a hand to stop me. "You're not thinking very clearly about it right now. You need to take some time to really consider that. If he spread a rumor so that the whole school would know you're gay, is that someone you want back as a friend?"

It takes me a minute, but I drop my chin and shake my head. "I guess not," I say.

"Maybe I'm misreading the situation—he's your friend, not mine—but you need to spend some time thinking about it before you know for sure.

"That third thing, about the boyfriend—it sounds nice. You can't be the only gay guy in school, right?"

"No but most of them are super skinny and don't play sports or anything. I like men," I joke.

Alex chuckles at that. "I get it."

"Just not my type, is all," I explain.

"So, what do you want?"

"I don't know. I think I just wanted to be heard—to be seen."

Alex reaches out and puts his hand on my shoulder again. "I see you, Derek. I hear you." I meet those green eyes with my own and he gives me a warm smile.

Then I hear footsteps coming up the stairs. My heart starts racing. "Oh shit! Someone's coming!" I breathe.

"I'll go," he whispers, standing to go to the window.

"There's no time!" I get the words out just as there's a knocking at the door. "Quick, hide in the closet!"

Alex rolls over on the bed, gently puts his feet on the floor and takes two agile steps to the closet that's standing open. He sits in my laundry hamper, which thankfully is mostly empty, and I silently shut the closet before opening my bedroom door to find my mom standing just outside.

"Is someone in there with you?" she asks, standing on her toes to try to see over my shoulder.

"No, of course not," I say, feigning exasperation from mistrust. Slimy move, I admit, but I was already in trouble.

"Thought I heard you talking."

"Yeah, I was talking to myself. You took away my phone. I have to entertain myself somehow."

She gives me a sideways glance and I hope that's the end of it. Then she says, "I need to talk to you about something super quick." She starts forward and I have no choice but to move aside for her. She sits down at the foot of my bed and I quickly sit exactly where Alex was sitting a moment ago, hoping my mom doesn't notice that there are two butt prints on the comforter. "So I called Brody's mom."

Oh shit.

"And apparently Brody also came home from school with a bruise on his face." She gives me a suspicious look. "Any idea how that happened?"

"No. Brody wasn't at practice today, so I didn't see him after lunch."

"Well apparently he told his parents that he dropped a weight on his face while he was doing skullcrushers."

Of course! Why would I go with dumbbell press when skullcrushers literally explain the injury with the name of the exercise? Damn, Brody's smart.

"So you two were in the weight room together, and you both dropped weights on your faces... in completely separate workouts... Independently... And you forgot about it between then and now?"

I give her a smug grin. "Crazy story, right?"

180

"Sounds like bullshit. You two got into a fight."

"No we didn't!" I say, waving a hand at her.

"I wasn't born yesterday, Derek. You two got into a fight over something from this weekend. Now I don't know what happened or who started it, and I don't care. Brody has been your best friend since first grade. I am not going to let you two throw that away over a stupid fight."

"Mom, please. It's more complicated than that," I say through gritted teeth. I pray I won't have to come out to her right here and now just to get her to shut up. It was hard enough telling Alex and I barely know him. Also, I really don't want to have that conversation while he's hiding just a few feet away. "You don't understand," I tell her.

"You're right," she says, a trace of a smug smile on her own face. Dammit, that's where I get it from. "The good news is I don't have to, but I *am* going to force you and Brody to make up."

"*Mom!*" I protest.

She raises a stern hand and silences me. "Enough, Derek. You and Brody are going to do yard work at his place this Saturday. You're going to work together and by the time you come home, the two of you will have buried the hatchet."

I hold my tongue. I'm already grounded, and for good reason. Fighting with her about this is either going to force me to spill my secret or get me into even more trouble. My mom stares at me for a couple more seconds and then turns to leave. As she does, her eyes catch the shoes between the bed and the window. Then she cocks her head curiously and freezes.

Oh crap. I know what she's going to ask. Quick, think of an excuse! Those are mine, they're new. No wait, they don't

181

look new. I've had them for a while, but I only wear them to practice and the weight room. Yeah, that's why she's never seen them.

She moves her gaze from the shoes to me and says, "Have a good night." She gives me that smile again. That smile that I know means a punishment is in the works. Does she know those aren't mine? Does she just think she hasn't seen those shoes before? Does she even know what my shoes look like? I don't know what her shoes look like, but then again I'm a guy so I don't really notice other people's shoes that much. But Mom's a *woman!* There's no way she hasn't noticed, right? Oh fuck, how did I manage to dig myself into an even deeper hole than the one I'm in now? All I can do is play it cool and hope that she just doesn't think anything of it. All I know for sure is that Alex has to be twice as stealthy leaving as he was coming in.

My mom walks out and doesn't close the door behind herself. Once she disappears down the stairs, I hurry over to the door and push it closed, then I wheel around to the closet and open one of the doors to find Alex still sitting in my laundry hamper. "You can come out now," I whisper.

"No, she'll be listening for a second voice," he says. He stands up from the hamper, tosses it into the middle of my bedroom, and sits back down on the closet floor. Thank God it's clean otherwise he'd be in a living hell right now. "Let's stay in here," he says.

"Good idea." I sit down next to him and pull the door closed so that just a slit of light is coming in. This would be like seven minutes in heaven if I wasn't completely distressed and Alex wasn't straight. On any other night, this would be great, but there's no sense in chasing after a straight guy. I only had to make that mistake once to learn my lesson for good.

In the darkness, I can only make out the edge of Alex's beard, the side of his cheek, the tip of his button nose, and a little twinkle in his left eye, the one closest to the door. "We'll just have to whisper."

He nods. "I can do that."

"I can't thank you enough for everything, Alex. For just listening to me. I really needed it."

"Of course." I feel his hand on my shoulder again. I jump a little bit. "Sorry," he breathes quickly.

"No no no, it's okay. I just couldn't see you reach out, it's so dark. My eyes haven't adjusted yet."

There's a moment of silence between us. "You don't need to leave anytime soon, do you?"

"No, why?"

"I think my parents are on high alert right now. My mom saw your shoes. She didn't say anything but she already heard another voice coming from here. I think you should stay for a while, at least a couple hours, just to be safe."

"Okay," he says. I'm a little confused. I thought he'd be frustrated or angry.

"I know it's a lot to ask. Like *a lot* a lot."

"It's okay, really," he repeats. His tone is so reassuring. "I don't have anywhere to be."

"Won't your parents get mad about you being out so late on a Monday night?"

He shakes his head. "I'll just explain that a friend needed me."

He called me a friend, and I feel like my heart is going to melt. "I do need a friend right now."

"Here I am!" Even in the dark, I can tell he's smiling. "If we're gonna be in here a couple hours, you wanna watch something on my phone?"

"Oh sweet. Hang on one second." I gently push open one of the closet doors, tiptoe across the bedroom, and steal a couple of pillows from my bed. I rush back to the closet and throw the pillows against the side wall so Alex and I can lean back. My closet isn't very deep or long, but it's enough for both of us to lean against the side with our legs extended, even if it's not enough to lie down completely.

I crawl over Alex's legs and sit down between him and the back wall. Our shoulders touch as he pulls out his phone. He plugs in a pair of earbuds and hands one to me. "My family just got a Hulu subscription," he says. "We can watch *Family Guy* if you want."

"Yeah! I could use a good laugh."

"Just keep it quiet," he reminds me.

The glow of his phone lights up the closet, and I try not to lean in too close. He doesn't seem very uncomfortable, but I also don't want to push it. I don't want him to think I have a crush on him.

Even though we're staring at the bright glow of the phone screen, I can feel my eyelids start to get heavy after half an hour. "Sorry," I whisper through a yawn. "I'm getting tired."

"I'm getting a little tired too."

"You can head home if you need to."

"No no, it's still kinda early. Your parents might catch me. I'll wait a little longer."

As the minutes tick by, I can feel my head start to nod under the newfound weight of drowsiness. I think about saying something to Alex, but next thing I know my head is on something firm, yet remarkably comfortable and I forget about trying to follow the show.

CHAPTER 14

The abrasive klaxon of an alarm jars me awake. The blaring horn stops after only a few seconds and I rub my face on my pillow, hoping for just a few more minutes of sleep. Then my pillow shifts. That's when I remember that I'm not in my bed, I'm in my closet on the floor with Alex. That must have been his alarm that went off just now. But that also means that he stayed over until the morning and that isn't a pillow my head is resting on—it's his shoulder.

"Whoa!" I say, sitting up straight.

"Oh, shit," he says groggily, dazed and disoriented. "Uh... I.... uh..." He and I are both immediately aware of the fact that I fell asleep with my head on his shoulder and he rested his head against mine, and that was how we spent the night. "Let's not speak of this again. Please."

"Yeah, no, absolutely," I say quickly.

"If my parents call your parents or... whatever... I slept on the floor and you slept on the bed."

"Yeah, works for me."

He pushes open the closet door and steps out, stretching. I stand behind him and check my watch. "It's only 5:30," I say. "Do you usually get up this early?"

"No, I set an early alarm just in case, so I could go home before my parents wake up and tell them I got home at

186

1 a.m or something."

"Damn, good thinking."

"Not my first time sneaking out," he says with a mischievous grin. He picks up his shoes from near the window and says, "You go back to sleep, on your bed, although you could go back to the closet—I won't judge."

I stifle a laugh and he gives me a triumphant grin.

"I'll get out of here."

"Go down the stairs and out the front door," I whisper to him. Just be super quiet."

"Deal."

"And Alex," I say before he walks out of my room. I almost grab his arm, but he stops and turns around. "Thank you. For everything."

He shrugs casually. "It's what friends do."

He slips out the door and tiptoes down the stairs. A few moments later I watch him walk across the lawn to the sidewalk and down to where he parked his car. It feels weird calling Alex a friend; I hardly know him. But still, as I lie down on my bed for another hour of sleep, my heart warms knowing that I do have one genuinely good friend in the world, someone who has my back no matter what.

It only feels like a few minutes have passed when my dad knocks on my door to tell me it's time to wake up. I change out of yesterday's clothes and throw them into the hamper that's in the middle of my room. When I pick it up to put it back in the closet, I notice an unfamiliar faded green shirt on the bottom.

It's Brody's. He gave it to me on Saturday night after

we were done swimming. Well, I guess that'll give me an excuse to talk to him later today, and I *am* going to talk to him today. I know what Alex said, and I know I'm not exactly in the clearest headspace right now, but a good night's sleep can work wonders. I at least want to say I tried to patch things up with Brody. Sure he started the rumor that I'm gay, but that's all it was—a rumor. After a few days, no one will remember it in the first place. It was a dick move, but maybe I deserved it after texting him while pretending to be Camilla. That was way out of line for me and this was way out of line for him. Maybe we're even now. Maybe we can put all of this behind us and go back to being friends again.

I pull the green shirt out of my hamper, fold it up into my backpack and head downstairs. My dad pours himself a cup of coffee and when he looks up at me, his eyes flick over to something on my left. "What is it?" I ask.

"Why is the front door unlocked?"

I turn around to see the handle on the bolt lock turned to the unlocked position, a minor detail I overlooked when Alex snuck out an hour ago, one that just might give me away. Damn my dad's eagle eyes.

"I must've forgotten to lock it when I got back from school yesterday."

"Oh... Okay..." he says, seemingly unconvinced. I can't help but wonder what my mom told him last night after she and I talked in my room.

I decide to just say goodbye and go to school before either of my parents can ask me any more questions.

Brody is still giving me the cold shoulder and silent

treatment, and I'm taking his silence as a hint that I'm banished from his presence. Or maybe I just think I'm unworthy of it. Either way, I choose a seat as far away from him in class whenever possible. Still, I'm determined at the very least to return his shirt to him today. I just need to do it in private. I think about meeting him in the locker room again, but that seems like a bad idea.

In English, I take a seat way in the back of the class in a desk that's usually empty, leaving the desk next to Brody unoccupied. A couple people glance my way at the beginning of class, but most forget about it by the time Ms. Cooper starts talking.

When English ends and Brody leaves, instead of moving to my usual seat, I just stay in the back of the room to make the seat change seem a little more casual. Much to my surprise, however, Logan notices that I'm in a different spot when he walks into the room, and decides to join me. "Whatcha doing back here?" he asks.

"Just waiting for class to start," I say, an annoyed tone clear in my voice.

"Something wrong?"

I'm about to tell him no, but then I remember Logan's status in the school. President of the LGBTQ+ club. He might have some wisdom to throw my way. "Yeah, kinda."

"What's up?" He furrows his brow in concern.

"I don't wanna get into it right now," I explain.

"What are you doing during study hall?"

After another uncomfortable lunch with the team, I meet Logan outside the library where he tells me to follow him. We walk down the hall, turn a corner, and Logan pushes open the door to the art room. It's twice the size of a normal classroom and its walls are lined with art supplies—paint, brushes, plaster, clay, pastel crayons. The mural for prom that we were painting just a few days ago is sprawled out on the floor. The yellow brick road has been completely filled in. The towers of the Emerald City have been given their gleaming coat of paint, and I see that Gabby has added flecks of white so that it looks like they're glimmering in the sunlight. The first band of a rainbow has been streaked across a white sky, which someone will turn blue later. Logan hands me a paintbrush and a little cup of red paint. "You'll be filling in the sleep poppies," he says, beaming at me.

"Oh… I don't think I'd be very good at painting flowers."

"They don't really need to look like flowers," he tells me. "Red splotches will do just fine."

We take a seat on the tile floor and begin painting. Logan is working on the yellow band of the rainbow; the red band hasn't dried yet and he knows not to paint wet next to wet.

"So… what's up?" he asks me again, giving me a curious look from the other side of the mural.

I breathe a heavy sigh. "What have you heard?"

"I heard that you're gay and in the closet."

"Oh, is that all?"

"And that you're crushing on Brody big time," he adds.

I don't want to explicitly confirm both of those rumors, but I also know that if I correct the second one (since I am no longer crushing on Brody) without correcting the first, then it'll seem like I'm corroborating the first. I think about denying both for a moment, but then I remember that I'm hoping Logan has some advice for me and lying to him won't help me out. I just remain silent.

"Look, I know what you're going through," he says without looking my way, focusing on the rainbow instead.

"Oh do you?"

"When I came out freshman year, there was a lot of talk, but over time it kind of blew over."

"I didn't come out, Logan. Someone outed me."

His face morphs into a perturbed grimace. "I know, and that's not fair to you. But I think people will accept it as time goes by. That's what happened to me."

"I don't want people to accept it—I want people to *forget* it!"

"That won't happen," he says, finally facing me and pointing the business end of his paintbrush at me. "Trust me. I know. Rumors like that are too juicy for anyone to forget."

"What should I do?" I ask him.

He shrugs. "Whatever you want."

"That's not helpful."

"Okay then how about this—instead of hiding it, let it out! It feels *so good* to let the gayness flow and just be yourself!"

"But I *was* being myself. I always have been."

"Then why are you so upset about this rumor?" He asks it with a somewhat aggressive tone. Damn, he got me. "Why do you think there's something wrong with being gay?"

"I don't. I just don't want people to know it about me."

Logan looks up from the mural again and narrows his eyes at me, thinking... "You know, we have someone coming to the school in a couple days to talk to us about something. I think you should come."

"What are you talking about?" I ask.

"Oh sorry, I'm talking about the Rainbow Club."

"The Rainbow Club? What's that?"

"It's the new name for the LGBTQ+ Club. We're re-branding."

"What's he going to talk about?" I ask.

"You'll just have to come and find out."

My blood starts to heat up. I don't like getting yanked around. "If you don't tell me, I'm not going," I snap at him.

"If I tell you, you'll decide it's stupid and doesn't apply to you and you won't go."

"You're not wrong about that," I growl, focusing again on the flowers I'm painting.

"Look," he says to me in a comforting tone. "You can't be the only gay athlete in the school. You're probably not even the only gay athlete on the baseball team. What about that new guy?"

"New guy? You mean Alex?"

"Yeah. Isn't he gay?"

I swallow the urge to roll my eyes and instead play it cool. I hadn't considered it if I'm being honest. Maybe there were clues last night, but I was more focused on Alex being a friend and giving me emotional support than anything else. "I don't know," I tell Logan. "Why don't you ask him?"

"*No!*" he whispers back. "You can't just ask people if they're gay. That's so *rude!*"

"What difference does it make who else is gay?"

"So you know who you can go out with!"

"I don't want to go out with anyone," I clarify. "Not

while I'm in high school. I just want high school to be over with."

"Okay, you *definitely* need to come to Rainbow Club on Thursday!"

I ignore him and go back to the mural. These poppies I'm painting look absolutely awful. "I'm surprised no one's kicked me out of the prom decorating committee," I say absent-mindedly. "I'm not going to prom and I'm terrible at decorating."

"Prom's gonna be a lot of fun this weekend. I really think you should go."

"I have no one to go with."

"You can take Alex," he jokes.

I give a humorless laugh. "Ha ha. Who are you going with?"

"Kelly and Bridgette."

"Last I checked neither of them are guys," I point out.

"Hey, I don't have to take a guy to prom. I'm already comfortable with who I am."

I want to punch him for that. I am comfortable with who I am, just not this one part of me. Right? Yeah. Wait... no, that doesn't sit well in my head. I know when I'm lying to myself.

I bolt out of Mr. Holtz's chemistry class at the end of the day, once again desperate to get to practice and away from school. I wheel around a corner and almost walk straight into Gavin Murphy. He stares at me a little too long and I know he's admiring my black eye. "Good to see someone gave you a piece of their mind, Milligan," he says with a sneer.

"Say hi to the other fairies on the baseball team for me."

I shove his shoulder as I walk past him, eager to get outside. Right now, I'd do anything to escape the real world and just have one minute at the plate, where Alex throws me a pitch—a challenge—and I once again knock it out of the park. I'd die just for that single moment of glory.

But there's something I still have to do. It's been in my backpack all day and the dugout will be the best place and time as long as he gets there soon enough. I have to give Brody his shirt back.

I dash down the dugout stairs a few minutes later and sit at the far end of the bench, waiting for Brody to come in, hoping he'll be alone when he gets here.

Before long, I hear footsteps in the dirt behind the dugout and I quickly turn my head towards the doorway to see Brody walk in. Our eyes meet. The shiner on his face looks almost as bad as my own. He immediately diverts his gaze, dropping his bag on the complete opposite end of the long bench and ignoring me entirely.

My heart sinks and I feel a little pang of guilt again, but I know I need to do this now before someone else comes in. I take the faded green shirt out of my bag and walk over to Brody.

I stop a few feet away from him and he looks over at me, then gives me an annoyed and expectant look, as if to spit at me an aggravated "What?"

"I..." my voice is shaky again and I clear my throat, starting over. "I realized last night that I still had your shirt." I stick out my arm with the shirt awkwardly. "Thank you."

He eyes the shirt, then me, then the shirt again. He takes it quickly, almost snatching it from my hand. Then faces the bench again. "Thanks," he says quietly. "Happy to help."

The words are all coming to me at once and I know I just need to spit something out before I vomit. "I'm sorry, Brody," I say, almost panting once the words have left my mouth. "I lied to you and I betrayed your trust and... and I kept secrets from you that I shouldn't have. I was a terrible friend and... I want you to know that I really am sorry."

Every word hurts because every word reinforces the painful truth that I hate to admit—I'm a bad friend. No matter how much I was there for Brody, I still used him and I still lied to him and friends don't do that to each other. But once it's out, I'm glad I said it. Even if Brody never does forgive me and never wants to talk to me again, at least I'll know that I gave him a sincere apology and that is worth the few extra minutes of sleep I'll get at night.

Brody exhales and turns to face me. "I'm mad at you. I still am, but thank you for apologizing." He faces his bag again and I take a step backwards to walk away when he shouts, "Why didn't you tell me!?"

"I thought you'd be mad," I mutter.

"I'm not mad that you're gay! I'm mad that you lied to me!"

I'm about to tell him to keep it quiet, but what's the point? Everyone's heard already.

"I've told you everything, Derek. I have never kept a single secret from you. Why would you keep this hidden from me?"

"I didn't know how to tell you."

"So you kissed me?"

"Well... now you know."

He glares daggers at me. "That's true. Now I know. Thanks for telling me in such an appropriate manner."

"Why do you even care anymore? You got even," I snap back at him.

"What are you talking about?" he asks.

"Don't play stupid with me," I shoot back with an annoyed voice.

"Derek, I don't know what you—"

"You told Kelly that I was gay and had a crush on you so that she'd spread the rumor around the school." I shake my head. "I know what I did was way out of line, but I can't believe you outed me to everyone for it."

Brody screws up his face. "Derek, what the fuck are you talking about?"

"Literally the whole school knows about me. They all know—uh, *think* I have a crush on you. You think I'm fucking stupid? I know it was you."

He doesn't say anything for a moment, but just keeps staring at me with that same perplexed expression.

"Whatever, man." I say. "I apologized and I meant it and I just hope I can get one of you someday." I walk back to the other end of the dugout as Parker and Alex enter, chatting about their last class.

Once I change into my practice clothes, Alex asks me if I want to warm-up with him again. I tell him yes and follow him into the outfield. "You didn't get in trouble for being out last night, did you?" I ask.

He shakes his head. "I just explained a friend needed me and that I got home a little after midnight. Both my folks were in bed by then, so they believed me."

"Okay, good. I'd hate for you to get into trouble because of me."

He shrugs. "I don't care."

As we begin to stretch out our legs on the grass, I say to Alex in a low voice, "I can't believe Brody told Kelly everything. What a dick."

"Kelly?" he asks.

"Yeah, Brody told Kelly about me and that I have a crush on him or something."

"Oh, that's weird," he adds, nonchalantly as he hugs his right leg close to his body to stretch out his hamstring. "I heard it from Bridgette."

"Yeah, they were both going around telling people, but I think it started with Kelly."

Alex nods in understanding. "I see them together all the time," he adds. "Makes sense they'd be spreading the same rumors."

"I just have to let it run its course. It'll blow over soon enough."

There's a lull in the conversation as we stretch, then Alex finally asks, "You going to prom this weekend?"

I shake my head. "I think Logan was trying to talk me into it today, but I don't know who I'd go with."

"All the girls taken?"

"Logan thinks I should take a guy. Are you going?"

"Nope. Don't know anyone. Except you, but I don't think I could take a guy to prom," he laughs.

"Not sure I can either."

That evening after dinner, I put the screen back over my bedroom window before either of my parents notice it's gone. I go downstairs and ask my dad for my laptop so I can print out the second draft of my short story. I think maybe Ms. Cooper and Logan were right: the main character does need to be gay. Luckily, I think I finally got the ending just right, polished to perfection. I give myself a little pat on the back as I print it out.

"Is that your short story?" my mom asks as the printer whirrs and spits out each page of double-spaced text, one at a time.

"...Yeah." My stomach trembles as I know what the next question out of her mouth will be.

"Can I read it?"

"No, it's personal."

"Well, you're gonna show it to your teacher. Why can't I read it?"

"Because it's my story and that's what I said!" I shout back before storming up the stairs to my room. I can't risk it. My parents can't know yet. That's a huge milestone I'm completely unprepared for. I just pray that the rumors at school don't somehow make it around to them. Oak Ridge is a small town and people love to talk.

I pant as I lean against my bedroom door. That was too close. Next time I need to print my story off at school where no one's gonna try to get into my business.

I push off the wall and breathe a final sigh of relief. I check my watch and decide it's time for bed. I undress and slide under the covers, but it feels off. I can't stop thinking about last night when Alex came over—how comforting it felt to have a friend here with me when I needed one more than anything else, not to mention how fun it was to be sneaking around on a Monday night. The thought of Alex hiding in the closet still makes me smile.

I roll over and face the closet. Nothing to stop me re-living it... *No*, I decide at last. *I should sleep in my bed tonight.* The memory of sleeping in the closet was special because I got to share it with Alex. Copying it on my own wouldn't be the same. It wouldn't give me the same comfort as falling asleep on Alex's shoulder.

I know Alex isn't gay, and after my last fiasco, I wouldn't trust myself to guess. He'd have to tell me and even then I'd be skeptical. Still, it's nice to reminisce, just for a bit. It's nice to imagine sitting with him on the couch down-stairs, just like I imagined the day after our teams played each other for the first time.

CHAPTER 15

When I wake up I somehow know that today is gonna be easier. Some other piece of gossip twice as juicy as me being gay is bound to take over the school today, and just like that, I'll once again fade into the background of the junior class.

I dress for the day, eat a quick breakfast, then head out the door. There's a light rain this morning and I can see my breath in the air as I climb into the cab of my truck. I'm running a little late and the traffic in the student lot starts to pick up as the bell for first period gets closer and closer. I take my usual empty spot towards the back of the lot.

The rain is coming down a bit harder now, and I didn't bring a jacket. I open up my truck door and the cold shock of the rain hits my arm. I power walk through the parking lot, the rain streaking through the lights from cars that are still cruising around for an empty spot. A car parks just ahead of me and a lanky guy in a heavy coat steps out. I squint and I can tell it's Logan. I look down to hop over a large puddle of freezing water, but when I look back up, someone else is approaching Logan. It's a tall guy with a wide frame and big arms. Then I realize it's Brody and I can tell from his body language that he's pissed. "Hey!" I hear him shout.

What's going on? I pick up my pace a bit more as Brody

gets close to Logan and starts talking directly in his face. Then Brody grabs Logan's collar and pins him against the side of his own car.

Oh shit. I break into a run, not caring about soaking my shoes, just trying to get to the two of them to stop whatever's happening before it escalates.

Brody shoves Logan against the car again. And again. "You fucking asshole!" he shouts.

"Stop!" Logan cries, hoping someone will help him as he fumbles around in his pocket. I know what he's groping for.

I'm only two cars away when Brody pulls back his fist and lets it crash directly into Logan's face.

I stop dead in my tracks right as I reach the bumper of Logan's car. "Brody!" I shout so he can hear me over the rain and the traffic. "What the fuck did you just do?"

He turns and gives me a powerful look, his eyes still filled with rage. He takes a couple deep breaths and I swear his gaze softens for a brief second before he storms off past me. "Leave him," he grunts as he passes. "Now we're even."

Logan is sitting on the ground, his face in his hands, his jeans completely soaked. A can of pepper spray lies on the ground next to him, unused; he couldn't get it out of his pocket fast enough. I kneel next to him and put a hand on his shoulder. "Logan?"

He turns around to face me and I have to fight the urge to recoil. His nose is dripping blood all over this mouth, and now his hands are smeared too. "Go," he says quietly.

"What? No, let me help-"

"GO!"

I jump back in shock. I slowly rise and turn around to

see Brody waiting for me. "Let's go."

As Brody and I walk to class, I can't hide the fact that I am immensely uncomfortable standing next to him. Why the fuck did he punch Logan? And why wouldn't Logan let me help him? "You saw nothing," Brody says to me in a low voice as we walk to calculus. "Someone's probably gonna ask you what you saw and what you know. The answers to those questions are nothing and nothing."

"Yeah... okay..."

He can tell I'm not convinced. "Derek, I don't have time to explain right now, but you have to trust me, okay?"

"Brody, how can I trust you after what you did to me?"

"I don't know, but I know that I can trust you even after what you did to me."

My heart aches with guilt as the memories of my betrayal rush back to me, but Brody gives me a smile. Not a forced smile, a genuine one, a smile that reminds me of the old days. "Okay," I say at last. "Okay." I glance down at his hand and there's some blood on it. "You should wash that off though." I gesture to it and he looks at his knuckles.

"Yeah. I'll go do that now."

I follow him into the nearest boys' bathroom and watch as he fills his left hand with soap and scrubs his right until the last bit of blood is scoured off and disappears down the sink drain. "Oh, by the way," he says to me as he grabs a handful of paper towels and delicately dries his hand. He tosses the paper towel into the trash can and fishes a pair of swim trunks and a t-shirt out of his backpack. They're neatly folded and smell like the same detergent that Brody uses on his clothes. "These are yours. I went ahead and washed them for you last night."

"That was nice of you." I accept them and stuff them unceremoniously into my own book bag before we leave the boys' room for Ms. Garcia's class.

"How long do you think before you're called to the front office?" I ask him as we make our way down the hall.

"Ten minutes into first period."

"I don't think you'll last five," I say.

"Bet you a beer?" he asks with a grin.

"Deal." I extend my hand for a shake and I feel my heart swell as Brody takes it. I think this means we're friends again. Not friends who aren't talking right now but might someday. Actual friends, back to normal... or as normal as possible all things considered. I'm not sure how I feel about our friendship being repaired over Brody punching Logan in the face, but I'll worry about that later.

We walk into Mrs. Garcia's class and I feel no trepidation or awkwardness in occupying my usual seat next to Brody. Logan's not here and Kelly and Bridgette are giving each other curious looks. Camilla still looks pissed at me, but that's the last thing on my mind right now. She shoots a dirty look over her shoulder at Brody too, who doesn't seem to notice.

Mrs. Garcia stands up when the bell rings. Brody and I look at each other to confirm that the time starts now. "Let's do a couple problems from last night's homework. Bridgette, you do number fourteen, and..." As Mrs. Garcia searches the room for her next victim, a voice from the intercom fills the room. I immediately recognize it as Principal Sampson's.

"Brody Hernandez and Derek Milligan, please report to the front office. Brody Hernandez and Derek Milligan to the front office."

Brody and I look at each other again and neither of us can keep from smiling. "That wasn't even sixty seconds!" he laughs.

"You owe me a beer," I say as we rise and grab our backpacks.

"Won't you be coming back?" Mrs. Garcia asks as she realizes we're packing up.

We both laugh. "No idea, maybe not!" Brody calls to her as we leave the room.

As we walk down the hall towards the front office, I realize Brody is right. We may not be going back to class after this. The school has pretty tough punishments for fights and someone had to have punched Logan in the face. There are bound to be consequences.

Brody kindly opens the door to the front office for me and waves me inside. Once we're in, we lean against the counter and grin down at the familiar face of the secretary. "Hi, Linda," Brody says, reading her name tag and clearly trying to flirt with the twenty-two-year-old woman. "My friend and I were just called to the office. Any idea what it could possibly be about?"

She gives us a look as if it were obvious. "Could it be about the bruises both of you have on your faces?"

Brody and I look at each other and burst into laughter.

The secretary looks more annoyed than amused as she checks a post-it-note on her desk. "Are you two Derek and Brody?"

"No, we're Brody and Derek," I correct her.

She gives a groan of frustration then points down the hall around the corner of her desk. "Just go sit down. Principal Sampson will be out shortly."

Brody and I walk around her large desk down a narrow, dingy hallway to the door that reads PRINCIPAL SAMPSON. There are three chairs adjacent to the door and Logan is sitting in the middle one. His nose is bruised and the skin around his mouth still has little blood stains on it. He's holding a pack of ice up to his face and brings it down to get a good look at us. He glares daggers at Brody, who then sits on Logan's left. I take the seat on his right.

"How's the nose?" I ask Logan. I'm in an awkward situation. I want to be on Logan's good side since he gave me some advice yesterday, but I also need to help out Brody. I know he fucked up—punching Logan was way out of line —but that doesn't mean I'm gonna tell Sampson what happened. She's a smart lady. She can figure it out herself.

Logan raises the pack of ice from the nurse's office back to his face. "It hurts. It's not broken, but it's gonna be bruised, which means I'm gonna have a bruise on my face for prom."

"Welcome to the club," I joke with him. He doesn't find it very funny. "You'll laugh at that later. Like, in a couple years."

Brody leans forward to catch my attention from around Logan. "Dude, you're going to prom?"

"No, but I'll have a bruise on my face *during* prom."

He and I laugh for a moment and then the door to Sampson's office swings open. She steps outside, puts her hands on her hips, and frowns at the three of us. With a heavy sigh, like she's tired of all the bullshit this school throws at her, she waves us inside her office. Logan is quick to take the chair on the right so he doesn't get caught between Brody and me again. Can't blame him. I sit in the middle and Brody sits on my left. Principal Sampson closes her office door, then slowly walks around her desk. The swivel chair gives a little bounce as she settles in and she folds her hands on her desk.

"Okay," she says at last. "So... What happened?"

There's a long silence as no one knows where exactly to start. Then finally Brody says, "This morning, or....?"

"Yes, Brody," she clarifies. "This morning. I'm wondering why one of you has a black eye, one of you has a bruised cheek, and one of you has a busted nose."

"It's not broken," I correct her.

"It's just bruised," Brody adds.

"It *hurts*," Logan says pointedly at Brody.

"Never said it didn't," he murmurs.

"What happened to your eyes?" Sampson asks Brody and me.

"Well, I dropped a weight on my face while I was doing dumbbell bench press on Monday," I explain.

"And *I* dropped a weight on my face doing skull-crushers on Monday," Brody adds.

She raises her eyebrows with skepticism. "You honestly expect me to believe that?"

Brody and I look at each other, then back at her. "Yes...?"

"So what happened to you?" she asks, looking at Logan.

"Brody punched me in the parking lot right before school!"

"Brody?" she asks.

I'm getting ready for whatever twisted logic Brody is about to whip out of his back pocket.

"Yeah, that's right."

I flinch in my seat. He admitted it? Just like that?

"Brody, we don't tolerate bullying around here, you know that," Sampson says.

"*Thank you!*" Logan exasperates as an aside.

Sampson continues as if she didn't hear. "There are gonna be consequences for this. I'm going to call your parents and I'll tell you what that punishment is as soon as I decide it. In the meantime, please take a seat outside my office."

Logan stands up, a smug grin on his face. I wonder if my smug grin looks that irritating, but then I remember I'm cuter than Logan and so probably not.

I reluctantly rise from my seat, wishing there was something I could do for Brody—wishing there was anything I could do for him, really. I'm about to leave when I realize Brody hasn't moved.

"Mr Hernandez?"

"Don't you want to hear *why* I punched Logan in the face?"

Principal Sampson narrows her eyes. Typically the answer would be no, but the way Brody phrases it seems to suggest to her that there is a piece of the story she isn't getting. "Why did you punch Logan in the face?"

"Because he was spreading rumors about Derek."

Wait. What? I glance in Logan's direction and I don't know if it's because he's glaring at the back of Brody's head or because he's afraid of meeting my gaze, but I get the feeling he's purposely avoiding eye contact with me.

Samson breathes a heavy sigh. "Brody, while that's not appropriate—and Logan, you can take a seat outside too so I can talk with you—punching someone is not the correct response to rumors."

Brody shakes his head. "Principal Sampson, you don't understand." He leans in close and lowers his voice. "These weren't just random stupid rumors that Logan was spreading. Logan outed Derek."

Wait. WHAT?

"To the whole school," he concludes.

That couldn't be true, right? There's no way that the president of the LGBTQ+ club was the one who started the rumor in the first place. How could he have guessed? Someone had to have told him.

Principal Sampson's face morphs from general disinterest in a rather run-of-the-mill student fight to outrage over a serious issue.

"You two, take a seat," she says pointing to Logan and me. "Brody, what exactly do you mean? I need you to be as specific as possible."

Brody takes his time, clearing his throat and sitting up straight. I can tell he's getting some perverse enjoyment out of this, and if what he says is true, I don't have a problem with it. "You see, ma'am, there has been a rumor going around the school that Derek here is gay. Now, typically this could be dismissed as nothing more than hearsay and adolescent gossip. *However*, if this particular rumor were true, then the person who started it is not guilty of some petty gossip, but rather publicly outing a closeted student, which, and I'm sure Logan, as the president of both the student body and the LGBTQ+ club, would agree is a much more serious offense."

"It's the Rainbow Club now," he corrects Brody without thinking. "We're rebranding."

Sampson turns her head to me. "Derek...?"

I don't know what to say. I don't know what to think. There's no way any of this is true, right? All three of them are looking at me, as if they expect me to confirm or deny right here and now. "Before I say anything, I want to ask Logan a question."

I turn in my seat to face Logan. He's holding the ice pack to his face. I wait for him to lower it, but he never does. "What do you think should be the punishment for someone who outs a classmate to the school?"

Logan should look down as he considers this. His eyes should flick to somewhere else in the room as the gears of his mind turn. But they don't. His eyes stay on me. Well, the one eye I can see does. The other is hidden behind the pack of ice on his nose. It makes his expression impossible to discern.

"Logan?" Sampson says. "That's a fair question. What's your answer?"

Logan drops the ice pack to his lap and says, "I'm not sure."

"While you think about it, here's some food for thought," Brody jabs at him. "That bruise on your face will heal and before long, your life will be back to normal. But Derek can never get his privacy back."

"*If* the rumor were true," I add quickly. "It's not. It was just a rumor."

Sampson's eyes narrow at me, then she turns back to face Logan. "Okay, Logan. It's just a rumor. Derek just said it himself. So if it were true, what should the punishment be?"

"Outing someone is a form of bullying," he says, sitting up straight. "I would never do it."

"Would it be fair to say that it should get the same punishment as getting into a fight?" Brody asks pointedly.

"Sure! Why not?" Logan shouts back. "I didn't do it and you know that!"

"Calm down," Principal Sampson says. "Everyone just calm down." She raps her knuckles on her desk as she thinks...

"Okay," she says at last. "Brody and Logan, go wait outside. Derek, you stay right here."

Logan and Brody rise from their seats and shuffle into the hall. I turn around in my seat and watch as Brody holds the door open for Logan, then shuts it behind himself, shooting me a wink just before he vanishes behind the crack of the closing door.

"Derek..." Principal Sampson says. I turn back to face her. "I'm sorry I have to ask you this, but I need to know if the rumor was just a rumor or something much more serious."

I feel a knot in the pit of my stomach. "Do you really?" I ask her.

"Yes."

"What difference does it make?"

"All the difference in the world."

I look down at my feet, afraid to meet her gaze again, her intense gaze that she's trying to make soft and friendly, but I know is underscored with serious concern. The longer I wait, the more I realize that I'm not leaving the room until I give her an answer. "I have to tell you, don't I?"

"Yes."

Should I be honest or should I lie? If I'm honest, then whoever started this rumor about me is gonna face some actual consequences for violating my privacy, and the school might look into it. But I'm torn because I want all of this to go away, to get swept under the rug. If the school intervenes, it will be specifically because I'm gay and the rumor is true and everyone will know it. The only way to seek justice is to out myself not only to Principal Sampson, but by extension every school board member she holds a meeting with about this very issue and everyone who helps the school with its resources. Then again if I tell her the truth, maybe Brody's punishment could get lightened. I have a feeling that getting in a fight to stand up for a friend earned a lighter sentence than punching a kid out of the blue. Ugh! Why did Brody have to do this? Why couldn't he have just talked to me first instead of going straight to punching someone? I can't be too mad at him when it was on my behalf, but maybe I should just lie now so this whole thing doesn't escalate even more.

Tell the truth. You have lied enough.

"All right, fine…" I say at last, my heart in my throat. "It's true. I'm gay. Happy now? I was outed to the whole school, but I can't prove that Logan was the one who did it."

"I want to thank you for your honesty, Derek, and I also want to thank you for your bravery in telling me this."

I know she's trying to flatter me, but I also just want to get out of her office now.

"Derek, if I can be honest with you," she says just as I'm about to ask to be excused, "I think you need to embrace this part of yourself, and let go of the people in your life who maybe aren't so accepting."

"What do you mean?" I ask. "Now I need *you* to be as specific as possible."

"I think Brody is a bad influence on you."

I shake my head with disbelief. That was the single

most ridiculous idea I'd ever heard. "What makes you say that?"

She casually shrugs as if the words that just came out of her mouth were in no way unreasonable. "Is he really someone who's going to accept you for being gay? I have my concerns."

"Well you don't know him like I do," I argue. "You don't know the first thing about him."

"All I know is that he walked into my office this morning and admitted to punching a gay student."

"Because he said he was sticking up for his best friend, who happens to be gay."

She raises her hands in an attempt to calm me. "I'm just trying to give you food for thought. In the meantime, you're not getting off scot-free."

"Excuse me?"

"I want you to attend the Rainbow Club for the rest of the semester."

"Why?"

"I already told you—I think you need to be more accepting of this side of yourself, and when I see the people you hang around with, I'm worried that might not be a possibility for you unless you branch out a little bit."

"My teammates aren't homophobes," I say, knowing I have no anecdotal evidence to suggest either in favor or against that statement.

"Maybe, maybe not. I hope the Rainbow Club will shed some light on that for you."

"How?"

"They help people like you see the homophobia that is a ubiquitous part of life," she explains. "That might do you some good—it might help you see who your real friends are."

"Is there any way out of that?"

"No," she says, with a tone of finality in her voice. "Now, if you will please let Brody in." She gestures towards the door and I know that our conversation is over. I rise from my seat, open the door, and when I poke my head into the hallway, I see Brody and Logan sitting a chair apart from each other.

"Brody, she wants to talk to you."

He stands and as we shuffle past each other in the narrow hallway, he gives my shoulder a friendly bump with his fist. My heart feels a half pound lighter, and I know I don't have to wait, but I can't leave until I know what's going to happen to Brody, so I take a seat in the chair he just left unoccupied.

I keep a seat between myself and Logan, letting my suspicion fill the empty air with a thick tension. I'm not sure how much I can trust him right now. I decide the best way would be to just ask him. "Logan," I say after a moment of strained silence. "Is anything Brody said in there true?"

"No, of course not!" he shoots back at me angrily. "Don't you trust me?"

I don't want to tell him no, so I don't respond.

"I thought—I hoped—you'd want to be my friend," he says quietly, shaking his head in frustration with his own foolish ambition.

"Well, you'll be seeing plenty of me because I'm going to LGBTQ+ club for the rest of the semester."

He looks at me as if I've gone insane, not even correcting me on the club's name. "What?"

"That's what Sampson said."

"Well… I'll be happy to see you there. I think it'll be good for you."

"That's what she said."

The door to Principal Sampson's office opens again and Brody steps out, looking down at Logan. "You're up, Mr. President," he says with a condescending tone.

Logan gives him a scowl and rises from his seat. "I know whatever punishment you get for your homophobia is nowhere near enough."

Brody, his face only a few inches from Logan's, scoffs at him and takes a small step closer, sizing him up. "Homophobia? I'm not a homophobe."

"You punched me in the face this morning—that's homophobic. It might even be a hate crime."

Brody laughs, then his voice changes to a growl. "Let's get something straight, Logan—I have nothing against gay people, but I really fucking hate you."

Logan takes a step back and awkwardly tries to scooch past Brody into Principal Sampson's office.

Brody sits down in the chair next to me and breathes a heavy sigh of relief. "Glad that's over with."

"What? No detention?" I ask in disbelief.

"No, no detention. I did get suspended for the rest of the week, though." He puts his hands behind his head to get more comfortable as if this were just a second spring break for him.

I stare at him, jaw on the floor. "Brody! This is bad! This is really bad!"

"Why?"

"Getting suspended is serious! Colleges are gonna find out about it when you apply!"

"I've already told you that I don't think college is right for me," he says. His tone isn't nonchalant, but it definitely sounds like he's trying to calm me more than himself.

"Your parents are gonna kill you."

"Probably. But I think I did the right thing."

I can't help it. I feel so overwhelmed. This all started because I couldn't tell Camilla to just text Brody herself and now Brody's been suspended, I have to miss baseball practice once a week, and Brody's gonna be in deep shit with his parents. I don't know what to say or what to think and all I can do is put my head in my hands and fight the urge to start screaming.

"Hey, hey, hey," Brody says, his voice going up half an octave as he sits up and puts his hand on my back. "It's okay. It's all gonna be fine, just not right away."

"This is all my fault, Brody," I say quietly. "I'm sorry."

"No it isn't," he says. "I punched Logan. You didn't make me do that."

"I'm sorry, Brody." I sit up straight to look him in the eye. "I really am."

He doesn't say anything. He just gives me a wan smile and then the door to Sampson's office opens again. Logan wastes no time storming down the narrow hallway back towards the front desk and out of the office. Brody and I exchange a curious look when Sampson saunters out. She faces us and says, "Brody, it's time to go."

Brody gives me a pat on the shoulder, stands up, and walks out of the office. Then Sampson looks at me again. "You can go back to class now."

CHAPTER 16

The rest of the day feels like the aftermath of a horrible car accident. How can it not? My best friend won't be around for the next few days and my plans for the afternoon have been completely scrapped. Every time I think the hole I dug for myself can't possibly get any deeper, I find I've already scooped out another ten shovelfuls of dirt.

I get to French class late and take my seat next to Camilla, who still gives me a stink eye at every available opportunity. I know I should, but I can't bring myself to apologize to her, not yet. I just ignore her scowl for now, delaying my overdue apology until I find the right words for it. She's my friend and she deserves better from me.

When I get to Ms. Cooper's room for English class, Kelly is glaring at me too. I've really learned how to make enemies these past couple weeks, haven't I? I give her a curious look and she rises from her desk to take the seat next to me. "I hope you're happy," she says sarcastically.

"I bet you don't really mean that," I say with a smug grin.

"Logan's been suspended."

"*What?*"

"Yeah. School policy is that whenever there's a fight, anyone involved gets suspended. Your asshole of a friend punched him and now Logan, the *victim*, is in trouble."

"So... how does that make *me* the bad guy?" I ask, confused.

"Because you're friends with Brody."

"...Okay?"

"Logan can't even go to prom now."

I give her a double take "How come?"

"Because he's *suspended!* You can't go to any school events if you're suspended."

"But his suspension ends Friday, doesn't it?"

She shakes her head. "No, it doesn't technically end until Monday. So now Bridgette and I have to go together and everyone's gonna think we're lesbians."

"What's wrong with that?" I ask with an amused grin. "Considering you hang out with Logan all the time, I thought you'd be cool with the gays."

"That doesn't mean I want people to think *I'm gay!*"

I roll my eyes, done with this conversation. "Calm your tits and go back to your seat. Maybe you'll get lucky and Bridgette'll dump you before Saturday."

She's about to yell something at me about how they're not together when Ms. Cooper begins speaking. Kelly has to force herself to shut up and go back to her desk.

In creative writing, Ms. Cooper asks us to partner up again for another round of peer reviews of our short stories. I scan the room and it looks like everyone else has already been taken. "Derek, are you looking for a partner?"

"Yeah, but it looks like everyone's already got one."

"Logan's gone today," Ms. Cooper explains, careful not

to reveal extra details to the other students. Then she extends an open hand towards me. "I'll read your story!"

I'm a little nervous, just like I was for the first draft, but then I remind myself that since Ms. Cooper will be grading the story, she's probably the best person to be revising my second draft. "The only real changes are at the ending," I explain. "That's where you and Logan said the story needed the most work."

She gives me a warm smile, and as she adjusts her glasses and skips to the end, I re-read the last paragraphs of my story over her shoulder so I can gauge her reaction to every detail.

> Dillian was sad. He had tried his best but it was not enough and Sarah was not going to prom with him. Just when he thought he would have to go home and sulk for the night, Brian turned to him and said "Hey, you!"
>
> "Me?" Dillian asked.
>
> "Yeah, you! You tried to take Sarah away from me! You tried to break my ankle by making me slip in that water you poured out! You tried to get me expelled by breaking everything in Mr. Smith's room! Sarah is going to prom with me and that's final!"
>
> Dillian was angry and he jumped to his feet. Then, as he thought about it more, he realized that his problem was not with Brian. He never had a problem with Brian at all. The truth was that Dillian secretly liked Brian. But how could he explain that to Brian now that he

was so angry?

"Brian! Wait! Let's not fight over Sara!"

"Why not?" Brian asked, fists ready to fight.

"Let's not fight over Sara because the truth is that I don't even like Sara. The truth is that I like you. I just never knew how to tell you."

"Well why didn't you say so?" Brian asked. "That's okay. I forgive you."

Then Brian and Dillian shake hands and hug and Dillian knew that they would be best friends forever.

THE END

Ms. Cooper scratches her head when she gets done reading it. "Well this is definitely a better ending. I can tell you worked really hard on it. It just seems a little light."

I was hoping she wouldn't notice that my new ending was about a hundred and fifty words shorter than the original.

"It needs some more length, for sure, but it also needs some more depth. I just don't quite know what that is yet."

She bites her lip as she thinks and I groan as I think about rewriting the ending again.

"I can't quite put my finger on it, but there needs to be a little more... something to this."

I force a smile and say through gritted teeth, "Thank you, I really appreciate the feedback."

"Your writing is definitely improving," she says with a

grin before walking back to her desk. "Just add a little something more for the final draft when you turn it in."

Lunch is painfully awkward. Brody's absence is immediately noticed at the table and the teammates who have already heard about his suspension have to fill in those that haven't. "Brody punched Logan in the face this morning before school," Parker tells Austin, whose eyes automatically flick towards me, then back to Parker. "They both got suspended."

"Why would Brody do that?" Austin asks.

"No idea," Parker responds.

Alex sits next to me and tries to distract me by changing the subject of the conversation. "You excited to play Emmerdale this Saturday?" he asks, running hand through his red hair. "I'm hoping to pitch three-up-three-down at least once!"

I give him a weak smile. I appreciate the effort, but it's not working.

I stay in the library during study hall. I don't see the point in going to the weight room when I won't be lifting with Brody; it'll just remind me that he's not here and make me think more about my role in this whole mess.

The rest of the day drags on, partly because I'm in such a bad mood and partly because I know I won't even have baseball practice to use as a release when the day is over —I have to go to the LGBTQ+ club. I can't help but look at the clock over and over again, even though I know it's only counting down the minutes to an event I'm dreading.

Finally, when the bell rings at the end of chemistry, I slowly pack up my things and leave Mr. Holtz's room.

I can feel them again, those damn butterflies. They build with every step I take down the hall towards Ms. Cooper's room, getting stronger and stronger until I feel like I'm going to be sick. This is what it felt like getting ready to kiss Brody. This is what it felt like coming out to Alex. Would I ever get used to this horrible feeling of my heart pounding and my stomach twisting itself into knots?

I casually wait by the water fountain about twenty feet down the hall from Ms. Cooper's room until I'm sure everyone has left. I walk by just to discreetly glance inside a couple times before I do this for real.

It's not hard. Just walk in.

I begin to bargain with myself. Maybe I can hang out here for a few minutes and act like I couldn't figure out where the club met. I still get to go to practice today, then if Sampson hears about it, I can play stupid and try again next week.

No. If you stay out in the hall then you will get in trouble. Part of the deal with Sampson was that you go in. Now move!

Just as I lean against a row of lockers, unsure how I'm ever going to find the courage to leave this spot, a small group of chattering students approach from the other end of the hall. They must be heading to the same place as me. That's it! If they all go in together, I can come in right behind them and they probably won't even notice. Sure it looks like I'm about a foot taller than most of them, but this is a better plan than hugging the lockers forever.

I calculate when I need to move and how fast I should walk. Wait... Wait... Now! I take a step forward and begin sauntering at a pace that is carefully calculated to appear casual. The three of them, two girls and a boy, continue chattering, oblivious to the fact that I've just used them as cover to enter Ms. Cooper's room less conspicuously. Once I'm inside, I see that Ms. Cooper has rearranged the desks to form a large circle, just like for the prom decorating committee. She says hello to the three students who walk in before me and takes a seat at one of the desks in the circle before her eyes fall on me.

"Hi, Derek," she says with a tone that makes it sound a little bit more like a question than a greeting.

I nod and give her a weak smile as I put my backpack down at a desk. The other students lower their voices and give me curious looks. They think I've made some sort of mistake.

Ms. Cooper rises from her seat and sits down next to me. "Hey, Derek. Um... so, this is -"

"I know what this is," I say flatly.

"You do?" Her eyes are still narrow as she tries to compute. "Because this is supposed to be a safe space..."

And just like that, I see my out. Yes!

"Oh. I understand," I say as I rise from my seat. "If I'm keeping this from being a safe space, then I can just leave, for everyone else's sake." I sling my backpack over my shoulder and lunge for the door, desperate to get out before Ms. Cooper can clarify and stop me.

"WAIT!" she shouts as I'm about to bolt through the

doorway. I stop dead in my tracks and peer over my shoulder. She's staring at her phone and holding a finger up to me. "I just checked my email; I've got something here from Principal Sampson." She opens the email and quickly reads it. "Take a seat, Derek," she says at last, striding over to the door to swing it shut.

Once it closes with a bang, Ms. Cooper spins on her heel and faces the rest of the room. "Okay, the door is closed, we have our privacy. Welcome to the Rainbow Club! As I say at the beginning of every meeting, this is a safe space and what happens within these four walls stays within these four walls.

"Looks like we have a new member today," she continues, indicating me.

"Oh, I'm not a member."

"You're here."

"Right, but... not a member."

She gives me an unconvinced nod, then addresses the other three students. "Why don't you all begin by saying your names, preferred pronouns, and a fun fact about yourselves?"

As Ms. Cooper takes a seat at the desk on my right, the first girl speaks with a quiet mousy voice. She's got black hair, wide blue eyes, and thin lips. "I'm Haley," she squeaks, barely audible over the ambient sound of the room's air conditioner. I have to lean in to hear her from across the circle of desks. "My pronouns are she/her/hers and... I don't know... I have an older sister."

"That's not a fun fact," the boy sitting next to her says. "Almost everyone has siblings."

"Well I don't know what to say."

"Tell him about your Star Wars obsession," he jokes with a prod of his elbow.

"*Tristan!*" she breathes, turning beet red with humiliation.

"Tristan, would you like to go next?" Ms. Cooper asks to save Haley.

"Hi, I'm Tristan, my pronouns are he/him/his, and I'm on a diet right now."

I look him up and down. I didn't know anyone could be thinner than Logan, yet somehow Tristan exists. He is about as tall as me, but only half as wide. His legs look like toothpicks, so he definitely skips leg day, although I doubt he's ever been to a gym for much more than cardio. I could throw him across the room if I had half a mind to do it, although it might be like throwing a tissue—as soon as he leaves my hand, he'd hit a wall of air and just float back down to the ground. Also throwing him across the room wouldn't make the club a very safe space. Not sure what good a diet would do him, but he seems pretty confident about it working so I won't ask about that.

Finally, everyone's head turns to face the second girl and she sits up straight to speak. She has a crew cut instead of the longer locks more typical for girls at Oak Ridge. She's wearing yoga pants and a tank top with a cardigan over it. "Hi, I'm Ash, my pronouns are they/them/theirs, and I'm the only nonbinary person at Oak Ridge! So that's my fun fact..."

I had a couple questions, as I'm sure Ash is used to receiving after an introduction like that, but I save them. There's probably going to be another time to ask them.

Then I notice that everyone's eyes are on me. Tristan raises his eyebrows, expecting to hear me say something.

224

"Derek?" Ms. Cooper says gently. "Why don't you tell us who you are?"

Okay, I tell myself. *I don't have to tell them anything I don't want to. Sampson didn't tell me that I had to come out to the club, just that I had to go.*

"Hi, I'm Derek... Milligan... My pronouns are he—is he... and I play baseball."

"Why are you here?" Tristan blurts out.

Again, seeing a slim chance to take an out, I respond. "Do you not want me here? I can go," I suggest.

"Huh-uh," Ms. Cooper says. "You're staying right here. Tristan, can you find a better way of asking that?"

Tristan rolls his eyes and crosses his arms. "Fine. What made you decide to join us today, Derek?"

"Logan mentioned it to me and I got curious. I've never been to the LGBTQ+ Club."

"It's the Rainbow Club," Ms. Cooper kindly corrects me.

"We're rebranding," the other three say in a bored, re-hearsed unison.

"Right," I say. "I was curious."

Ash speaks up. "It's just that this is supposed to be a safe space for LGBTQ+ folks and if a straight cis person walks in, folks might feel like they're being gawked at a bit—that could make them uncomfortable."

"Again... I can go."

"Derek, stop." Ms. Cooper says with a tone of finality.

"Wait, I think I heard something about you..." Haley whispers, but I think I'm the only one who hears.

"Ash, he's not gawking and he's not leaving," Ms. Cooper continues. "Why don't we let Derek explain why he's here today?" She turns to me and raises her eyebrows, clearly expecting me to take over from here.

Not much of a warning, is it? How much time can I waste dancing around this? "Well, I spoke with Principal Sampson today and she suggested that I come to this meeting."

"Did that have anything to do with what happened to Logan?" Tristan asks.

Oh good, a change of subject. "Uh... yes it did."

"Why would someone do that?" Ash asks in disbelief. "He's such a nice guy!"

"I... I agree. I don't know why someone would do that." Brody went too far this morning. It was getting harder and harder to justify it.

"Who was it that punched him?" Ash asks.

"It was a football player."

"I thought it was a lacrosse player," Haley adds quietly.

"No no no, it was a *baseball* player."

All three of them glare at me.

"I didn't do it!"

Ash gives me a suspicious look up and down, then says, "I bet you know who it was, though."

I have to distract them for as long as I can so I don't have to talk about myself or why I'm here. "I do know who it was. I don't know if you've ever heard of the baseball player Randy Fischer, but he plays shortstop for us and he's a really great guy—"

"Doesn't sound like a great guy if he punches an innocent gay kid," Ash growls.

"Well he didn't. He just plays shortstop. I play third base, so I'm always on Randy's right, because shortstop is in between second and third base." I decide to throw in that little tidbit because something tells me that no one here knows anything about baseball. "Anyways, the guy on Randy's *left*, the guy who plays second base, is named Brody. When he was walking into school this morning, he ran into Logan and I'm not entirely sure what happened—I only saw it from a distance and it was dark and raining so, you know—but it ended with Logan having a bloody nose and Brody having a black eye, so clearly some punches were thrown."

"What happened to *your* face?" Tristan asks bluntly.

Not a subtle one, is he? "I was in the weight room and accidentally dropped a weight on my face."

Tristan exhales with resentment and sits back. "That's why I stick to running."

"...Uh-huh."

"Derek," Ms. Cooper jumps in. "In that long, meandering story, I noticed that you never got around to telling us why exactly you're here."

"Well... After Brody and Logan beat each other up, they wound up in Principal Sampson's office and they both said that I was nearby, so I was asked to go and tell Sampson what exactly I saw. While I was there—"

"Derek, I'm gonna stop you right there because I know what you're doing."

I sit in an awkward, uncomfortable silence for a few seconds as she looks straight into my eyes.

"Just tell them."

"Do I have to?"

"Yes."

I breathe a heavy sigh, and I decide to say it fast before the butterflies get too intense. Now that I'm looking at all three of them and all of them are looking back at me, I can't find the words. I'm too nervous. How did I do this the other day with Alex?

Wait. That's right. Alex was so kind and gentle and understanding that night. I take a moment to go back to that mental state, to remember what it was like to sit on my bed with him and whisper the burden off of my shoulders.

"I'm gay. That's why I'm here. Principal Sampson thought it'd be good for me to come here instead of going to baseball practice today."

"*Oooooh!*" Ash cries. "Why didn't you just say that?" The other two are nodding in sudden understanding.

I shrug. "What makes you think it's something I can just say?"

"Well it should be."

I'm about to say something back, but Ms. Cooper cuts in. "I think Derek is having a little trouble accepting his sexuality."

"No I'm not," I say. "I'm fine with who I am."

"Then why were you nervous to tell us?" Tristan asks back.

"Because it's personal. What makes it your business?"

I think I have them, but the three of them give each other the same smug grin as if it were the most predictable response in the world. I look at Ms. Cooper for help, but she's wearing the same annoying expression. "Derek, we usually only meet on Wednesdays, but I have a friend who's coming in tomorrow to talk to us about some issues facing the LGBTQ+ community. Why don't you come back in a day? I think you'll get a lot out of it."

"Do I have a choice?"

She smiles and shakes her head. "No."

I suppress a frustrated groan and settle on rolling my eyes instead. Great. Another day stuck in here instead of out on the baseball field practicing with the team. We have a game this Saturday and even though Brody can't play, I still can. I'd like to get some practice in before that so we at least stand a chance of beating Emmerdale. Unfortunately, I know there's no changing Ms. Cooper's mind. My fate has been sealed and I have to accept it.

"So... What are we doing for the rest of today?" I ask tepidly. As soon as the words leave my mouth, I'm afraid of the punishment I may have just invited upon myself.

"We're going to talk about prom!" Ash shouts. "Who's going? Who is everyone taking? Give me details!"

"I still don't have a date," Tristan laments. He glances at me, I think to remind me that I'm technically part of the conversation too. "I was thinking about going with Logan, but he never asked me. I guess I should have asked him."

"Doesn't matter now," Haley whispers.

Tristan hunches over his desk, staring straight at Ash. "She's right. He can't go now, even as someone's date. Who are you going with?"

"Haley and I are going, but just as friends." Ash tacks on the last half of that sentence to stifle any questions Tristan has.

"Wooo...." Haley says to herself. Something about her expression suggests to me it's a last-minute thing.

"That'll be fun!" Tristan says to try and keep Haley from sinking into a funk. "What do your dresses look like?"

"Mine is green," Haley says. "It has a really poofy skirt and lots of feathers around the bodice."

"Oh that's cute! You'll look like a swiffer!"

Smooth, Tristan, I think to myself.

"What about you?" he asks Ash.

"Oh I'm not wearing a dress. I'm gonna wear a tux. Blue bowtie and cummerbund, and instead of dress shoes I'm gonna wear matching blue Converses."

"That's such a good idea!" Tristan exclaims. "I'd steal it from you but I know I'll see you there." They both laugh at that and then Tristan continues. "I'm just gonna wear a boring black tux with a red bowtie. Had to go with school colors."

"Makes sense," Ash says. Then all of their eyes fall on me. "What about you?"

It takes me a second to remember what exactly they were talking about—I was on the sidelines for the whole thing. "Oh! Right. No."

"No?" Tristan asks. His tone makes it clear that he isn't satisfied with my answer.

"I'm not going to prom."

"Why not?"

"I have no one to go with," I explain. "Plus I have a baseball game earlier that day and I know I'm gonna be wiped out." Then another excuse pops into my head. "Plus I have a black eye! Don't want prom pictures with this thing, ha ha."

"Are you uncomfortable with the idea of going to prom with a boy?" Ms. Cooper asks politely.

"Well... Kind of... Again, I just want to keep some parts of my life private. I'd be fine going with a girl as friends, or with a group of friends, but I haven't bought a ticket yet and I don't have a tuxedo to rent."

"Is that why your short story for my class is about two boys fighting over a prom date?"

"Well, no that wasn't how the story went until this last draft."

Ms. Cooper nods in understanding. "Because you were uncomfortable writing that before," she explains to me.

"What? No. You and Logan told me to write it that way."

Right? I think that's right. Or maybe what she's telling me is actually what happened and I'm just remembering it wrong? It would make sense. How many other times have I done something entirely driven by my sexuality and used a conveniently-located plot device to explain it away?

"Jeez, textbook case, isn't he?" Tristan whispers to Haley and Ash.

"What?"

"Nothing," he says with a wave of his hand. "We'll talk about it more tomorrow."

CHAPTER 17

So we beat on, boats against the current, borne back ceaselessly into the past.

I finally close my copy of *The Great Gatsby* and toss it carelessly into my backpack. Hopefully the rest of the reading assignments this year will be shorter and a lot less sophisticated. I have no idea how Brody can bear, let alone actually enjoy, this high-minded self-righteous crap.

I wish I could get the story out of my head, but I keep thinking about it again and again as I drive to school and park my truck in the back of the student lot. No wonder Ms. Cooper begrudgingly assigned us to read that stupid book. It's so pompous and egotistical and smug. I'm allowed to be smug because at least I'm cute. Fitzgerald, not so much.

I scoff to myself as I hop out of my truck and begin walking towards the school. *Pretentious. That's all that book is. Pretentious.* Dead white guys writing books for their dead white friends, imploring them to consider how serious life is, how important every single instant of life is. Why hadn't anyone ever told them to get over themselves? That's what they needed. They needed to play a sport. They needed someone to put a baseball bat in their hand and say, "Good luck, kid. You're gonna strike out." They needed to lose. Just once. They needed to feel like the greatest, most important, most

232

respected player on the team just so that when they lost they'd feel an overwhelming sense of shame at how dumb they looked the whole time. That way they might learn some humility. That way they could understand why people like me refuse to take anything seriously.

I drop my backpack at my usual spot in Mrs. Garcia's room, still fuming from the ending of *Great Gatsby*, then I leave to roam the halls. With Brody suspended, and without my phone to distract me, I really can't stand the thought of sitting in Mrs. Garcia's room and just waiting for class to start.

I walk past the art room, which is still locked with the lights turned off. I try to spot the prom mural through the safety glass on the door, but it's too dark to see anything. I do however catch a glimpse of my reflection. My black eye is still prominent, demanding attention from every other feature on my face. I notice people looking at it instead of me.

With a shrug and a quick, careless thought to myself, *Who cares? It'll heal and everyone will forget about it*, I check my watch and slowly start making my way back to Mrs. Garcia's room. When I turn around, I almost walk right into someone. I instinctively apologize until I notice who it is. "Sorry! Wait...."

It's Camilla, and then it dawns on me. Who else knew that I was flirting with Brody? Who else knew that I was hiding something? Who else had an axe to grind? I was so quick to eject Camilla from the equation that I completely forgot that she had access to all of the text messages and she knows just how much of a gossip people like Logan can be. As soon as the pieces fall into place, my face contorts into a vengeful glare and I growl, "You fucking bitch!"

She turns around and tries to power walk away from me. I dart in front of her and stop her in her tracks. "It was you! You told Logan that I'm gay!" My voice is still low so no one overhears, but it's coming out as a furious hiss. "You started the rumor about me and Brody!"

"No, I didn't," she murmurs, her eyes wide and downcast in a completely unconvincing lie.

"Don't lie to me! I've known you too well for too long for you to get away with it."

"Well I thought I knew you!" she fires back. "But apparently you were keeping a giant secret from me for your entire life, so I guess we weren't really friends in the first place, were we?"

I reel after that shot. It hurts because I know she's got a point. I hid it from her because I was afraid of how she would respond, of how her family might respond if they ever found out, if I'd be allowed back in the house. How else was she supposed to take that other than me purposefully keeping her at a distance? "You know it's not that simple," I say back.

"Oh no, I'm sure lying to your friend is very complicated."

"Well that doesn't give you the right to go telling everyone about it. You know Logan's been suspended? He's been suspended because Principal Sampson thought he was outing me to the school. If I told her that the rumor actually started from you, I'd guess that Logan would be back in school tomorrow and you'd be the one spending prom at home."

Camilla turns red and I can feel the heat radiating off of her. "No no! Please don't do that!"

"What do you expect me to do, Camilla? After what you did to me, do you really expect me to cover for you?"

She doesn't say anything and I know I have her cornered.

I take a step backwards and before I turn around to storm back to class, I tell her, "Don't talk to me again. Ever."

Calculus is especially lonely today with Brody gone and Camilla sitting in the back of the room to keep her distance from me, but I feel vindicated in my solitude, which makes it way more bearable than the isolation I felt on Monday.

Camilla avoids me in French class too. Madame Miller asks why she's sitting on the opposite side of the room from her usual spot. She mutters something incomprehensible and Madame Miller gives her a confused nod, resigning to let her sit by herself if that's what she really wants.

Ms. Cooper is a little too friendly to me when I walk into her class before English starts. "How are you doing today, Derek?" she asks with a grin.

"Fine…?"

"Don't forget about the after school group discussion we're having," she says with a wink.

'Right. I won't forget."

"Great! Looking forward to it!"

I take my seat as Ms. Cooper stands at the front of the room and says, "All right! What did you all think of the ending?"

After lunch with the team, it's time for me to go to the library for study hall, but first I go to the front office. The secretary flashes me her rehearsed smile, then drops it and replaces it with an annoyed frown when she recognizes me for my black eye. "Oh. It's you."

I walk up to her desk and stand there, waiting for her to ask me what she can help me with.

"What?"

"I need to speak with Principal Sampson," I say with a polite smile.

"She's busy."

"Oh I bet she is, Linda. But this is very important and it should only take a second, so when she's done with whatever it is she's doing now, let her know I'm out here."

"You shouldn't be missing class."

"I'm in study hall right now. I've got an hour." I walk over to the nearest chair and sit down, putting my hands behind my head to get comfortable.

Linda gives me stink eye from across the room for a solid ten seconds. I grin back at her until she finally picks up the phone, presses a button on it, and says something too quietly for me to hear.

I instinctively reach for my phone to entertain myself until I remember it's not there anymore. Will I get it back tomorrow or Saturday? Or Sunday? Jeez, I can't wait to have it back again, although I have to admit that the silence has been a relief and one I definitely need more of when I'm finally connected to all my friends again.

I'm about to lose myself in thought when Principal Sampson comes out of her office and waves for me to join her from down the narrow hallway. I'm surprised she's already free. As I walk past Linda, I give her another grin and I think she knows that there is a middle finger implicit in my smile.

"Hi, Derek," Principal Sampson says as she pushes open the door to her office, ushering me inside. "Linda said you have something important to tell me?"

"Yes, I do," I say as I take a seat in front of her desk. I explain my conversation with Camilla earlier in the morning. She listens attentively, jots down a note to herself, and five minutes later I'm standing to leave her office. "Thanks for taking the time," I tell her, shaking her hand. "I really do appreciate it."

She smiles and waves a hand. "Not a problem, it's been a slow morning around here."

I put my hand on the door knob and freeze. "It has been?" I ask. "That's weird. Linda said you wouldn't have time for me because you were super busy."

She gets a confused look on her face and then I shrug casually.

"Whatever. She probably says that to everyone. I'll see you around."

I leave her office, walk back down the narrow hallway, and as I pass Linda I lean on her desk and slap on an obnoxiously cheerful smile. "You have a *wonderful* day, Linda!"

"Yeah you too," she says without looking at me.

I leave the front office and breathe a heavy sigh as I walk towards the library for the rest of the period. I finally feel like all of the pieces are falling into place. The pieces of what, I'm not exactly sure, but I can't deny that I'm feeling a growing sense of closure.

I quietly slip into Ms. Cooper's room after school and find I'm the last one to arrive at the party. The desks are already in a circle, Haley, Tristan, and Ash are already in their usual spots, and Ms. Cooper is sitting next to someone new. He's a man in his mid-twenties with a short, well-groomed beard and a pair of circular glasses. He looks like a young professor and I feel an immediate thump in my chest when I look at him. I can't lie, he's pretty dreamy. I tell myself to calm down. He's probably not gay, and even if he is, he's about eight years older than me. I can daydream but I also know what is and isn't illegal.

"Hi, Derek," Ms. Cooper says as I walk in. "Have a seat."

"Is this everyone?" the man asks.

Ms. Cooper shakes her head. "No, we have one more coming—oh, there he is."

The door opens and Logan pokes his head in. "Hey, everyone!" he shouts.

"Logan!" Ash and Tristan cry.

"How's it going?" Logan asks me as he picks a seat.

"I thought you were suspended," I reply, ignoring his question as I sit down in the same spot as yesterday.

"Principal Sampson called today to apologize and to say that my suspension was ending immediately, which means I'm allowed in the school again *and* I can go to prom!"

The three other regulars cheer and I remain silent. I can guess what happened to Camilla.

Once the commotion dies down, I turn to face Ms. Cooper and the guest speaker. He looks at me and his gaze is so warm, so kind. The others thought I was in the wrong room when I came here yesterday. He looks like he's excited that I decided to show up.

"So, everyone, this my friend Matt. We've known each other since college. He works at the Oak Ridge community center and leads an LGBTQ+ group there every week. Matt, welcome to the Rainbow Club."

"The Rainbow Club?"

"We're rebranding," everyone else in the room says in unison.

"Oh... Cool," Matt says with a nod of approval. "So Ms. Cooper asked me to come today to talk to you all about a topic that I think is more persistent in the queer community than people realize—is it okay if I call it the queer community?" he asks hurriedly. "The longer title is just a mouthful."

"Yeah, that's fine," Ash says. The others nod along. I have to take a moment to think about it. I suppose I belong to this community now, although I never considered myself a member. I guess that means my opinion matters now, but I can't get past the fact that I really don't care.

Matt continues. "So the issue I'm referring to is internalized homophobia." His eyes flick to me, then scan the rest of the crowd. "Show of hands, who's heard of that term before?"

Ms. Cooper raises her hand, as do Ash, Tristan, and Logan. Haley and I give each other a confused look. We have no idea what's going on.

"Internalized homophobia is when someone in the queer community basically hates themself for who they are. Now, you may be thinking that you don't hate yourself and that's that, end of story, no internalized homophobia here."

Damn, this guy is good.

"But you'd be wrong," Matt says. "Internalized homophobia is a little more pervasive than that, which is why it's so hard to identify when you're the one who's experiencing it. It's funny because, kind of like the joke that gay people are the last to figure out that they're gay, people who experience internalized homophobia are typically the last to realize it. Everyone else around them can see it and they think, 'Oh wow, that guy has problems. That guy really hates himself,' but he himself doesn't recognize what's going on."

"Do you have some examples?" Logan asks.

"Yes! So, if you think of internalized homophobia as kind of like a disease, then these are all symptoms that might come along with it. The most common symptom that I see in my small group is being selective about who you're out to."

All of a sudden, I feel like he's talking directly to me. I'm only out to a couple of friends, and not even by choice. I'm only out to Logan because Camilla told Kelly who told him…. I think. I'm only out to Camilla because she figured it out on her own, and I'm only out to Brody because I drunkenly kissed him on Saturday night. The only person I've willingly come out to is… Alex. And now that his name has popped into my head, there's nothing I want more than for him to be sitting here next to me as I try to figure all of this out.

"So…" Haley speaks up, which I can already tell is somewhat out of character for her. "Who should we be out to?"

"Ideally, everyone," Matt answers. "You shouldn't be lying about being gay or bi or trans or whatever you are to anyone. You should be comfortable discussing your sexuality or gender identity with everyone."

My blood runs cold and my stomach drops. How the hell am I supposed to do that? That sounds like an impossible task. Be out to *everyone?* Even my parents? That's a big step— it's a big step for anyone. I was hoping to get around to it by the end of college in five years, maybe sooner if I bring a guy home for Christmas. This Matt character is telling me that I need to be out to my parents *now?*

"How does that mesh with high school?" Ms. Cooper asks, reading Haley's pained expression. "Because not everyone is in a position where they can be out to their parents."

"That's a great question, and a real concern," Matt replies. "But the thing is that you should ideally be open and honest with your parents about your sexuality and your gender identity. If they punish you for it in some way, then I think it's safe to say your parents are toxic and you need to find somewhere you can go where you will be safe, protected, and accepted. Maybe that's a relative's house, maybe that's a friend's house, maybe it's our community center where we can help if you're put in a situation like that."

"What other 'symptoms' of internalized homophobia are there?" Tristan asks.

"Fear of associating with other members of the queer community," he says bluntly. "I see it a lot, particularly in young men who are just figuring out that they're gay. Maybe it's because they've been raised in a religious home, maybe their parents or their friends are homophobic, who knows? But they tend to think that the "gay scene" is something that everyone in the community does and they decide that they're not comfortable with it, even though they've never ventured into it themselves."

Is that *me*? It's not that I've ever been *afraid* of associating with Logan or Tristan I just never felt inclined to do it. But is that because I'm afraid of how it will make me look?

This is messing with my head. Maybe Matt has a point. Maybe my I'm just reluctant to join the queer community because it's different and I like my life the way it is now. Change is always a little scary, but that's no reason to run from it, is it?

"Another one I see—and again, I see it a lot among young gay men who are just discovering themselves—is the excuse of 'I'm only into straight-acting dudes' or 'manly men.'"

Logan scoffs on my left and Tristan shakes his head on the other side of the circle of desks. Something tells me they've heard that one before.

Matt smiles with them. "I know, right? Honestly, I think it's a defensive mechanism to, again, not associate with the rest of the queer community. I think it's really because they're afraid of what liking femininity will do to them. This is the most destructive of all the symptoms of internalized homophobia because what it leads to is a fetishization of straight and heteronormative men. So these young gay men over and over and over again idolize, romanticize, and fall in love with straight men, especially their friends, and they justify it by saying that they're attracted to 'manly men.' They end up sabotaging their friendships and any potential at a real romantic relationship because they refuse to accept the fact that their straight friends will never like them back. It's very sad and when you realize that someone is stuck in that loop, you wanna do everything you can to break them out of it."

And just like that, I know he's talking about me. Just like that, I know what waking up feels like. I know what it feels like to realize that your entire life is a lie. I know what it feels like when you finally realize that you were the butt of a joke that had been going over your head for years.

Even to my own surprise, I raise my hand. Ms. Cooper

242

lifts her eyebrows in astonishment and Matt calls on me. "Where do you think internalized homophobia comes from? Like, what makes gay people hate themselves like this?"

"Society. The implicit homophobia that's inherent in every aspect of our society. Think about it—how many times have you been treated differently because of your sexuality or gender identity?"

The others nod along and I immediately think of Linda in the front office. Up until now I've had the benefit of my sexuality being secret, but word has gone around over the last few days. Was it possible that Linda was acting the way she was because she was uncomfortable talking to a gay guy?

"Open your eyes and you'll see it—there's homophobia everywhere. If society were more accepting of the queer community, particularly queer youth and queer people of color, then this epidemic of internalized homophobia would end in a heartbeat."

"I know exactly what you mean," Logan says. We all turn to face him. "When I first came out as gay, I definitely noticed people starting to treat me differently. I knew I wasn't acting any differently. The only thing that changed was that word had spread that I was gay. As soon as I realized that it was the environment around me that had changed, and not me, I knew that *that* was the source of that new discrimination I was dealing with."

Logan's words hang in the air as we all retreat into our own thoughts. He was absolutely right. *I* haven't changed, but the secret that I was hiding for so long had been shared with the whole school. The world I now live in is very different from the one that existed just a week ago.

"Thank you for sharing that, Logan," Ms. Cooper says

at last.

"So what should we do?" Haley asks, barely audible. "If we think we might... you know... have some... internalized homophobia?"

"It's sort of like exposure therapy," Matt explains. "If you're afraid of snakes and you want to overcome that fear, then you need to start small—look at pictures of snakes. Then go to the snake exhibit at the zoo. Then go to a pet store and look at the snakes, because that's a less controlled environment than the zoo. Then ask the pet store owner to hold one of the snakes. What you'll find is that each step makes you braver and stronger because at the beginning of that process you were afraid to even look at a picture of a snake, but by the end you're holding one in a pet store. Not many people would ever do that.

"So, what can you do? Well, you can start by coming out to more people. Come out to a stranger you meet in a coffee shop. Come out to someone you see around school a lot but don't actually know that well. That'd be a good place to start. It's all about exposing yourself to the experience of coming out so that you are more comfortable doing it to a friend or your parents, until eventually you don't care and you'll be open about it to everyone."

I sit back in my chair, exhausted. So much to take in and so much to think about. I have a lot of work to do and no idea where exactly to begin. After a moment of silence, I raise a trembling hand.

Matt sees it and calls on me. "Yeah, Dillian."

"Derek," I correct him. I think Ms. Cooper blushes, don't know why.

"Oops, sorry. Derek. What's your question?"

"So… I guess I'm just a little confused on where to get started… That's not really a question, but…"

"I have an idea!" Logan jumps in. "Matt said you should start by coming out to people you see a lot but don't really know personally. That'd be a good place for you to start," he suggests.

"Okay… so, who would that be?"

"What about the teachers?" he asks, raising his eyebrows at Ms. Cooper for approval. "A bunch of them are still here, they won't go telling other people, and they're people you know but don't have personal relationships with."

My face instantly heats up and I can feel beads of sweat start to form on my forehead. "Oh yeah…" I say, attempting to hide my obvious revulsion. "There's an idea… Ms. Cooper, what do you think?"

Please God, just say no!

"I think that's a really good idea, Logan," she says with a smile.

Fuck!

"Derek, what do you say? Are you up to it?" Matt asks.

"I don't know. That sounds really scary."

"I think that's a sign that you need to do it."

"Is anyone else going to be doing this?" I ask, turning to face the other three students opposite me in the circle of desks.

"I'm already out to everyone," Tristan says. "So is Ash. Haley is out to everyone except her parents."

"Guess I know what I'm doing tonight," she breathes.

"So it's just me? Cool. Can't wait."

I start racking my brain, frantically looking for an excuse to delay this. I come up empty-handed.

Ms. Cooper looks at me with a smile. "Derek, who do you have for first period?"

"I can't do this, Ms. Cooper," I say with my back pressed up against the wall. We're standing just outside Mrs. Garcia's room as she grades papers at her desk inside. I'm hyperventilating and my heart is pounding in my chest. "Why does she need to know?"

"Because if you want to accept yourself for who you really are, you need to be open about being gay." She doesn't say anything for a moment as I try to catch my breath. "Count of three. Ready?"

"No."

"One... Two... Three." She puts her hand on my shoulder, leads me away from the wall, and guides me with a gentle nudge into Mrs. Garcia's room.

Mrs. Garcia is hunched over a stack of exams, her reading glasses sitting low on her nose. She hears my footsteps and looks up with surprise. "Derek. What are you doing here so late?" Her eyes flick over to Ms. Cooper by the door, then narrow in confusion as she fixes them back on me.

I immediately resort to my old habit of making a joke out of something I have to do but absolutely dread. "I could ask you the same question! Shouldn't you be at home grading papers? You know leaving these lights on costs taxpayer dollars and—"

"Derek..." Ms. Cooper scolds from the corner of the room, forcing me back on track.

"Right... Mrs. Garcia, I came by because... I just wanted to let you know... that I'm gay."

Mrs. Garcia doesn't take her eyes off me. I can see she's trying to figure out what the hell is going on and if I'm serious or not. "Oh," she says at last. "Okay. Thanks for sharing, Derek."

I stand awkwardly in front of her desk for a few seconds. "Well... I'll see you tomorrow," I say before turning on my heel and walking for the door.

"I'll see you tomorrow, Derek. Allison!"

Ms. Cooper pokes her head back in the room as she ushers me out.

"Can I have a word?"

Ms. Cooper looks at me. "Just wait right here," she says quietly before going back inside the room.

I wait with my back against the wall, same place I was just a minute ago, and I try to hear what exactly they're saying inside. Their voices are hushed and I can only pick out small pieces of the conversation.

"...accept himself."

"You mean so you..."

"...on his own."

"... you know it. What makes it..."

"...understand?"

"...understand... exactly why you're doing this."

The whispering suddenly stops and Ms. Cooper comes storming out of the room. When she sees me, she puts her arm on my shoulder and guides me by her side down the hall.

"What was that about?" I ask innocently.

"Nothing, sweetie. Don't worry about it. Some people are just assholes."

I glance back at the door to Mrs. Garcia's room as we walk away. As we move down the hall to Madame Miller's

247

classroom, my mind can't help but change the light with which I see Mrs. Garcia and how I think about her. "Ms. Cooper, what should I do if people don't accept me?"

"Just ignore them," she responds firmly. "All that matters is that you accept yourself."

That night, I finish typing up the new ending for my short story. It's due tomorrow and I made a tough change but one that I knew needed to happen. Overcome with mental and emotional exhaustion, I lie down on my bed and stare up at the ceiling. I feel like a completely different person than who I was when I woke up this morning. I don't know if it's in a good way or not. Am I more comfortable with myself than I was yesterday? I guess. Coming out this afternoon helped me. I was so scared to come out to Mrs. Garcia, but with Ms. Cooper by my side, each time was easier than the last. Eventually when we got to Mr. Holtz, who was in the process of locking up his classroom and lab for the night, the words flowed out of my mouth instead of being forced through gritted teeth. That was a good sign, right? Maybe I'd just become numb to the feeling, it's hard to tell.

I keep thinking about everything Matt told us today. How much had internalized homophobia affected me and my life? I definitely have a type and that type is what I consider to be masculine men. I always thought it was just because I play sports and I'm surrounded by athletes all the time. I've never given Logan a second thought, although I guess he is kind of cute. Alex is cute too, though. But Matt warned us about falling for straight guys. Do I have some sort of weird straight fetish? Ugh, thinking about me having a fetish makes my skin crawl. I always thought my sexual desires were pretty standard, you know, for a gay guy.

But I do like Alex, as a friend at least. He was there for me when I needed him. If I had my phone, I'd ask him to come over right now and I know he would. Do I find him attractive? Yes. I don't know if that's a new revelation or if I always thought he was hot. I do so much retconning of my own thoughts it's hard to remember what I thought and why. I've seen him shirtless and I liked what I saw. Wish I could see it again. I really like his beard too; it makes him look just a little bit older than seventeen. And how could I forget his button nose? All I want to do is reach out and pinch it.

Is this wrong? Should I not be thinking of Alex in this way? Matt was right—falling for straight guys over and over again is going to be a destructive habit. I need to break it. Still, I guess there's nothing wrong with appreciating beauty when I see it, and damn is Alex beautiful. I'll just think about him, but I won't romanticize him. I put my hands behind my head and close my eyes as I think one more time about the night he and I spent together. It was right here on my bed. What if I wasn't an emotional mess? I wonder what it would have been like to kiss him.

Stop. That's a slippery slope.

Damn, I'm right. Alex isn't gay, I shouldn't be imagining a relationship with him. But I could at least think about the time we've already spent together. Maybe he and Brody could be friends. I hope so, because Alex really is a great guy. Maybe Alex can come over the next time Brody and I hang out, although who knows when that's gonna be. Brody's parents may have grounded him until the end of time for getting suspended. I may not see him before summer.

Wait a minute. Brody and I are supposed to do some yard work at his place this Saturday. So I will see him! I breathe a sigh of relief. I've been missing him this week, not just because I really need a friend, but also because we just patched things up only a few minutes before he got suspended.

Why the heck does Principal Sampson think he's a bad influence on me? She has to be wrong. She doesn't know Brody like I do. Then Matt pops into my head again, and something he said about idolizing straight men. I shrug it off. Matt had some good advice, but he doesn't know everything about my life.

As that thought crosses my mind, I can't help but recognize an all too familiar lopsided satisfaction. Something isn't sitting quite right, I just can't pinpoint exactly what it is.

CHAPTER 18

It's finally Friday. For the first time in a week, I don't feel like lead weights are keeping me in bed. I rise and somehow can't keep the smile off my face. *Today isn't going to matter,* I think. *Just like old times.* I quickly dress and hurry downstairs for breakfast. My mom's in the kitchen pouring herself a cup of coffee. "Morning, sweetie," she says when she hears me walk in. She turns around and gives me a smile. I can't help but think it looks a little wan. I immediately begin to wonder what she's heard and what she knows.

"Morning, Mom."

"Do you know where I put my car keys?" she asks.

"I do not."

"Huh.. We need to get a key bowl."

"Sure do, Mom."

There's a moment of silence when I can feel her studying me from across the kitchen. She sips her coffee, then says, "Isn't your prom coming up soon?"

"Yeah, it's tomorrow."

"Oh. Are you going?" I can hear a tiny bit of futile hope in her voice. It's all in the upward inflection she puts at the end of the question.

"No."

"Oh… Okay."

Is she expecting me to say something more? Should I tell her the truth? Is this even the right time, when my dad's upstairs probably still in bed? Shouldn't I wait until we're all in the same room?

I open my mouth to say something, and then I shut it again. It just doesn't feel right, not yet. I don't have butterflies, my heart isn't pounding, my stomach isn't in knots. Those are all signs I'm about to do something that I'm dreading but should probably do. This just feels off. It doesn't sit right. I'm not even out to all of my friends yet. A hasty coming out to my mom in the kitchen on a Friday morning seems short sighted.

"I just don't have anyone to go with is all," I explain, trying to put her at ease.

"What about Camilla?"

I almost laugh. I can't tell my mom that she's suspended because then she'll ask why. "She was planning on going with Brody, but since he isn't going anymore she doesn't really want to go either."

"Oh, that makes sense." She puts down her cup of coffee and takes a seat at the table. "Derek, I want to talk to you for a minute." She pats the chair next to her.

Oh no. Did someone at work say something to her? What does she know? Please, Mom, don't put me on the spot about this.

I take a seat, hoping the nervous sweat on my forehead isn't too obvious.

My mom takes in a deep breath. "I don't know if you should be spending time with Brody anymore."

"*What?* Why?" I ask angrily.

"Derek, he's been suspended from school. He punched

some poor kid in the face, he punched *you* in the face. Look at your eye!"

"It's fine, Mom. I punched him too. We got into a fight. It's not the first time I've been in a fist fight."

"The last time was the summer after your freshman year and you weren't in school. This is different. There are consequences."

"We've already made up. I don't see what the big deal is."

"I just think he's a bad influence on you," she says flatly.

"Why do you think that?"

"Because he's been getting into trouble."

"He's been getting into trouble because he's been standing up for me!"

"Derek, I know that's not true," she says. "If that were the case, he wouldn't have been suspended."

"Mom, it's way more complicated than that," I try to explain.

"I don't think it is. After the two of you do yard work tomorrow, I don't want you hanging out with him anymore." She pats the table, punctuating the end of the conversation. I stand to leave, but before I go, my blood begins to boil and I turn around for what I know will be an act of defiance.

"You know what, Mom? I don't really care what you want. Brody's my friend and if I want to spend time with him, that's what I'm going to do."

She raises her eyebrows in surprise. "Oh is it? Well then maybe you don't need your truck privileges anymore."

"Oh yeah? Have fun picking me up from baseball every day. Have fun driving me to and from every weekend game, getting there an hour early and leaving thirty minutes after they end.

"You want me to be mature? You want me to act like an adult? Let me start by saying this—I'm seventeen and you will not choose my friends for me. You don't want Brody in your house? I can respect that, but you will not decide who I hang out with in my free time."

She stares daggers at me, maybe hoping that her motherly fury will get me to take back everything I just said. Instead I pick up my backpack and head for the door. "Good luck at work," I tell her before I leave the house.

Calculus is lonely without Brody or Camilla by my side, but I know it's the last day like this. Come Monday, Brody will be back in his usual seat and Camilla will be in the back of the room, pretending not to exist.

When Mrs. Garcia looks at me, her expression looks a little pained, a little contrite. It's hard to think of her in a kind way after yesterday afternoon. Maybe I misunderstood something? Maybe the way she acted came across differently than she intended? But then what Matt said yesterday pops into my head, about society's ubiquitous homophobia, and I let out a disappointed sigh. I always thought Mrs. Garcia was a tough woman with a big heart. Apparently I was wrong, although I still don't understand how I could have been. I guess people are just messy.

It's time to turn in the final draft of my short story in creative writing. I approach Ms. Cooper's desk with the stapled bundle of papers in my hand and she beams up at me. "Finally get the ending right?" she asks.

"I think so."

Before I hand it over, just to make sure I'm comfortable with it, I read the last page one more time...

Dillian was angry and he jumped to his feet. Then, as he thought about it more, he realized that his problem was not with Brian. He never had a problem with Brian at all. The truth was that Dillian secretly liked Brian. He wasn't mad that Brian was going to take Sara to prom. Dillian was mad that Brian wasn't taking him to prom. But how could he explain that to Dillian now that he was so angry?

"Brian! Wait! Let's not fight over Sara!"

"Why not?" Brian asked, fists ready to fight.

"Let's not fight over Sara because I'm not mad that you're taking her to prom. The truth is that I'm mad you're not taking me to prom!"

"Well why didn't you say so?" Brian asked, his anger disappearing. "I want to go with you to prom too!"

"Why didn't you say something sooner?" Dillian asked Brian.

"Because I was afraid. I didn't want you to tell me no."

"Of course I'll go to prom with you!" Dillian shouted.

Then the two of them went to prom that weekend and they had a really good time. They danced a lot and even Sara was happy that they were happy even though she went to prom by herself. She even danced with Dillian and Brian and the three of them had a lot of fun together. Then when they announced the prom elections, Brian won prom king. Dillian was very happy, but felt a little left out. Then the principal announced that instead of a prom queen, the students had voted for a second prom king and they voted for Dillian. Dillian jumped on the stage with Brian and they were crowned kings and they danced together in front of everyone. Dillian and Brian were very happy and knew they'd be together forever.

THE END

I place it on Ms. Cooper's desk right next to the tiny pride flag. Unable to help herself, she immediately picks it up and giddily turns to the last page.

A minute later, she looks up at me with a grin. "I think you should be proud of it."

I shrug. "It's weird. It doesn't really feel like it's mine anymore. It feels like it kind of belongs to... well... everyone."

She gives me a nod of approval and a big grin. "I think that's how you know you got it right."

I sit down at my desk next to Logan and he whispers

to me as class begins, "Hey, the prom decorating committee is hanging up the backdrop during study hall today. Meet me in the art room later."

At the beginning of study hall, I follow Logan to the art room and when I walk through the door I see Gabby standing over the completed mural. "Just got done with the finishing touches this morning," she says, placing her hands on her hips in pride.

I walk around the backdrop to stand next to her. The yellow brick road has been completely painted and detailed. It leads over a hill to a glimmering Emerald City, its towers rising high into the sky and glistening in the sunlight. A rainbow frames the entire image and in the field I try to remember which of the poppies I painted myself.

"It looks amazing!" I tell Gabby.

She gives me a smile. "Well it was a team effort." Her smile fades as she turns her gaze back down to the masterpiece on the floor. "...Yeah."

"That's right. We all helped!" Logan shouts from the other side of the backdrop. "Now we need to go hang it up."

"Where exactly is it going?" I ask.

"By the front office," Logan answers. "On prom night, people will come in through the front doors, walk by the office, and stand in front of the backdrop for a quick picture, then go to the gym for the actual dance itself."

I squat to grab a corner. "Well, let's go hang it up!"

We prudently carry the large paper through the hall, careful not to let the ends wrinkle or tear. Gabby insists that we walk very, very slowly through the empty halls, probably too slowly if you ask me, but then again I didn't spend nearly as much time on this as she did.

When we get to the front office, we see Principal Sampson standing in the middle of the waiting area in front of Linda's desk. She has her hands on her hips and I think she looks a little irate until she sees us through the windows and puts on a smile. "Hey, folks!" she sings, her eyes falling on the painting in our hands. "Oh *wow!* That looks amazing!"

"Thank you!" Logan says. "We're finally putting it up!"

We walk to one of the floor-to-ceiling windows and Logan takes a roll of duct tape off of his wrist. He hands it to me. "You're taller than me, Derek. Can you put some pieces high up on the window for me?"

"Yeah, no problem," I reply, accepting the roll of tape from him. I pull out a long strip with a satisfying rip, then tear it off and connect the ends to form a loop. I go to the window and guess how high I should put it. "This good?" I ask Logan over my shoulder, my left hand a few inches over my head.

"A little higher," Logan says.

I raise my hand more.

"A little more."

The bruise on my back protests with a stitch of pain as I stretch out my arm as high as it will go.

"Okay, that's good."

I slap my hand against the wall and hop a couple times to smooth it out. As I grab the roll of duct tape and tear off another long piece, I glance at some movement inside the front office. Linda is moving around a lot behind her desk, and when she finally stands up I see that her eyes are red and she's dabbing her nose with a wadded up tissue. I frown as

I watch, wondering what's wrong, and then before I can ask Logan or Gabby if they know, I see her put a cardboard box on top of the desk. Linda lifts a picture frame off of her desk and carefully places it among the contents of the box, then drops a coffee mug inside too. She slides the box off the desk and into her arms, hugging it to her body, awkwardly carrying it with one hand while dabbing her nose with a tissue in her other.

She holds her head high, then strides across the office waiting area to the door. Principal Sampson pushes the door open and holds it for her. I watch as Linda walks down the hall and vanishes out the door. Before I can ask what's going on, I look back at the now empty desk in the office and catch Principal Sampson's eye. She gives me a resolute smile and comes back out to the hallway just as I turn the second length of duct tape into a loop and stick it high on the window.

"Looking good, folks," she says.

"We're almost done," Logan says, handing me the top corner of the painting.

"So I just gotta jump and try to stick it?" I ask, unsure I can do it without tearing the backdrop itself.

"Hang on," Principal Sampson says. She grabs two chairs from the office waiting area, and returns with one in each hand. "These would probably be useful."

"Yes!" Logan says, taking the chairs from her, placing one on my end of the painting and taking the other to Gabby.

I step onto the chair's cushion and my shoe sinks in, throwing me off balance. I lean against the window for support and raise the corner of the backdrop until its lower edge is flush with the ground. Then I stick it to the loop of duct tape already on the window and Gabby does the same on her side. Logan and Principal Sampson watch from the ground, making sure it's straight and at the right height.

Once it's up, Gabby and I climb down from the chairs and join them to gaze at it.

"This is wonderful," Principal Sampson says. "People are gonna love this at prom tomorrow night."

I sit in chemistry class wishing Mr. Holtz would hurry up. Well, really wishing time would hurry up. I haven't been to baseball practice since Tuesday and I'm dying to get back on the field. My foot won't stop tapping impatiently under my desk, a mind of its own, just like on opening day.

Mr. Holtz turns his attention towards me in the middle of his lecture when he hears the incessant tapping. "What is that?" he asks.

I force my foot to stop, pressing it hard against the ground to crush its will.

He listens for the sound but can't hear it anymore, so he shrugs and continues with his lecture.

Every class today has been slightly uncomfortable. Knowing that every teacher knows I'm gay is... bizarre. They now know some part of my private life, an intimate part at that, which was handed over to them without warning or context. I wonder if this is how teachers feel when students run into them in public.

Finally, the bell rings and I dart out of the room before Mr. Holtz can wish me a good weekend or good luck at tomorrow's game.

I'm apparently not the only person excited about practice today because when I shuffle into the dugout, I find Austin and Parker already changing into their clothes for practice. Parker beams when he sees me coming down the short staircase. "Derek!" he shouts. "You're back!"

"Yes!"

"Where were you the last couple days?"

I freeze. I can't tell him the truth. I'm not ready for that. I make up a quick lie. "Remember how Coach told Brody and me to join the prom decorating committee? Well I had to go to that the last couple days. There's a lot we had to get ready for tomorrow night."

"Oh, gotcha." He doesn't seem entirely convinced, but I know better than to oversell my story. If I overqualify it, he'll know it's a lie.

A couple more of my teammates jump into the dugout and say hello to me, and before any of them get the chance to ask about my absence from the last two practices, I take my glove and climb out of the dugout. Just as I'm about to run to the outfield, Alex almost walks right into me.

"Derek!" he exclaims, stopping on a dime.

"Alex!" I can't keep the corners of my mouth from curling into a smile.

"You're back today!"

"I am! Wanna warm up with me?"

"Yeah, just let me drop my stuff in the dugout first."

A few minutes later, we're in the outfield stretching our legs out for the scrimmage game we're about to play against the JV team. "Here they come," Alex says, looking past me towards the visitor dugout. The same dozen scrawny kids from just the other day shuffle inconspicuously onto the field, some of them visibly afraid of us, keeping to the dugout and the first baseline for their stretches. Only a couple intrepid sophomores journey into right field near Alex and me. They wave hello to us, a friendly smile on their faces. I know most varsity, especially seniors, would give them stink eye. They'd take the opportunity to shoot them nasty looks and say something about how they're gonna get their asses kicked, or maybe just ignore them all together. Alex and I, we just smile back and give them a wave. A truce.

Was I that small just a year ago? I wonder what Alex looked like a year ago. Did he still have that beard?

"So," Alex says to me after a few minutes of silence. "Where've you been the last couple days?"

"I had to go to the Rainbow Club."

"The Rainbow Club?"

"Yeah, we're rebranding."

He looks slightly flummoxed, then shrugs it off. "So... Why did you have to go?"

"Principal Sampson thought that I could learn something from it."

"Did you?"

I think one more time about what Matt told us yesterday about internalized homophobia, how it felt like he was speaking directly to me. "Yeah, I think I did."

Alex squints his eyes and looks over my shoulder for a second, then back to me. "Who's the faculty sponsor of that club?"

"Ms. Cooper, one of the English teachers."

"Is she a skinny blonde woman?"

"Yeah, why?"

"She's in the bleachers."

I spin and stare across the baseball field, over the pitcher's mound and past home plate to see, sure enough, Ms.

Cooper sitting in the middle row taking in the sun and chatting with Coach Cole. What the fuck is she doing here? This is my turf. This is a sacred space, strictly off-limits from whatever she plans on doing.

"Oh shit," I say loud enough for Alex to hear the stress in my voice.

"Maybe she just came to watch?" Alex suggests.

I give him a skeptical look.

"Yeah, not super likely," he says.

We play catch for a few minutes before Coach Cole walks onto the field and waves us over to the dugout. He's about to give the team a short pep talk before the game starts. As I approach, Ms. Cooper walks to the fence along the third baseline and calls me over to her with a wave of her hand. I know I have to go to her.

"Come to watch a scrimmage game?" I ask.

"Well, yes, but..." she says with a playful tone in her voice. "I'm here for something else too."

"Okay..."

"Considering what we talked about in our club meeting yesterday," she says in a low voice so no one overhears, "I thought it'd be a good idea to encourage you to come out to your teammates."

My heart stops. I'm at a complete loss for words. She can't be serious.

"What do you think?"

"*No!*" I growl, quiet enough so only she can hear . "There's no way I'm coming out to my teammates. I don't want them to know!"

"Derek, remember how we talked about internalized homophobia being about hiding your sexuality from your

263

friends? I think this is a good step for you."

"You can't be serious."

"I am, *and*, may I also point out that this was your exact reaction yesterday afternoon when I suggested you practice coming out by telling your teachers."

That shuts me up. She's right, and the butterflies in my stomach and my racing heart tell me that this is the next step, that this is something I have to do if I want to avoid going down a self-destructive path. It's gonna be a long process and every step will be a hard one, but that doesn't mean I can give up. Even though I hate to admit it, I hate it with every fiber of my being, I know that Ms. Cooper is right.

"God *dammit!*"

"Watch your language, Derek."

"You can tell me to watch my language when I'm in your classroom, thank you very much. We're on the baseball field. You're in my house now." I take a deep breath to calm myself. "Fine. I'll... tell the team. But you have to stay for the whole game."

"Deal," she says. "I was planning on doing that anyways."

"Why?" I ask, but before she can answer me, Coach Cole comes over.

"How's it going over here?" he asks, as if it's not at all bizarre that the English teacher is on the baseball field talking to his third baseman.

I open my mouth to answer when Ms. Cooper says, "Just fine. Derek has something to say to the team, FYI."

"Okay, I can give him a minute before the game starts."

My head is reeling. I'm missing something, some very large piece of a puzzle. Just as I'm about to ask the two of them to clear things up, Ms. Cooper plants a kiss on Coach Cole's cheek. "Thank you, dear," she sings happily, putting an arm around him and holding on to his opposite shoulder.

Coach Cole and Ms. Cooper are dating! That's why he wanted Brody and me to be a part of her prom decorating committee when she suggested it! He knew it would make her happy! He also probably didn't like the fact that we were shit-talking his girlfriend behind her back.

"No problem," Coach responds, a dull tone in his voice. It sounds like he's bored, but he's just more of a distant person. Apparently he's even distant in his intimate relationships. I'd believe it. He barely shows us a glimpse of his true self and we spend at least twelve hours a week with him.

Coach Cole shrugs off Ms. Cooper and puts a hand on my shoulder, guiding me back to the front of the dugout where the rest of the team is waiting for him to say a few words before the game. We arrive at the small circle together and all eyes are on me, even though Coach is the one speaking.

"All right, guys. It's the JV team and I know you might think this game is gonna be a walk in the park, but that's not a guarantee. They have some strong players who are gonna be your teammates next year for those of you who aren't graduating in a few weeks. Don't make the mistake of underestimating them. That's exactly what they want you to do."

He takes a short, uneasy pause and I know what he's about to say. I feel like throwing up.

"Now before we play ball, Derek has something he'd like to say... Derek, the floor's yours."

I look around the group. My eyes meet Parker's and Austin's and Ryan's and Randy's and Blake's and Josh's and finally they meet Alex's. All these players—all my friends, staring at me with nothing but reverence and I know it's time to come clean.

"Uh... hey, everyone. You know, I think we're gonna play really well today. We're gonna crush the JV team. I mean, have you seen those guys? They're like a foot shorter than us and -"

"Derek..." a voice says from behind me. In the moment, I can't tell if it's Coach Cole's or Ms. Cooper's.

"All right, all right... You guys are my best friends and... it's time that I open up to you about something... something I've been hiding for a while... and that's that I'm gay..."

Silence. Total silence.

"So... that's that... and now you know."

"...Okay," Parker says at last.

"I think we should give Derek a round of applause for being so brave," a voice says right over my shoulder. I turn around to see Ms. Cooper standing just behind me. She starts clapping and the rest of the team waits for a few seconds before slowly joining in, their applause trickling in like reluctant rainfall.

"Uh... thanks," I say when the clapping dies down. I thought I'd feel relieved. But I don't. If anything, I just feel numb and drained, exactly the way I did yesterday afternoon by the time Ms. Cooper and I made it down to Mr. Holtz's room. Maybe that's because I'm starting to get used to coming out. I guess that's a good sign.

"Okay," Coach begins again when I'm done speaking. His eyes are a little downcast, a little confused. He must be trying to figure out how I feel. I don't quite know either, but

I know I should be happy. I force a smile on my face, hoping it'll kickstart an emotional response.

"Good for you, Derek," he says at last. "All right, Trojans. Let's play ball!"

We destroy the JV team. I know Coach said not to underestimate them, but Alex's pitching scares them half to death. We can tell who the strong players will be next year because they are the only ones who manage to hit anything Alex throws at them. We end up winning 8–2, which I appreciate, but I also wonder how well this is preparing us for our game against Emmerdale tomorrow morning.

After the game, I jog back to the dugout and as I descend the stairs to join the team, I can't help but feel a little removed, like an outsider in my own home. My teammates, they're smiling at me, and I know I should feel happy— I should feel accepted—and yet I can't help but feel like the whole charade is a little forced. What did I expect? A parade? I know there's a lot of progress that they need to make, but at least this is a good start. I have to admit that my heart swells with pride, even if I will miss the old days of having my own little secret. Still, there's one person who treats me exactly the same as before.

"That was easier than I expected," I tell him.

Alex looks up from his bag and smiles at me.

I take off my practice shirt and reach for the shirt I wore earlier today. "Yeah, I know Coach tried to warn us, but still. Not that hard."

After I change, I walk out of the dugout to find Ms. Cooper sitting on the bleachers. I'm surprised she stuck around this long. "I'm very proud of you, Derek."

"Thanks," I say, my voice void of any emotion. I still feel a little emotionally exhausted.

"You got a minute to talk?" she asks.

"No. I just want to go home." I walk away, heading back for my truck across the street. About ten yards later, Alex catches up to me.

"I didn't expect her to make you come out to the team," he says.

"She didn't *make* me," I point out. "She *pushed* me to do what I knew I had to do. Sooner or later."

Alex furrows his eyebrows. "Okay," he says. "Well... Good for you... I'm glad you're happy."

"I am." Or at least I will be when this strange emotional stupor wears off.

"You doing anything tonight?"

I shake my head. "Just being grounded." I realize he was probably about to ask me to hang out and I add, "I'd definitely be down to chill if I was allowed."

"That didn't stop us last time."

I shower when I get home and eat a quiet dinner with my parents. When we're done eating and I've washed the dishes, I climb the stairs back to my room and lie on my bed. Can't believe this week is finally over; this insane, roller-coaster of a week. I check my watch. 8 p.m. I peer out my window just in time to see a crappy red convertible coast down the street and park a few houses away. I hurry over to my bedroom door and gently shut it, then go to the window and remove the screen again.

Minutes later, Alex is pulling himself up from the windowsill and climbing into my room. "It's the weekend!"

"Finally!" I reply with a grin. "Keep your voice down, my parents are downstairs."

"Sorry," he whispers back.

It's only then that I notice he has a backpack. "What's that for?" I ask as he takes it off.

"I hear you like beer," he says, ripping open the zipper and handing me an ice cold can of ale.

"I do!" I say with a laugh, ignoring my own advice to stay quiet. "This is awesome! Thank you!"

He wears a smug smile as he sets his backpack on the floor and sits on the window seat. He runs a hand through the orange flow on his head and says, "I have eight beers that we need to take care of tonight."

"How are you gonna get home?"

"I thought I could just crash with you until I'm sober enough to drive, if that's all right."

I nod and Alex cracks open his beer as quietly as he can. I open mine as Alex raises his for a toast. "Here's to new friends!"

"To new friends!" I echo, before taking a swig of the cold, blonde beer.

My first beer is gone as night sets in and my second is gone as the cicadas start to sing. Alex outpaces me and finishes his third just as I'm opening mine. We hold our breaths as we hear my parents climb the stairs for bed, then let out a stifled laugh as we sit on the windowsill and drink our fourth beers together.

In the morning, Alex nudges me awake so he can sneak out of the front door and we can both get ready for our game against Emmerdale.

CHAPTER 19

I fit into my white baseball pants and button up my jersey. Damn. I look sharp.

I leave home for the baseball field and as I bring my truck to a halt in the parking lot a few minutes later, I notice a familiar black Subaru just a few spots away. When I get to the dugout, I find Brody sitting in the bleachers behind home plate. "You came!" I shout when he waves hello.

He hops to his feet and walks over to me with a grin. "I had to beg my parents to let me come. Even if I can't play, I gotta show up for the team."

A surly roar hits my ears and I turn around to see a bus pull into the baseball field parking lot. It lets out a belch and its brakes squeal as it comes to a stop. Off march the Emmerdale Alligators, dressed in green jerseys and white pants. "They look intimidating," Brody says.

I shrug. "Yeah. We'll show 'em who's boss. I'm gonna go get warmed up. I'll see you later today for our punishment." I shoot him a wink and he smiles back as I hurry to the dugout. I drop my bat bag on the bench and jog to the outfield for my warm-ups, shooting a wave to Alex as he throws practice pitches to Austin in the bullpen. He waves back and once again, a shy smile creeps over his face. I try to hide the one growing on my own.

I stretch my legs, rub the tender spot on my back, and do some suicide sprints before playing catch with Parker. He starts laughing at something by the bleachers and when I turn around I see Brody doing his standard dozen cartwheels before the game starts. I can't help but laugh.

Coach Cole shows up right on time in his standard, slightly grouchy mood and a clipboard in his hand. He shows us the batting lineup just a few minutes before Kev's voice blares out of the speakers and he declares that it's time to play ball.

We lose to the Alligators. I don't know if it's because their right fielder hit a grandslam in the bottom of the fourth, because Brody wasn't playing, or if it's because I forgot to eat my peanut butter and jelly sandwich before the game. That last theory is my strongest. There's no way I'd have only hit a double in the sixth inning if I'd had my sandwich.

In the dugout after the game, once we bump fists with the Alligators and begrudgingly tell them good game, the guys check their phones to learn that their girlfriends and prom dates are already getting ready for tonight. "I'm not picking her up for another three hours," Randy says. "The fuck is she doing that takes so long?"

"My girlfriend started getting ready before the game," Parker tells him. "I'm gonna text her ten minutes before I pick her up and say I still need to shower."

Laughter erupts from the dugout and for a moment, a brief moment, I can't help but feel like an outsider. Something about everyone knowing I'm gay distances me from the rest of the team. I can feel it, and I wish that for just a second I could join in the joke. I wish I was going to prom, even if I was taking a guy. Even as Alex gently nudges his elbow into my ribs to get me to smile, I know I'm just masking some deep, nebulous contrition.

I shower after the game and when my mom tells me it's time to head over to Brody's for yard work, I find myself oddly excited for my punishment as I leave through the front door. The afternoon sunlight filters through the canopy over the street and a pair of birds fly right past my head. Spring is already off to a good start and I can't wait for summer. Of course, I'm still in trouble and so is Brody, but my punishment ends tomorrow and Brody will be back in school on Monday. I know Principal Sampson and my parents think he's a bad influence on me. Maybe he is, maybe he isn't, but as I knock on his front door, I know that the time has come for me to slowly start distancing myself.

Brody's mom answers the door and I'm afraid she's going to be irate with me, but instead she beams and says, "Derek! Come on in!" Her gaze lingers on my black eye for just a second as she waves me in. "Brody's out back. He'll tell you what you two are doing today." Very professional. She knows I know I'm in trouble. The physical labor is a reminder of that. No need to hurt feelings in the process. This is strictly business.

I walk downstairs to the basement and out the patio door to find Brody sitting at the table by the pool. He stands up when I see him, and I can see the shiner I put on his cheek is healing nicely. "You're here! Welcome! Ready to get to work?"

"Yes! I get my phone back when this is done. I can't wait!"

He points around the yard as he explains what we need to do. "The storm on Wednesday morning threw a bunch of leaves everywhere, so we need to clean those up. Getting them out of the pool is the most important thing, but we also need to rake the yard. The swing on the gazebo needs to be rehung; my dad bought some chain and a pair of bolt cutters for that. We just need to take off the old, rusty chain and cut the new chain to the same length. Any questions?"

I shake my head. "No, I'm ready to go."

He hands me a skimmer net on a long aluminum pole. "You can clean the pool. It's the easier job. I'll start raking the leaves in the yard."

I'm about to turn towards the pool when he says, "Wait wait wait. Before we get started..." He takes the net from my hands and chucks it into the grass. Then he disappears into the basement, grabs two beers from the deep freeze, and hands one to me when he returns.

I know I shouldn't, but when it's Brody offering, I can't refuse. I accept the beer and pop the tab. "They can't see us from here," Brody says, looking straight up the rear wall of the house to the living room window. "But we shouldn't take too long."

I pull two chairs away from the patio table and place them next to each other. Brody drops into his seat and I sit down carefully so I don't bother the bruise on my back. We sip our beers in unison and breathe a heavy sigh.

"Look, Derek," Brody says, "I just want you to know that you're still my best friend and nothing's gonna change that."

"Thank you, Brody. That means a lot."

"And if anyone ever gives you shit about being gay, let me know and I'll kick their ass."

I laugh and take a sip of my beer. I'm glad that I'm still Brody's best friend, but I don't think I can call him mine anymore. Too much has happened that can't be taken back.

I think again about our night together last week and everything that's happened since; about the kiss, the punch, the suspension, and now the beers. Deep down, some part of me knows that my friendship with Brody is temporary, that if I really want to grow up and grow out of my own self-hatred, I'll have to put some distance between the two of us. Just last weekend I was dreading the thought of Brody and I gradually becoming strangers. But now I know it's for the best. As I take a sip of the cold beer in my hand, I know that this afternoon with Brody is the first step of a very long goodbye.

Brody and I cast our gaze around the backyard. Leaves everywhere, a dirty pool, and a gazebo swing that's hanging at an odd angle on a rusty chain. A gargantuan task lies ahead of us, and before I can say anything, Brody takes a swig of his beer and says, "Man... we've got a lot of work to do."

THE END

ACKNOWLEDGEMENT

Thank you to my editor, Amber Hatch
Thank you to my friend and cover artist, Gracie Buelow
Thank you to my friend, critique partner, and fellow Oarscar winner, Josh Buelow

ABOUT THE AUTHOR

Seph Pelech

Seph Pelech was born in 1901 in Snina, Czechoslovakia. He immigrated to America in 1917, where he quickly earned his fortune by becoming an early investor, and later owner, of the Trans-Mojave Railroad, shuttling passengers and goods from Albuquerque to Zediker.  He died of tuberculosis at the tragically young age of 24. His estate is publishing his works today to raise awareness of Slavic people everywhere.

Made in the USA
Las Vegas, NV
01 June 2022

49631831R00166